An alarm beeped. Silenc... "Something big, coming fast. I don't believe these readings. It's the size of a city! Look at those weapons and speed readings!"

"Going for *Implacable*," said A'Tir from her battle-station.

The main screen blurred, the view shifting from *Implacable* to a black blur.

"Dump visual," said K'Tran, frowning.

An instant later the tactical projection occupied the entire screen.

A'Tir whistled softly. "Ten times our mass," she said, reading the scan. "Weapons batteries the size of our engines. Citadel-class shielding." She looked at K'Tran. "We don't make anything like that. What is it?"

"Something we made once, long ago," said K'Tran quietly, watching the screen. "It's a mindslaver."

As they watched, red beams sprang from the center of the projection. "And it's about to wipe *Implacable*!"

Look for these Tor books by Stephen Ames Berry

THE BATTLE FOR TERRA TWO
THE AI WAR

STEPHEN AMES BERRY

THE AI WAR

A TOM DOHERTY ASSOCIATES BOOK

THE AI WAR

Copyright © 1987 by Stephen Ames Berry

First printing: May 1987

A TOR Book

Published by Tom Doherty Associates, Inc.
49 West 24 Street
New York, N.Y. 10010

Cover art by Ron Walotsky

ISBN: 0-812-53193-0
CAN. ED.: 0-812-53194-9

Printed in the United States of America

0   9   8   7   6   5   4   3   2   1

ORDER OF BATTLE

Fleet of the Republic

Admiral Second S'Gan—Senior field officer leading the hunt for the corsair K'Tran.

Commodore H'Lor A'Wal—A subordinate of Admiral S'Gan, also hunting K'Tran.

Commodore J'Quel D'Trelna—Commanding officer, the Trel task force; aboard *Implacable*.

Captain Y'Kor—Commander of Admiral S'Gan's flagship.

Captain T'Lak—Commander of *Glory Run*, a ship in S'Gan's task force.

Captain His Excellency H'Nar L'Wrona—Commanding officer, the L'Aal-class cruiser *Implacable*.

Commander T'Lei K'Raoda—First officer, *Implacable*.

Commander Y'Gal T'Ral—Tactics officer, *Implacable*.

Commander S'Tyr T'Lan—Alien Artifacts Officer, assigned *Implacable*.

Commander N'Trol—Engineer, *Implacable*.

Lieutenant S'Til—Senior Fleet Commando officer, *Implacable*.

Medtech Q'Nil—Senior Medical officer, *Implacable*.

Colonel R'Gal—Fleet Intelligence officer, assigned *Implacable*.

Lieutenant T'Laka—Master gunner, *Implacable*.

Zahava Tal—Ex Mossad agent. A guest aboard *Implacable*.

John Harrison—Ex CIA officer and Tal's husband, also on board *Implacable*.

Symbiotechnic Control Unit 7438 (Replicant), or **Egg**—One of a series of machines used as the primary inorganic computers aboard mindslavers.

The Corsairs

Y'Dan K'Tran—Ex-captain, Fleet of the Republic—A

man of many talents and no perceptible morality. He commands *Victory Day,* a stolen Fleet cruiser.

S'Hlo A'Tir—Ex-commander, Fleet of the Republic—K'Tran's second-in-command.

K'Lal—*Victory Day*'s bridge officer.

The R'Actolians

Alpha Prime—First of the mindslavers.

The D'Linians

Major S'Ta L'Kor—Commanding officer, 103rd Border Battalion, D'Lin.

Captain S'Yin G'Sol—Executive officer, 103rd Border Battalion.

Exarch Y'Gar—Ruler of a small archipelago on the planet D'Lin.

Lieutenant S'Lat—A line officer of the 103rd Border Battalion.

The AIs

Admiral Binor—Commander of the AI's invasion vanguard.

U'Kal—AI commander on D'Lin.

The Biofabs

Guan-Sharick—Illusion Master of the Infinite Hosts of the Magnificent.

Lan-ASal—A comrade of Guan-Sharick's.

Others

Crew and officers of the Fleet of the Republic, Planetary Defense Command—S'Tak, *Victory Day* and the 103rd Border Battalion; men, machines and creatures of Combine T'Lan, the Fleet of the One and *Alpha Prime.*

1

THE FAINT CHIRP roused D'Trelna from a light sleep. Lifting the long-barreled blaster from the night table, he slipped to the side of the door, bare feet silent on the carpeting.

The chirp sounded again, closer. D'Trelna clicked off the weapon's safety.

The door hissed open. Someone came into the bedroom, features and clothing indistinguishable in the dark. Moving with feline grace, the figure stole to the bedside, steel glinting dully in its upraised hand.

The lights flared on. "Drop it!" snapped D'Trelna. He stood blocking the door, a short, fat man in a rumpled red sleep gown, blaster leveled.

The broad-bladed commando knife fell with a thud to the floor.

"Turn—slowly."

The intruder was young and wiry-framed, wearing the black uniform of a Fleet commando, corporal's hashes on his collar. D'Trelna noted the callused palms and wary, balanced stance of a fighter. Calculating gray eyes gauged the distance to D'Trelna. Too far. "How'd ya know?"

Combine production world, thought D'Trelna. Slum kid, grew up tough. He touched an ear. "If you were a real commando, you'd know—every sound on a starship is self-tagging. A lock on override is like a battle klaxon. You're not crew. Who are you? Who sent you?'"

A noise from behind sent D'Trelna stepping to one side, half turning to cover both sides of the doorway. As his eyes flickered toward the office, the killer leaped—and died, shot through the heart.

1

A second black-uniformed figure, a woman's, lay sprawled on the office floor, knife in her hand, a neat hole in her forehead.

"Two out of two," said the man facing D'Trelna across the woman's body. He held a Terran pistol pointed at the floor—a blue-chromed Italian automatic capped by a round cast-aluminum silencer.

"Two what?" said D'Trelna, blaster centered on the man's chest.

"Assassins, Commodore. These two were for you." Thin and balding, he wore an engineering tech's white jumpsuit.

"And who are you?"

"Colonel R'Gal, Fleet Counterintelligence Command. I came in with your replacements last watch. As did those two." He nodded toward the bodies. "Shall we step into your office?"

R'Gal turned and walked to D'Trelna's big traq-wood desk. Laying down the pistol, he took the commodore's chair, swiveling about to look through the armorglass wall at Terra and the North American continent, eight hundred miles beneath. A low front was moving across the Midwest—a cottony, gray-white mass busily adding another foot of snow to the Great Plains.

"Nice view," said the colonel, swinging back around. "There're no windows in the engineering techs' bay."

"I'll have some put in," said D'Trelna, standing in front of his own desk, and not liking it. "You got an ID, CIC hotshot?"

R'Gal smiled sarcastically. "A covert agent, carry an ID? Really, Commodore."

"And the Terran weapon?"

"Ship's internal security is not programmed to read a gunshot. Had those thugs come for you with pistols, we wouldn't be talking now."

"Why were they after me?"

The colonel stared past D'Trelna at the gray bulkhead. "D'Trelna, J'Quel. Officer commanding, Task Force One

2

Nine Seven, currently standing off Terra. Born S'Htar. Mother engineer, father merchant. Was himself S'Htarian merchant for a number of years, engaged in independent trade. Served in prewar Fleet as fighter pilot during the A'Ran Action. Awarded the Meritorious Commendation. Offered services during the third year of the S'Cotar War. Appointed captain, commanding the L'Aal-class cruiser *Implacable*. Figured prominently in discovery and destruction of the main S'Cotar citadel. Promoted commodore. Figured prominently in the discovery and destruction of a S'Cotar fallback point in an alternate universe. Eight battle ribbons, four unit citations, the Valor Medal, with cluster, the Cross of S'Dal, with cluster.''

R'Gal looked at D'Trelna. ''You must be as competent as you are fat—they're pretty stingy with the Cross. Cool, too. Murderers come for you in the night, but the only thing you seem upset by is my sitting in your oversized chair.''

''I'm impressed by the way you killed those two'' —D'Trelna jerked his head toward the bedroom—''not by your memory or your manners. And the chair is standard issue,'' he lied. ''Who sent them?''

The colonel shook his head. ''You line officers. You really don't know, do you, D'Trelna? Sit down.''

''I'll stand.''

R'Gal shrugged. ''Important people want you out of the way, Commodore. Dead, brainwiped, disgraced—whatever. An order for your arrest is being sent from K'Ronar to Admiral Second S'Gan. The fact that I stopped our fun couple here will only hasten the order.''

D'Trelna sat, bulk perched on the edge of the small office sofa, blaster beside him. ''Arrest? On what charge?''

The intelligence officer shrugged. ''It doesn't matter. Suspicion of sabotage, I think. It's political—an excuse to imprison or brainwipe you.''

''Political?''

''Haven't been home for a long time, have you, D'Trelna?''

The commodore shook his head.

3

"You and Captain L'Wrona came out of the war as our chief heroes—there's a docudrama based on your exploits running in four quadrants." He smiled, bemused by other's blank look. "You didn't know? Surely someone approached you for the vid rights?"

"My wife holds full writ on my behalf. She mentioned something about vid rights, but . . ."

"You're popular and not an Imperial. Oddly enough, neither is L'Wrona."

"The margrave's an enlightened aristocrat," said the commodore, smiling faintly.

"Well, the Imperial party's afraid of you both. You, they want home to brainwipe."

"Not L'Wrona?"

"No. As Margrave of U'Tria and Hereditary Lord-Captain of the Guard, he can't run for Council—it's against the Second Covenant. Alone, he's no threat.

"Historically, no candidate with both the Traders' Guild and the aristocracy behind him has ever failed to take and hold a Council seat. Run with L'Wrona supporting you, D'Trelna, and projection is for enough votes to take the Council Chair."

D'Trelna stood, face resolute. "I'll submit to arrest and be exonerated."

"You'll submit to arrest and be brainwiped! The court-martial would be secret, the tribunal paid off. People who send out assassins don't blink at rigging a trial, Commodore."

"This is insane! I have no political ambitions!" Hearing himself shout, he sat back down. "What do I do?"

"Leave. Now. Head out on the Trel Expedition, just as you're supposed to. Before that arrest order arrives. S'Gan is a combat officer—order acknowledged and you'll be headed home, shackled, the watch after that order reaches the command ship."

"But . . ."

"You want to spend the rest of your life drooling in front of a vid screen, D'Trelna? Then just sit on your cheeks and wait."

Both men stood.

"Why is CIC intervening?" asked the commodore.

"Because if they arrest you, they'll scrub the Trel Expedition. We don't want that—Pocsym's warning must be investigated."

D'Trelna made up his mind. "We'll jump at firstwatch."

R'Gal shook his head. "Leave now."

"Very well. And you?"

The colonel slipped the pistol into his jumpsuit. "I'll be around—I have my work . . . Get this ship underway."

Implacable's bridge was quiet. Thirdwatch—the starship's equivalent of nightshift—was ending. The first officer looked up as the armored doors opened. "Good morning, sir," he said, relinquishing the conn.

"Morning, T'Lei," said L'Wrona, taking the captain's chair. "Are we ready?"

"We're ready." K'Raoda stretched. "The last of the supplies are on board, and S'Gan's finally sent over the rest of our replacements."

"About time." L'Wrona scanned the ship's status report. "Anything from the admiral?"

"Leaving us alone for now."

Both looked up at the main screen. Five long, gray ships hung above Terra—resurrected Imperial cruisers, bristling with weapons batteries and instrument pods.

"The less I see of that cheery face . . ." said K'Raoda.

The doors hissed open again. D'Trelna came onto the bridge, a tired-looking man in a wrinkled, brown duty uniform and holstered blaster.

"Morning, J'Quel," said L'Wrona, turning toward D'Trelna.

The commodore nodded absently, standing beside the captain's station, eyes on the screen. "H'Nar," he said quietly, "an order's being issued for my arrest. S'Gan will be directed to execute it."

The captain frowned, adjusting the resolution on a telltale. "The Imperial party?"

5

"Does everyone know this but me?"

"You're not for them, J'Quel, therefore you're against them. You could be a grave threat to them if you ran for Council."

"You're out of your mind, H'Nar."

"Am I?" The captain stood. He was a sharp contrast to the older officer: tall, thin, with aquiline features, his uniform impeccably cut, silver inlaid blaster grips protruding from the gleaming v'arx leather holster.

"Those slime profited from the war—they and their friends in the industrial combines. And now they're profiting from the cleanup. Billions dead, millions brainwiped, scores of planets in ruins. The restoration contracts will run for years. And this talk of keeping Fleet at wartime strength, 'reclaiming' the old Imperial quadrants. Inspired by greed, all of it."

"Greed and glory lust," said D'Trelna. "Here's something you don't know, H'Nar." Quickly, he told L'Wrona about the assassination team and R'Gal. The captain showed surprise only at R'Gal's name.

"You know what R'Gal is, J'Quel?"

The commodore shook his head.

"He's a Watcher."

D'Trelna's eyes widened. "A Watcher? A S'Cotar hunter on this ship? Gods of my fathers."

"Admiral S'Gan for the commodore," said the comm officer, K'Lana.

D'Trelna smiled tightly. "Perhaps it's about the supply requisitions.

"Put it on the board, K'Lana. You should all hear this."

The five cruisers vanished from the main screen. A woman looked out at them, her graying hair tied back in a severe bun, the golden triangle of an admiral second on her collar. Watchful green eyes scanned *Implacable*'s bridge. S'Gan sat at a traq-wood desk identical to D'Trelna's, backdropped by a slab of armorglass and a view of Terra's

6

moon. Her gaze settled on the commodore. "J'Quel," she said.

"Admiral." He nodded, sweaty hand gripping the leather back of the empty command chair.

"Important people want your ass in the brig, Commodore," she said, raising a steaming cup of t'ata to her lips, sipping.

"Really?"

"You don't seem very surprised."

"I had some warning."

She shrugged. "No matter. This"—she held a pink commsheet disdainfully between thumb and forefinger—"has the wrong sign-off. Fleet Security can only issue orders of arrest over the signature of a FleetOps flag officer. This bears the signature of a Councilman and is thus not a lawful order." The paper fluttered to the desk top.

"I've requested clarification, D'Trelna. It'll take a while, going deferred priority. Meantime, I've received orders to reinforce Commodore A'Wal. The corsair K'Tran's base has been located. I'm leaving one ship on station off Terra. The rest of us are joining the blaster party."

D'Trelna and L'Wrona exchanged glances. "May we join the fun, Admiral?" said D'Trelna. "We owe K'Tran."

"No." She put her cup down. "The instant I receive that corrected order, I'm sending a shuttle for you. Head out on your mission—now."

"Thank you, Admiral."

She crumpled the cup, tossing it off scan. "Don't thank me, D'Trelna. Just do your job—find out if there's anything to this Trel thing. I'll deliver your compliments to K'Tran." Something tugged at her lips—it might have been a smile. "Will a Mark Eighty-eight fusion salvo do?"

"It will," said the commodore.

"Luck. You're going to need it, out there in the Blue Nine."

7

"Luck to you, too," said D'Trelna as the view of space and S'Gan's flotilla returned to the screen.

L'Wrona turned to his first officer. "Make for jump point at flank, T'Lei. You have the Trel coordinates plotted?"

"Jump plotted and set, Captain," said the young commander.

"K'Lana, all-band communications silence till after we jump."

"Yes, sir."

"Mission briefing, J'Quel?" asked L'Wrona.

The commodore shook his head. "Not until after the last jump." He turned for the door. "Let's keep the good news to ourselves for a few weeks, H'Nar."

"Where will you be?"

"Seeing to the cleaning of my quarters. Have medical send a casualty team there."

The gray doors hissed shut behind him.

"Make for jump point, Commander K'Raoda," ordered L'Wrona, taking the command chair. "Shield to battleforce. Flank speed."

K'Raoda touched a key. Far amidships and deeply armored, the computer responded, executing the first of a series of mission commands. "Making for jump point at flank, sir," said the first officer.

Surrounded by the faint blue shimmer of her shield, *Implacable* slipped out of Earth orbit.

"Blue Nine?" said T'Ral as the captain spoke to K'Lana.

"They haven't gone shipwide with that," said K'Raoda dryly, watching the jump approach figures thread across a telltale.

"When do they tell us?"

"Briefing, I imagine. By which time everyone will know." He nodded at the main screen. "Want to say good-bye to Terra, Y'Gal?"

"We almost got killed there half a hundred times, T'Lei." He looked up as S'Gan's flotilla vanished and Terra shrank

8

to just another small light. "It was wild, wasn't it?" he smiled.

"Sure was. Will we ever see it again?"

T'Ral returned to his chores. "You know what they used to say, when a man died on Fleet duty?" said K'Raoda, returning to his instruments.

K'Raoda watched the light disappear, then looked at T'Ral. " 'Shipped into Blue Nine,' " he said quietly.

Neither said anything until they reached jump point.

2

"THERE ARE OTHER contractors in this quadrant with your skills, K'Tran," said B'Rol with a smile, setting down his drink. The hard blue points of his eyes belied the laugh lines crinkling them. To the uninitiated, B'Rol was just another restaurant owner—a jovial man, grown round on his own rich food and the easier times since the war's end.

K'Tran knew what lay beneath that facade: a man as hard and as cold as himself. "There aren't any in this quadrant with the resources your client needs," he said. "If you think you can do better—luck." He started to rise.

A surprisingly strong hand gripped his arm, pulling him back to his seat. "Let's not be hasty, Captain. Another drink?"

"It's your liquor."

Catching the server's eyes, B'Rol held up two fingers.

There were three restaurants worthy of the name in S'Tak. B'Rol's was atop the Bureau of Agriculture building and boasted a view of S'Takport. Sitting at the bar, the two watched as an agro freighter came gliding in on silent

9

n-gravs, two miles of oblong black hull against a perfect blue sky.

"It's just that since you failed your last mission," said B'Rol as the drinks came, "my client's uneasy about employing you again."

"A fluke." K'Tran sipped his drink—a tart, yellow wine from the southern hills of S'Tak. "If my ex-commander's brother hadn't been aboard *Implacable*, the mission would have succeeded." He glanced approvingly at himself in the bar glass—a wiry, light-complexioned man with thinning hair and the casual, well-cut clothes of a prosperous merchant.

"Yes. But he was aboard. And it did fail." B'Rol held up a hand as K'Tran started to protest. "Because of your prior efforts on his behalf, my client is willing to forget that fiasco."

"Generous. What does he want?"

"As usual, I wasn't told." Reaching into his pocket, he took out a small white cylinder and handed it to K'Tran. "It's all in there. Mission and delivery specs. Same terms as the last venture—less my client's deposit on that debacle, of course."

"Of course." K'Tran slipped the commwand into his shirt pocket. "We won't be seeing each other again."

"Just as well," said B'Rol as fresh drinks arrived. "Fleet wants you dead, and I don't want to be in the same system with cruisers shooting it out. Rumor has it they pulled four task groups out of relief and recovery to hunt you down."

K'Tran sipped his wine, watching the freighter. "Six task groups. Four in this quadrant alone. Flattering, but unwanted attention. We'll lift ship for a new base port as soon as my business with you is finished."

"I'll drink to that," said the drugger.

K'Tran lifted his glass. "Your health, B'Rol. I don't suppose your client's available for questions, once I've read this?" He tapped the pocket holding the commwand.

B'Rol shook his head. "That came to me circuitously,

like the rest. I've no idea who the client is—though I'm sure if I found out I wouldn't live to tell." He smiled, shaking his head. "Almost, I'm sorry to see you go, K'Tran. It's brought in some nice side money—my personal account always swelled the day after you lifted." Setting down his drink, he frowned, staring at the agro freighter. "Odd."

"What?" said the corsair, following his gaze. The ship had landed, but without any of the usual port bustle. It sat alone, port center, locks closed, dwarfing the port buildings and government towers—a ship big enough to feed a world.

"Any freighter pulling into S'Takport, Captain, has about ten other ports to reach as fast as possible. We're a designated provision planet. What we don't eat is sent to the liberated planets—fast. Freighters come in, off-load, on-load and upship. One, two, three. Millions are starving. Time is life."

"So?"

B'Rol looked at the corsair. "So, why is that ship just sitting out there, not locked into the docks, no haulers approaching?"

"They're opening up." K'Tran nodded toward the ship. A forward lock the size of the restaurant was cycling open. The two men watched as a broad, gray ramp extended from the ship. Eight dull, black vehicles sped out onto the duralloy.

B'Rol spilled his drink. "Combat cars!" he cried, staring wide-eyed at the turret-topped assault vehicles. Spreading into a long line, they raced toward a series of dun-colored warehouses along the field's northern edge.

"Standard ground assault formation." K'Tran nodded approvingly. "Aren't those your warehouses?"

B'Rol watched ashen-cheeked as three utility haulers hurried from the warehouses, away from the combat car. "Cowards," he said hoarsely. "Stand and fight!"

11

"Not even for dopers' wages," said K'Tran. "Not with hand weapons against Mark Forty-fours and battlesteel."

The drugger looked toward the distant gray block of Planetary Defense Command, now encased in the shimmering haze of a forcefield. "Why aren't the port defenses firing?"

"Perimeter's penetrated," said K'Tran. "The batteries would have to be reconfigured and reranged. Two, three days work."

"They'll hit her as she leaves."

"Comforting."

The combat cars had reached the warehouses. Assault ramps dropped. Squads of heavily armed troopers scrambled up the loading docks and charged into the warehouses. The restaurant was too far from the action for the men to recognize the uniforms.

From the freighter, five silver shuttles flew on n-gravs to the loading docks, landing unchallenged.

The few other people in the restaurant had gathered in small groups by the glass wall, drinks in hand, chatting quietly as they watched the raid.

K'Tran checked the time. "Very professional," he said. "Not a shot fired, either. Wonder when the Planetary Guard's—"

First from the spaceport, then from every direction, alert sirens began warbling.

The vidscreen over the bar flashed on. "Attention! Attention!" The head and torso of a green-uniformed Guards captain filled the screen. He looked haggard—there was some shouting going on off scan. "A corsair raid is in progress. A corsair raid is in progress." The officer's voice boomed through the restaurant at max volume. "All military personnel and reservists to rally points. All emergency services personnel report for duty. All others to bombardment shelters."

The restaurant emptied quickly as the announcement continued, accompanied by the siren's wail. Only the two men at the bar heard the rest: "Be advised. Be advised.

12

Fleet units are insystem and are responding. Fleet units are insystem and are responding." Evidently recorded, the alert began repeating.

K'Tran took out a slim communicator. "A'Tir, got anything on those Fleet units?"

"Three heavy cruisers, coming in at flank," replied a woman's voice, crisp and efficient.

"Can we make it?"

"If we load only four shuttles."

"Do it. Send the fifth for me, now. Straight in, commlink vector."

"Acknowledged."

Setting down the communicator, he faced B'Rol's baleful gaze.

"You," said the drugger. "That's *Victory Day* out there—your ship!"

K'Tran nodded.

Heavy blaster fire echoed through the port. The combat cars were sweeping the rooftops with bursts of red fusion bolts, answering a scattering of sniper fire. Flames sprang up as the sniper fire died.

"Why, K'Tran?"

"I'm a thief and a killer, B'Rol, like you," said K'Tran casually. "The only merchandise worth stealing on this dustball world is yours—so I'm taking it. You have eight h'kals of narcotics in those warehouses. Six of them are now mine. The other two will burn. I'll make two and a half million credits. Not bad for an afternoon's work."

"Dead men don't spend," said B'Rol, his voice low, hard and cold. "Run. Hide. Bury yourself in a citadel. Nothing'll save you, K'Tran. You'll die under torture. That's a vidscan I'll enjoy for the rest of my life."

The corsair shrugged. "No doubt." A palm-sized blaster appeared in his hand. "But your life is over."

"*Waa . . .*"

The thin red bolt flashed into the drugger's open mouth and out the back of his head.

"Stupid," said K'Tran as the body tumbled onto the polished hardwood floor. It twitched briefly, then lay still.

A shuttle appeared, silver hull filling the broad sweep of glass on the spaceport side of the restaurant. Pocketing his communicator, K'Tran walked past the corpse and tables to the window. Standing opposite the shuttle's open side port, he adjusted his weapon and fired.

A wide hole blossomed in the glass. Taking a helping hand from the shuttle, K'Tran leaped aboard, the updraft tousling his hair. The lock closed behind him.

"Status?" he asked.

"Last shuttle's loading now, Captain," said the big red-bearded corsair. The two men stood alone in the cargo bay. They grabbed for the crashbars as the shuttle rose and banked.

"And those cruisers?"

"We'll be gone before they're in range."

A moment later and they were on the ship's cavernous hangar deck. K'Tran jumped out as the lock cycled open, and ran past crew hastily unloading white duraplast shipping containers.

Reaching the bridge, he stepped to the main screen and its view of S'Takport. The last shuttle was coming in, the combat cars following.

"Enemy disposition, A'Tir?" he asked his first officer.

"Coming in like the Wrath of S'Halak," said the slight brunette, watching her telltales. "Their shields are up, all transmissions are highspeed and battlecoded. Computer identifies as two P'Tan-class heavy cruisers and a R'Sal-class command dreadnought."

K'Tran looked over her shoulder at the tactical readouts. "R'Sal class." He nodded, impressed. "That one alone could wipe us."

"All shuttles are berthed, all combat cars secured," reported K'Lal, the third officer.

"Atmospheric fighters approaching," said A'Tir, pointing at the telltale to her left. A phalanx of lavender crosses

14

were moving across her left telltale. K'Tran read the intercept projection, then took the captain's chair.

"Upshield, upship," he ordered. "Stand by all batteries, A'Tir, but don't jettison camouflage."

"Lifting ship," said A'Tir, engaging n-gravs.

The cruiser rose silently, S'Takport shrinking on the screen. "Coming within range of port defenses," said K'Lal. "They're waiting for us with all shields up."

"Detonate series one blastpaks," ordered K'Tran.

A circle of small, mushroom-shaped clouds sprouted around the port as preplanted charges atomized fifteen missile and fusion batteries.

"Give me forward tacscan, A'Tir," said K'Tran.

She entered a command, fingers flying over her keyboard. The green hills of S'Tak vanished from the main screen, replaced by a tri-dee tacscan of surrounding space. A profusion of green blips were moving out from the luminous white orb representing S'Tak. Farther out, beyond the third of the system's five planets, three red blips were coming in—headed for S'Tak much faster than the green blips were leaving it.

Computer had flagged *Victory Day* yellow. It lay closest to the planet, moving toward the green blips.

"We spooked lots of traffic," said A'Tir. "Looks like every ship insystem's heading for jump point, trying to get clear of any fighting."

K'Tran nodded. "Let's join up. Plot for jump point, but keep our speed that of a respectable old agro freighter." He turned to K'Lal. "What's the civilian commtalk?"

"Confusion. Questions directed at those Fleet units. Wild rumors." The young corsair smiled. "According to the latest, S'Tak was just taken by a S'Cotar nest."

K'Tran shook his head. "How did those idiots win the war?"

"Add our voice to the confusion, K'Lal."

"Task force commander is calling Planetary Defense Command," said A'Tir, head slightly cocked as she listened to the thin, distant voices in her earjack. "Current sector PDC code, which we have."

"Asking for an update and our description?"

"Yes. Time for series two?"

He nodded. "We don't want our description out till after we jump."

She entered a second remote firing command and pushed Execute.

"Shut up!" snapped Commodore A'Wal.

The Planetary Guard officer shut up, face reddening.

"I don't care about your pissy little port, Major," said A'Wal. He leaned forward in the flag chair, thrusting his large, squarish face into the pickup. "I care about K'Tran. Tacscan shows ships everywhere. Some are headed for jump point, some for your sister planet, some for those two moons.

"K'Tran's ship is undoubtedly camouflaged. I need a complete description to distinguish it from the merchanters. You will provide that description, Major. Now." He leaned back in the flag chair, waiting. Around him, the dreadnought's bridge bustled with activity.

"Yes, sir." The major looked down at something outside the pickup. "We'll transmit a complete recording of the corsair and the raid."

"You couldn't shoot them, but you took their picture?" said A'Wal, incredulous.

The major nodded miserably.

"Send it over," sighed the commodore. He looked at J'San. "Captain, give the—officer—on five channel a new datacom freq—"

The screen with the major on it went blank. As A'Wal watched, a line of text flashed onto the bottom: CARRIER FAILURE.

"J'San," said the commodore, "I've lost that idiot. Get her back, please."

The captain ignored him, intent on a readout. "We're

16

receiving a satellite scan of S'Takport, Commodore,'' she said. "Coming up on main screen.''

A'Wal looked up. S'Takport's control spire was now a scattered pile of burning debris. Nearby, across a shattered access road, a huge crater smoldered, almost obscured by a layer of thick, black smoke.

"Planetary Defense Command and Guard Headquarters,'' said J'San.

"He must have infiltrated their security and blastpaked it, maybe months ago,'' said A'Wal. "Then blew it up with his usual exquisite timing.''

No one asked who *he* was.

"Well, the slime's not out of this yet,'' said A'Wal. "Let's see if we can flush him.''

"All-ships order from task force commander,'' said A'Tir. "All ships to rendezvous with task force for inspection.''

"Fine.'' K'Tran glanced at the plot. "Make for the rendezvous. We should be one of the first there.''

"They're scattering like m'arka hens!'' said Captain J'San, staring at the screen. All but a few ships were fleeing the task force, heading outsystem at max. "Why? There's only one corsair.''

A'Wal ran a tired hand over his eyes. "I should have remembered. This is a drugger system—always has been. They grow and refine heavy duty stuff down on S'Tak, then jump it out all over the Confederation. Climate and location are ideal. Small garrison—not enough to control it.''

"All of those ships are druggers?'' said J'San, looking at the screen.

A'Wal nodded. "Probably all have at least some contraband, stashed with regular cargo. Retails at three, four hundred credits a shot in some combine slum.

"Divide the task force, Captain. Intercept as many as possible.''

"What about the ships coming to rendezvous?"

"Proof of innocence," said the commodore. "Let's get after the others—we may get lucky."

"There they go," said K'Tran, watching the tacscan. The three Fleet ships were scattering, headed out on complex intercept vectors.

"Rendezvous and inspection order cancelled," said K'Lal.

K'Tran stood, stretching. "Well done, all. K'Lal, make for jump point. Ploddingly."

"Acknowledged."

"A'Tir, my quarters now—let's see what's on this." He held up the commwand B'Rol had given him.

Together, they left the bridge.

Clearing jump point, Admiral S'Gan watched as the system-wide tacscan came up on the board. It looked like a training exercise: three Fleet vessels busily pursuing a score of slower moving craft. "Get me Commodore A'Wal."

She interrupted his report. "K'Tran is one of the law-abiding ships now moving toward jump point, Commodore." She'd been watching the screen as A'Wal spoke. "There are eleven of them. We are eight. Priority blue plot those ships nearest your force. Once you've determined intercept vectors, order each of those vessels to rendezvous with one of our ships."

A'Wal saw it. "And whichever one runs . . ."

"Is the corsair."

"He can jump at any time, though."

S'Gan shook her head. "He won't. He'll go for optimum. I know K'Tran well." Before the war, for about two years, K'Tran had been one of S'Gan's captains—her best captain.

"I should have seen it," said A'Wal.

S'Gan allowed herself a bit of compassion. "Don't blame yourself, H'Lor. K'Tran's one of the finest tacticians to ever graduate from the Academy. Hell, he fought

18

far inside S'Cotar space for seven years—and prospered. He thinks three moves ahead of everyone else.''

"By all reports, a very competent commander,'' said A'Wal stiffly.

"Yes. Now let's go kill him.''

K'Tran gave a low whistle. "The Trel Cache.''

"Pre-Fall myth, isn't it?'' said A'Tir.

"Pre-Fall,'' nodded K'Tran. He leaned back in his chair, fingertips pressed thoughtfully together. "The Trel were the masters of much of this galaxy, perhaps a million years ago. They had it all, A'Tir—hyperdrive, interstellar matter transmission, limited psi powers.'' He tapped the screen. "At least according to Imperial survey, as faithfully recorded by Pocsym. And *Implacable*'s going in after it.''

"How many jumps?''

He called up another part of the specs. Reading it, he shook his head. "Our client couldn't get the last two jump sets. We're to folllow her from the last known position.''

A'Tir laughed mirthlessly. "We do that, we'll be spotted and wiped. Just like the Trel.''

"Yes.'' K'Tran frowned. Twelve years together and she'd never shown anything but a cursory knowledge of Imperial culture and history. "You've read about the Trel?''

"It's in ship's computer,'' she said. "I came across it on a file run, just after we took over.''

Took over: killing the crew, they'd seized *Victory Day* as it stood off Terra. The cruiser was the latest from the yards of Combine T'Lan—a sleek, gray killer almost as deadly as stasis-found Imperial ships like *Implacable*.

"This ship was going to join D'Trelna,'' said K'Tran, reaching for the complink. "How's the file logged?''

" 'Mission Summary,' '' she said, stepping around the desk to look at the screen.

K'Tran pushed a small, green button. "Computer, last logged Mission Summary. Enter to screen and scroll.''

A'Tir read over K'Tran's shoulder as the unical green script rolled down the screen. K'Tran skimmed the text until a long series of jump coordinates appeared. "Freeze," he said. The scrolling stopped. "Comparison screen—jump coordinates just entered from commwand, this terminal, with those now on screen."

The Mission Summary had two extra sets of coordinates. Otherwise they were identical.

K'Tran leaned back, nodding. "We've got the full run. We can be waiting for D'Trelna instead of trying to follow *Implacable* through"—he counted—"twenty-five jumps."

He looked up at her. "Well done, Number One."

The commlink chirped. K'Lal's worried face appeared on the scan.

"What?" said K'Tran.

"Five heavy cruisers have just cleared jump point," said the second officer. "They're moving insystem at flank."

"Any ID?"

"S'Gan's personal squadron."

K'Tran swore. "We're on our way."

Admiral S'Gan was on the bridge—a rarity. She stood to Captain Y'Kor's right, watching the tacscan come up on the main screen. "There he goes," she said as a single point of yellow suddenly sped toward jump point.

Y'Kor punched up a projection. "Probability of intercept: twenty-eight percent," he said. "He's way out."

"Get me *Glory Run*, please," she said, turning to her station.

"Captain T'Lak," she said to the round face in her screen, "the corsair will reach jump point before we can intercept. Your vessel has an unmodified Imperial jump drive, doesn't it?"

T'Lak was prematurely bald. Perhaps as compensation he'd grown a beard: black, neatly trimmed and flecked with gray. The beard bobbed as he nodded. "Mark Seventeen—late High Imperial drive. Want us to tight-jump him?"

"Yours is the only ship present that can jump intrasystem,

Captain. But it's only a thought—not even a suggestion. The decision is yours.''

Imperial engineering remained unequaled. Toward the end, five thousand years before, the Empire had stasis cached some of its warships. During the S'Cotar War, many of those ships—*Implacable* and *Glory Run* among them—had been found and pressed into service, virtually untouched. Only the old Imperial drives could jump insystem—at some risk. About a third of all tight-jumping ships emerged either as scattering fragments or not at all.

"I'll meet him at jump point, Admiral," said T'Lak, "all batteries firing."

"Jump at will, Captain," said S'Gan. "Luck," she added as the image disappeared.

"They're not pursuing," said A'Tir, reading a telltale. "Intercept probability's too low." They were almost at jump point.

"Not like her," said K'Tran, "just to sit there and watch us slip away." He stared at the screen for a moment, watching the red points designating the Fleet units. "Computer," he said, "enemy jump drives. Are any of them Imperial?"

"Not a programmed category," said computer in its asexual contralto.

"The hardware gets better, the programming gets worse," said A'Tir, eyes still on those eight red points.

"Computer," said K'Tran hurriedly, "advise if any enemy vessel has five jump transponder nodules along the engine hull."

"One vessel has that configuration," reported computer.

"Current jump point deviation?" asked K'Tran.

"Eight percent of ideal," said A'Tir.

"Let's do it now. Stand by to jump."

"Ready to jump," said K'Lal after a moment.

"Initiate on my command," said K'Tran. He punched into the commnet. "Gunnery."

"Gunnery," said a voice from his chairarm.

21

"Fire a full shipbuster salvo, tight-grouped, at our initial jump point. Take your mark from the navheading—fire when set."

"Missiles away," said the voice a moment later.

A flight of silver needles flashed by on the outside scan. K'Tran slapped his chairarm. "And jump, A'Tir!"

A nanosecond after *Glory Run* emerged from its jump, ship's computer read the absence of a ship target and the presence of seventeen multimegaton missiles. It instantly fired a blocking salvo. Seven incoming missiles were destroyed by beam hits in less than a second. The rest detonated.

Overwhelmed, *Glory Run*'s shield failed. Miles of battlesteel and men flared into evanescent gases, the center of a blinding atomic vortex.

Captain T'Lak had time for a final thought: brilliant.

S'Gan stood in front of the big board for a long time, watching the pulsing red circle marking a destruct point, then turned and left the bridge. Y'Kor wanted to say something as she walked by him. Seeing her expression, he said nothing.

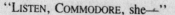

3

"LISTEN, COMMODORE, she—"

"No!" snapped D'Trelna. "You listen."

The young officer closed his mouth, staring fixedly past D'Trelna at the armorglass and the swirl of alien stars beyond.

"You've requested I review the captain's decision in this . . . incident," said D'Trelna, temper ebbing. "That's

your right. Frankly, I think you and she should be spanked."
He glanced at the complink, recessed into his desk top,
then looked back at T'Lan.

"You and our senior commando officer, Lieutenant S'Til,
met in Recroom Four, secondwatch, four days ago. After a
few drinks, she asked you to her quarters. You went
willingly, and had what Captain L'Wrona delicately de-
scribes as"—he peered at the screen—" 'an intimate period.' Neither of you deny this."

T'Lan stood at parade rest, hands clasped behind him.

"After this—period—you offered Lieutenant S'Til thirty-
two credits—'for your time,' you said. Lieutenant S'Til
firmly rejected your offer, dislocating your left patella with
a combat kick. Q'Nil fix your knee?" he asked, glancing
down.

"It wasn't my knee she was after, sir," said T'Lan,
eyes meeting the commodore's.

D'Trelna suppressed a smile. "No, I suppose it wasn't.
The facts stated are correct, Commander T'Lan?"

"Yes, sir."

"Have you anything to add?"

"Where I'm from, sir, we pay for what we get."

D'Trelna sighed. "You're from a subtropical paradise
larger than our capital, Commander. You were raised
in a garden—everyone in your father's employ, no one
except tutors and guardians about to deny you anything.
And you had a generous allowance, no doubt. That's what
you mean, isn't it?"

"Yes, sir."

The commodore nodded curtly. "Where we are now,
Commander T'Lan, is a big chunk of space that's probably
hostile and is certainly a long way from home."

"I'm aware of that, sir."

"You're aware of it, sir. But do you know what it
means? There's just this big old ship and a few hundred of
us. To succeed, to even survive, we must work together.
That means, T'Lan, a minimum of friction, a low level of
animosity. There should be some friendship, some good

23

feeling." He waved his hands. "Whatever. But I insist—
any competent commander would insist—that there at least
be mutual respect. To offer a shipmate money for an act of
friendship is disrespectful. Clear?"

"Clear, sir. Sir, I am due on watch in—"

"You transferred aboard off Terra, Commander. You
have been condescending, petulant, lazy and certainly in-
sensitive. That will change. Clear?"

"Sir . . ."

"Is that clear, Commander T'Lan?"

"Yes, sir."

"You are heir to a rich and powerful dynasty, Commander. Although of combat age the last two years of the
war, you were medically deferred for . . ." His eyes
searched the screen. "What is 'severe melancholia,'
Commander?"

"Sir, it is a condition of dysfunctional depression
occasioned—"

"Never mind. You were directly commissioned and
assigned as this expedition's Alien Artifacts Officer over
many others far older and far better qualified than you. To
date, you've shown yourself unworthy of the trust reposed
in you by Fleet and Confederation." And the enormous
bribes it must have taken to get you here, he added
silently. "That will change, won't it?"

"Yes, sir."

"The watch preceding your duty-time for the next four
weeks will be spent as part of a team, replacing some of
the older hullside sensor clusters. It is tiring, tedious work.
It can be dangerous if you don't cooperate with your
teammate. Space"—he jerked his thumb over his shoulder—
"forgives nothing."

"Yes, sir."

"I hope for your sake and ours, Commander T'Lan, that
your attitude and performance change. Quickly."

"I assure the commodore—"

"Don't assure me. Show me. Dismissed."

D'Trelna touched the commlink as the door hissed shut. "L'Wrona," he said.

The captain's face appeared in the scan. "Did you chew on him, J'Quel?" he asked with a smile.

The commodore nodded. "Surprised me and took it well. Who knows? There may be hope."

"And you?"

"A sharp homily to S'Til—tempering anger with reason. She didn't protest the detail."

"Does she know who her teammate will be?"

"She will secondwatch, when they suit up."

"I'd like to see that." They both chuckled.

"We're about to make the final jump," said L'Wrona.

"Ominous."

"You know what I mean."

"Fine. Sound briefing call as soon as we jump and we'll give them the happy news."

"How far from home, any idea?" asked Zahava.

"Over three hundred light-years," said John. High atop *Implacable,* they had the small observation dome to themselves. Outside, the hull swept past them, a mile to the bridge, another mile back to engines, half a mile to either side: a gray expanse of battlesteel broken by weapons turrets and instrument pods.

"Earth's not even a point of light anymore," he said. The stars were few and scattered in this part of the galaxy. The brightest object was a swirling red nebula, thousands of light-years away across the interstellar rift.

"One month," said Zahava, "and I've had it with the majesty of space."

On Terra, they'd been an odd couple: John, a slim, blue-eyed WASP; Zahava, a petite, olive-skinned Israeli. On *Implacable,* no one looked twice at them. The crew was from twenty-three different worlds, each with its own very distinct gene pool.

"Sorry we came?" he asked, putting his hand atop hers on the padded handrail.

"You will be," said a third voice: a woman's, a familiar voice.

They whirled, drawing their blasters.

The blonde stood opposite them, wearing a red jumpsuit, long silken hair soft-burnished by the starlight.

"How . . . ?" said John, staring beyond the S'Cotar. Outside was the reassuring shimmer of the shield.

"With us since . . . when?" said Zahava.

Both blasters were leveled at the Other's stomach.

"Long time," said the S'Cotar, gaze shifting between the two. "Since the Lake of Dreams."

"You're one of the crew," said John. His finger tightened around the trigger.

The blonde pointed at him. "You fire one of those cannons in here, Harrison, and that laser-bonded ion stream will deflect off the armorglass until its potential's spent. You two will look like you've been through one of your quaint food processors. And I'll have left." The elegant fingers snapped. "Like that. Teleportation's a wonderful gift."

"We'll find you, green slime," said Zahava. "D'Trelna will—"

"Yes, yes, I know," said the transmute wearily. "D'Trelna will take the ship apart. Probably with his bare hands. Not to mention Colonel R'Gal."

"Who?" said Zahava.

"Oh, I'm sure you'll meet," said the S'Cotar. "The three of you are . . . implacable."

"Why've you exposed yourself?" said John.

"It's imperative," said the biofab. "You've far worse to contend with here than slimy green bugs." The blonde was replaced by a green, six foot insectoid. It stood erect on four thin legs. Twin antennae grew above its bulbous eyes, two tentacles from its shoulders. The spectacle lasted only a second, then the blonde reappeared.

"Am I a bug dreaming that I'm a woman, or a woman, dreaming that I'm a—"

"What's so damned imperative, bug?" said Zahava.

"Commander T'Lan," said the S'Cotar urgently. "Watch him. He endangers everything you're trying to prevent, everything I'm trying to accomplish."

"Explain," said John.

The S'Cotar's head shook. "You wouldn't believe me. And I'll be missed in a moment. But don't let T'Lan out of your sight once we reach our coordinates."

"He's just a jerk kid," said John. "A K'Ronarin preppy."

"Harrison," said the S'Cotar intently, "it costs you nothing to watch T'Lan, much if you don't."

A chime sounded three times. "Stand by for jump," warned computer. "Stand by for jump."

"Luck," said the S'Cotar, and was gone.

"*Trust* him . . . it?" said Zahava.

The S'Cotar reappeared. "Oh. Congratulations on your marriage," it said, then vanished again.

The final warning sounded, six chimes repeating three times. "I need a drink," said John as they grabbed the handrail.

Outside, the stars changed. *Implacable* had moved ninety-seven light-years.

Zahava swallowed hard. "I think my stomach's back on Rigel or wherever that was. Are we going to tell D'Trelna about Big Green?"

"How do we know D'Trelna isn't Big Green?"

"Shit." She looked stricken. "Who can we trust?"

"You and me, chum. Unless, of course, it can project two illusions at once. After all, we were both at the Lake of Dreams." They eyed each other warily, then burst into laughter.

"They should make more bugs like you," said John, kissing her.

"Was that as good as the real Zahava?" she asked a moment later.

"Better," he said.

"Pig," she said as their communicators chirped.

"Briefing call," came K'Raoda's voice. "All desig-

27

nated personnel report for mission briefing, deck four, briefing room seven.'' The message repeated.

"Here's where they tell us what we already know," said Zahava as they clambered down the duralloy ladder to deck one.

"Rumor has it we're going into the galaxy's Bight of Benin."

"The what?"

"Pestilential West Africa slavers' port." He chanted in a passable baritone as they walked:

> "The Bight of Benin,
> The Bight of Benin,
> Few come out, though many go in."

"What are we going to do about the S'Cotar?" she asked as they reached the lift.

"Easy," said John, pressing the call tab. "We find him, have an engaging chat and kill him."

The briefing room—*Implacable*'s smallest—was full: fifty-eight officers. John Harrison and Zahava Tal stood in front of the red-cushioned traq-wood chairs. Conversation stopped as D'Trelna and L'Wrona entered and walked down the center aisle and up to the podium. "Sit, sit," said the commodore, waving them to their chairs. "You'll note," he said as the noise died, "that we've been in Quadrant Blue Nine for some time and are still alive. We're now proceeding to mission coordinates furnished by Pocsym."

"The Trel Cache," said Zahava.

"No," said D'Trelna, "not the Trel Cache."

L'Wrona broke the stunned silence. "We're to rendezvous with the first in a series of remote navigation markers placed by Imperial Survey, just before the Fall. We give it the access code furnished by Pocsym, it gives a new set of jump coordinates."

"We do know there's more than one navigation marker," said D'Trelna. "Beyond that—nothing."

"Leading us where?" asked N'Trol, the ship's engineer. N'Trol had been drafted from his well-paid job as chief engineer for a merchant line. His contempt of things military was as deep as his sarcasm.

D'Trelna shrugged. "We've no control over this process, Mr. N'Trol. Instructions and coordinates were sent by Pocsym in his final moments."

"We're touring the galaxy on the whim of a mad cyborg?"

"Is that you, T'Lan?" said L'Wrona.

Four rows back, Commander T'Lan stood, muscles rippling under his closely tailored uniform.

Dionysus, thought John, looking at T'Lan. With his perfect body, fine-chiseled face and flawless bronze skin, the young commander might have been a demigod out of Euripides. A prettyboy, certainly, but dangerous?

"It's too bad, Commander," said L'Wrona icily, "that you weren't with us when we assaulted the S'Cotar citadel on Terra's moon. Surviving that, you'd have appreciated that though Pocsym's instructions might have been mad, he executed them with flawless logic."

Mad's the word, thought John. Pocsym had been programmed in the Late Imperial age, five thousand years ago—programmed by social scientists who believed that right about now their descendants would be facing hordes of killer machines pouring into this galaxy from an alternate reality. Monitor human progress, they'd ordered Pocsym, and prepare mankind for that ultimate battle.

Deciding that only man could save man, Pocsym had created a race of biofabs—biological fabrications—dubbed them the S'Cotar, and sent them against the K'Ronarins. They'd almost destroyed the Confederation and claimed the galaxy for themselves. Almost. Only *Implacable*'s stumbling into the Terran system and her discovery of the biofabs' home base, deep beneath the surface of Terra's moon, had saved humankind—that and a hurried alliance between the K'Ronarins and the Terrans, ending in a desperate commando assault on the S'Cotar citadel.

29

That crazy cyborg started the war, reflected John—and finished it, blowing up the biofabs' citadel, most of the biofabs—and itself. The commandos and the few Terrans with them had barely escaped in time.

Is L'Wrona through with the twit? he wondered.

L'Wrona wasn't.

"Just before we left Terra, Commander, we went up against some hideous machines."

"I've read the report, sir."

"Then you'll know that though we stopped them in one parallel reality, they may well be coming into a separate part of this universe. Our part. Right now. We have the point in space at which they're supposedly entering. First, we go to the Trel Cache for a weapon to use against them."

"We only have Pocsym's word for this," said Zahava.

"A word that we'll soon confirm or refute," said the commodore.

"We're a sacrifice mission," said N'Trol flatly.

"No Fleet ship is ever intentionally sacrificed, Mr. N'Trol," said L'Wrona.

"But all ships are expendable," said the engineer.

"Depending on the mission—yes."

John stood. "No one's asked it. Let me be the one. What is there about this part of the galaxy, this Quadrant Blue Nine? According to the computer, no ship that ever came here alone has returned—not in over four thousand years. And," he continued as L'Wrona tried to interrupt, "any inquiries for data older than that gets a 'Non-Available.' "

"I know," said D'Trelna, leaning on the podium. "All information regarding this sector is proscribed and available only if we're under attack."

"That's an awful burden to operate under," said John.

"I protested," said D'Trelna. "S'Gan protested. To no avail."

"What do we know?" asked N'Trol.

"Just this," said L'Wrona. "Something happened here

that wiped the colonies in this sector and shook the Imperials down to their battle boots. They put this whole quadrant—that's two hundred cubed light-years, gentlemen—under interdict and never came back again.''

"The Confederation probed Blue Nine infrequently, John," said D'Trelna. "Computer gave you those results."

"Could it have to do with the Trel?" asked Zahava.

"May we soon find out," said the commodore.

"And survive the experience," said N'Trol.

"Here comes Fats," said A'Tir, putting the forward scan on main screen.

Looking up from ship's status reports, K'Tran read the tactical data threading across the bottom of the screen. On her present course, *Implacable* would pass close to where *Victory Day* drifted, not a light showing, her engines cold.

"Select down to auxiliary power, K'Lal," K'Tran ordered. "They've got Imperial-grade sensors."

"Selecting down," said the corsair, entering a command. The lighting and instrumentation dimmed.

"Their sensors will read our hull," said A'Tir, watching *Implacable* grow large on the screen.

"Fine," said K'Tran, dialing a drink from the chairarm. "Spectroscopy's going to show we're a meteor—nickel-and-iron."

"The camouflage baffling," she said.

"The camouflage baffling." He sipped his t'ata and grimaced. "K'Lal, this is ice-cold."

"Beverage warming's not a priority on auxiliary, skipper," said K'Lal dryly, adjusting a telltale.

"Hazards of combat." K'Tran dropped the cup into a disposer.

Implacable was moving off now, the menacing weapons batteries and sensor clusters shrinking on the screen.

"What concerns me," said K'Tran, "is our symmetry. If her computer considers that an anomaly, alarms are going to sound."

"Not to worry," said A'Tir, turning from her console.

"When they pulled those L'Aal-class cruisers from stasis they modified the shit out of the sensor package—slapped a restrictive overlay on it."

"What are you saying? They downgraded it?"

She nodded. "Right down to the primaries. It's our old unreasoning fear of artificial intelligence."

"Not all that unreasoning," said K'Tran. "The Machine Wars—AIs almost wiped the Empire. Fleet doesn't take chances, especially with resurrected Imperial systems."

"She's stopping," said A'Tir. *Implacable* was now stationary, screen-center.

"She's reached the last set of coordinates, and only one watch after us," said K'Tran. "Not bad." His eyes swept the sensor readings. "At last"—he leaned back in his chair—"after fifty centuries, a ship of K'Ronar is at the legendary Trel Cache. One would expect something dramatic—the universe trembling, stellar pyrotechnics, the end to life as we know it. Music. Certainly there should be music." He spread his hands. "Nothing. Not even the Trel Cache."

An alarm beeped. Silencing it, K'Lal read the new data. "Something big, coming in fast." He frowned. "I don't believe these readings!"

Nine long strides brought K'Tran to the tactics console. His eyes widened as he read the scan. "Big? It's the size of a city! Look at those weapons and speed readings!"

"Going for *Implacable*," said A'Tir from her station.

"Slowing," said K'Lal. "Just at the edge of visual." His fingers flew over the complink, trying to firm the pickup.

The main screen blurred, the view shifting from *Implacable* to a black blur.

"Split it," said K'Tran. "Tactical projection."

The space view shrank to the top half of the screen as the bottom half blanked. Data slowly threaded along the margins as a three-color, tri-dee projection began to form with agonizing slowness. "What are you running, one sensor array?" asked K'Tran, frowning.

"Even that's a risk. Counterscan could still pick us up."

"Dump visual, then."

An instant later the tactical projection occupied the entire screen.

A'Tir whistled softly. "Ten times our mass," she said, reading the scan. "Weapons batteries the size of our engines. Citadel-class shielding." She looked at K'Tran. "We don't make anything like that. What is it?"

"Something we once made, long ago," said K'Tran quietly, watching the screen. "It's a mindslaver."

As they watched, red beams sprang from the center of the projection. "And it's about to wipe *Implacable*," he added.

4

THEY'D TOLD K'RAODA what they were going to say at the briefing, taken a final look at the tacscan and left him in command. It had been quiet for a while, just he, T'Ral and a handful of others on the big bridge. He rose, stretching, then stepped to the nearest food server, dialing up soup.

"Incoming vessel," said the computer.

K'Raoda was back in the command chair, soup forgotten. "K'Lana," he said to the comm officer, "challenge. Y'Gan, give me a tactical work up."

"Incoming vessel does not respond," said K'Lana after a moment.

"What have you got?" he asked, swiveling the chair toward T'Ral.

"Huge," said T'Ral. "No current tactical configuration. Wait. Archival match. It's . . ."

He stood, seeing his death on the screen. "It's a mindslaver, T'Lei."

It flashed onto the screen as K'Raoda thumbed the battle stations' tab—twenty dark miles of battlesteel, instrument pods and weapons turrets.

"Command staff to bridge!" K'Raoda called above the klaxon's din. "Command staff to bridge!"

"Full evasive pattern, Y'Gan. Everything she'll do."

"Implementing," said the commander, fingers flying over the complink.

"Engineering," continued K'Raoda, turning to the white-uniformed tech at the engineering station, "cycle to drive. Gunnery, stand by."

Thick as a shuttle craft, cobalt blue fusion beams lashed out from the mindslaver, striking midpoint on *Implacable*'s shield, buffeting the cruiser like a gale.

"Shield power down four point eight percent," said the engineering tech.

The mindslaver ceased firing.

"Just probing our shield," said K'Raoda.

"Slaver holding position relative to our own," said T'Ral. Different constellations were now on main screen—the black ship still sat screencenter. "We're almost at light one!"

"That's not astrogation," said K'Raoda. "It's magic."

The battle klaxon stopped.

"All battle stations manned," reported K'Lana. "Damage control reports compiling. Gunnery requests permission to fire."

"I'll take your damage control," said the engineering tech.

"T'Laka," said K'Raoda over the commnet, "hold fire. We need everything for the shield. He's going to pour it on. Jump us out of here!" he ordered the engineering tech. "Now!"

The mindslaver fired, over a hundred batteries working

34

Implacable in a carefully predetermined pattern. The shield began to glow, a sullen burnt umbra.

"We can't jump," said the engineering tech, turning from the console. "Not and hold shielding."

"Shield failing, sections one, five, seven and twelve," said the computer. "Failure imminent. Failure imminent."

"K'Lana," said K'Raoda hollowly, "transfer ship's logs to drone pod and launch."

"Pod launched," said K'Lana.

A round ball of silver flashed by on the screen. Piercing the shield, it wove between the blaster beams and was gone.

The shield was turning an eye-searing white. The glare eased as the computer filtered the pickup. "Shield failure," it said, "mark fifty. Forty-nine . . ."

"I'd blow us up, right in its teeth, Y'Gan," said K'Raoda above the computer's death count, "but we need another senior officer to implement destruct."

"Let's not be hasty," said a new voice. D'Trelna stood behind the command tier.

"Commodore!" cried K'Raoda. "It—"

"I know," said D'Trelna as the count reached thirty. "Picked you up at rendezvous point. I've been listening on the tactical band."

He turned to the comm officer. "K'Lana, give me broad band linkage to that horror."

"Linkage established," she said at twenty.

"Commodore D'Trelna to mindslaver," he said, dropping into the flag chair. "Acknowledge."

"We hear," hissed a cold whisper from chair and wall speakers.

"Fifteen," said the computer.

"Here's a hideous poem you should like—Necropolis School—Late Empire:

"Sad-eyed S'Hra laments no more.
For as the metra petals drift down from
Q'Nar's rough hills . . ."

D'Trelna paused, fingertips pressed expectantly together.

"Six," said the computer.

"Proud Death slips gently to her side," came the cold whisper. "Welcome, Commodore. Proud Death is at your side. We are the last dreadnought of R'Actol, *Alpha Prime*—your navigation beacon."

"Zero," said the computer. Outside, the shield died even as the mindslaver ceased fire.

"We have a commwand for you, Commodore," said the mindslaver. "We will await your courier."

In a single fluid movement, the engineering tech rose from his console, drew his blaster and fired through the back of D'Trelna's chair.

The briefing ended abruptly as the battle klaxon's *awooka!* sparked a rush for the door.

John and Zahava were just behind D'Trelna and L'Wrona, running for the lift as the battle klaxon continued.

Zahava grabbed John's arm. "T'Lan," she said, pointing to where a door marked Ladder Access 17 was sliding shut.

"Maintenance and emergency use," John shouted above the klaxon. "Goes to every deck." Crew members ran past them, heading for battle stations.

The Terrans pressed against the wall, moving toward the access door. "Think T'Lan's battle station is on the ladder?" said John.

"No."

The battle klaxon stopped as they stepped through the doorway.

They were on a round apron of gleaming duralloy. A ladder of the same material ran as far as they could see in both directions, narrowing to a distant smudge. A warm air current tousled their hair.

There was no sign of Commander T'Lan.

John touched the communicator at his throat. "Computer. Advise if any doors from the access ladder seventeen have been opened in the last three t'lars."

"Deck seven twice," said the machine. "And hangar deck once, one z'lin later."

The two Terrans looked at each other. "That's five decks in about a minute," said Zahava. "What'd he do, fly?"

"Let's get to hangar deck," said John, stepping onto the first rung.

D'Trelna and L'Wrona burst onto the bridge, then halted, staring at the frozen tableau: Colonel R'Gal, in engineering white, standing with his weapon pointed at the charred, empty ruins of the flag chair, half a dozen blasters leveled at him; the great black bulk of the mindslaver filling the main screen; K'Raoda looking uncertainly at D'Trelna.

"What's going on here?" said L'Wrona.

Animation returned. Everyone tried to speak at once.

"Silence!" snapped the commodore. "You first, R'Gal." He pointed to the intelligence officer. "And put that thing away," he added. He looked around the bridge. "All of you, back to your posts."

Nodding, the colonel holstered his M11A. "I was manning the bridge engineering station. A person we believed to be you entered the bridge, assumed command and saved us from that mindslaver, using an authenticator only you, I and L'Wrona know. As a Watcher, I felt a growing conviction it was a S'Cotar transmute. I allowed it to save us, then drew on it. It flicked away as I fired. I'll need a force of commandos to scour the ship. It's probably—"

D'Trelna cut him off, pointing to K'Raoda. "Next."

The commander gave a succinct report, adding, "What's happening, Commodore?"

"Good question," said D'Trelna. "We were sent to meet a navigation beacon. Instead, we get a mindslaver." He looked at R'Gal. "Fleet Intelligence prepared our mission specs." He turned to the bridge crew. "Gentlemen, this is Colonel R'Gal, of our illustrious Fleet Intelligence.

"You slime set us up, didn't you, R'Gal?"

The colonel nodded, nonplussed. "Would you have

gone if we'd told you what Pocsym actually said? That you'd have to face a slaver?''

"We go where we're sent, R'Gal," said L'Wrona, turning from the damage control reports. "We do what we're told."

"What is that?" D'Trelna jerked a thumb toward the mindslaver.

"Let's let the computer tell you," said R'Gal, touching a complink. "Computer. Tactical-Imperative. Authenticator Prime One Four Nine. R'Actolian biofabs, history."

The computer's pleasant contralto spoke for a time.

"*Alpha Prime*," said K'Tran, almost to himself. "Of course." He swiveled the command chair. "A'Tir, Blue Nine's the R'Actol Quadrant."

"The what?" she said, busy trying to drift them closer to *Implacable* and the mindslaver, now almost back to their original positions.

"The Empire suppressed the information. So did the Confederation." He shook his head. "Had I known this assignment was in the R'Actol Quadrant, A'Tir, we'd have done something safer—like raiding FleetOps."

She turned from her work. "You going to tell me what a R'Actolian is?" she asked, pushing a strand of hair away from her eyes. "And what it has to do with that monstrosity?" She nodded at the screen.

"What do you know about mindslavers?"

"Built and abolished by the Empire. Run by brains ripped from living bodies. Twenty miles of magical death, capable of engaging and destroying a modern sector fleet. Weapons, navigation and computation systems far in advance of anything we have now."

"And all made possible by those living human brains," said K'Tran. "Brains preserved in variable stasis and bathed by a constant nutrient flow."

"And the R'Actolians?"

"You won't read it in Archives, but the R'Actolians

built the first mindslavers. And a woman, Number One, made the R'Actolians.''

"S'Helia R'Actol," said *Implacable*'s computer, "was the sector governor of Quadrant Blue Nine under the Emperor H'Tan. She was also one of the finest of the High Imperial geneticists. A woman with Imperial ambition, R'Actol took advantage of her position and the relative isolation of her post to conduct illegal genetic experiments on a grand scale. She wanted a superior, self-propagating warrior race, obedient to her. She was able to achieve all but the last goal. Never more than a thousand, the R'Actolian biofabs quickly dispatched R'Actol and her forces, then went on to invent the symbiotechnic dreadnought—''

"Mindslaver," said K'Raoda.

"Mindslaver," agreed the computer. "A fleet of mindslavers that almost toppled the Empire, striking without warning from Blue Nine. Only when the Empire built their own mindslavers in overwhelming numbers were the R'Actolians believed exterminated."

"And this quadrant, Blue Nine?" asked D'Trelna.

"Abandoned," said the computer. "Some one hundred and forty-three inhabited planets had been stripped of their people by the R'Actolians, the people then stripped of their brains for use in the mindslavers.

"By the time the last R'Actolians sought the braincased immortality of their last mindslaver, the struggle had all but bankrupted the Empire. The R'Actolian War marked the end of the High Imperial epoch and the beginning of the Late, with its decay and decadence."

"We are waiting," whispered the mindslaver.

"What is manning that ship, R'Gal?" demanded D'Trelna, turning from the screen to the colonel.

"The disembodied brains of psychotic geniuses sixty centuries dead," said the colonel.

"And we have to send someone over there," said L'Wrona.

"I'd go, but I've a S'Cotar to catch," said R'Gal.

"Go catch it then," said D'Trelna.

R'Gal headed for the door.

"Sometime between this crisis and the next, Colonel, you and I are going to have a long talk," added the commodore. "Clear?"

"Clear," said the colonel with a curt nod. The doors closed behind him.

"I'll go, sir," said K'Raoda.

"Actually, it's my turn, sir," said T'Ral.

Other voices vied with his as the whole bridge crew volunteered.

D'Trelna help up his hands. "Wait. The only fair thing is to draw—"

An alarm beeped. "Weapons fire, hangar deck," said the computer. "Weapons fire, hangar deck."

"Commandos are responding, Captain," said K'Lana after a moment. "I'm unable to contact flight control."

"Keep trying," ordered L'Wrona. "You and you"—he pointed at the two black-uniformed commandos flanking the doors—"with me. J'Quel?"

"Go," waved D'Trelna. "I'll entertain *Alpha Prime*."

"Won't . . . budge," grunted John, pulling with all his strength on the recessed door grip. Hangar deck lay just the other side.

The descent down the ladder had seemed interminable. It's got to be less than a mile, John had kept assuring himself.

"Unless you've a better idea . . ." said Zahava, drawing her blaster.

"Do it."

She twisted the muzzle as they stepped back, aimed carefully at the center right edge of the door frame and fired. The red bolt lanced through the metal with a satisfying crack and shower of sparks.

"Now try it."

The door groaned open. They eased through, blasters held high and two-handed, eyes searching for movement.

Hangar deck was almost a mile long and half a mile wide. Stars twinkled through the faint shimmer of the atmosphere curtain at its launch end. Silver shuttles, stub-winged fighters and squat, black assault craft nestled in soft-lit berths beneath the distant ceiling. The vaulted silence was as deep as a cathedral's.

Nothing moved the length of the deck. There should have been at least ten crew on duty—maintenance techs, flight control personnel, commandos pulling security detail.

Flight control was behind a concave sweep of black glass, set above the deck.

John touched Zahava's shoulder, pointing toward the stairway running to flight control. A body lay crumpled at the bottom.

Approaching cautiously, they saw it was a crewman—young, half his face torn away, his weapon holstered.

John jerked his head toward the top of the stairs. "Alert the bridge," he whispered. "I'll check around."

Nodding, she bounded silently up the stairs, disappearing into flight control.

John turned at a ripple of movement in one of the berths. A distant, brown-uniformed figure was slipping into a shuttle. Caution aside, he ran for the shuttle, boots ringing on the gray battlesteel.

It was a good hundred yards. He was halfway there when the n-gravs whined on. The ship lifted, passenger hatch slowly cycling shut.

Lungs bursting, he dived through the closing hatchway, sliding into the passenger section as the craft slid from its berth.

Bodies were sprawled throughout the small flight control area—three dead by blaster fire, two with their larynxes crushed, eyes bulging, tongues black and protruding.

Zahava was oblivious to the corpses. She stood watching helplessly as the shuttle silently traversed the length of the deck, pierced the atmosphere curtain and was gone.

After a long moment she called the bridge.

41

*   *   *

"There's a shuttle headed for the slaver," said T'Ral.

D'Trelna's head jerked up, looking at the screen. The silver craft was a quarter of the way out, heading for the darkened mass of *Alpha Prime*.

"Tal is on hangar deck," reported K'Lana. "The deck crew is dead. Commander T'Lan appears to have slaughtered them and stolen a shuttle. Harrison infiltrated the shuttle. His condition's unknown."

"Slaughtered?" said D'Trelna.

"That's what she said."

"Advise Captain L'Wrona. And respond a medical team to hangar deck."

"Do you want gunnery to . . ." began K'Raoda.

"No," said D'Trelna, shaking his head slowly. "I don't want to excite the mindslaver. But I'll bet you a month's pay, Mr. K'Raoda, that that hideous relic isn't through with us." He stared at the mindslaver and the shuttle for a moment, then touched the commlink. "N'Trol. D'Trelna. What's shield status?"

The engineer's worried face filled the pickup. "No status," he said. "No shield. Five major components are fused lumps. Some of the grid links are ash—never seen anything like it. And the hullside relay clusters . . ."

"How long?"

N'Trol shrugged. "Two, three days."

"You have the balance of this watch, Engineer." He silenced the other's protest with upraised forefinger. "Maybe. Once whatever is about to happen on *Alpha Prime* happens, N'Trol, that monster's coming for us. Believe it. Work on that shield as if all our lives depended on it. They do."

D'Trelna switched to the complink. "Computer. I want everything you have on tactical operations against mindslavers by non-symbiotechnic vessels—priority one to be L'Aal-class cruisers, if any. Run it to hard copy, print to bridge flag station."

Waiting, the commodore sat brooding, eyes on the shuttle. Even at highest magnification, it was almost lost against the mindslaver.

R'Gal's face appeared on the commlink. "The news about Harrison and T'Lan is all over your tactical network. What are you doing about it?"

D'Trelna glared at the screen. "Nothing, Colonel. There couldn't be a better person on that shuttle if we'd run through the whole Fleet order of battle—except maybe Zahava Tal. Both were covert operations specialists on Terra. One or both of them always fought beside us, almost from the moment we entered the Terran system."

"Then your pet Terrans could be S'Cotar, D'Trelna."

"R'Gal, I haven't time for your paranoia. Vanish."

The printer stopped as the commlink beeped off. An ensign brought D'Trelna the printout—it wasn't long, but he lingered over it, reading it three times. Finishing, he saw the shuttle was gone.

"She's inside the slaver, Commodore," reported K'Raoda.

Nodding, D'Trelna touched the commlink. "H'Nar, have you secured hangar deck?"

"Not much to secure." The captain stepped back, letting the wall pickup scan the deck. Blue-uniformed medtechs were wheeling away eight green-shrouded carts. "Just us, Zahava and the dead down here, J'Quel. Whatever T'Lan is, he's a very efficient killer."

"Smart money says he's not human, H'Nar. Our Alien Artifacts Officer is an alien."

"Agreed. What now?"

"Meet me at the lift, outside Armory One. Alone. We're going to see a special friend."

The captain's eyes widened. "Your little souvenir?"

D'Trelna nodded solemnly.

"You get that thing started, J'Quel, there's no telling . . ."

"There's no other way, H'Nar."

"Very well," nodded the captain. "I'm on my way."

5

THE SHUTTLE HAD an aft storage compartment, accessed from either the passenger section or from outside, through a hatch. John hid there in the dark, pressed against the bulkhead, waiting for whatever had just exterminated ten crew to leave the pilot's cabin. He was going to wait until T'Lan had passed by, then empty the M11A's chargepak into that perfect body, holding the trigger back until the reload chimed. Forget John Wayne, the Army had taught him a million years ago—kill the enemy with the least possible risk to yourself. Although, he recalled with a faint smile, that wasn't quite the way Drill Sergeant Eddy had phrased it.

The pitch of the engines changed, climbing an octave. Must be almost to the slaver by now, thought John.

From below came the faint whine of landing struts deploying, then silence as the shuttle landed and the n-gravs died. The Terran drew his blaster and waited, a hand on the door switch.

Hurried footsteps followed the distant hiss of a door opening. The footsteps stopped in front of the storage area.

John clicked off the safety and leveled his weapon at whatever was beyond the thin slab of steel.

There was a faint click, then the whir of the passenger airlock cycling open. John counted to three, pressed the door switch and stepped squinting into the harsh light, his finger curled around the trigger.

The shuttle and the ramp were empty.

He had a glimpse of the darkness beyond the circle of

44

light thrown by the shuttle, then T'Lan's voice spoke softly from behind. "Put it down, Harrison."

"Not following the antics on the bridge?"

Zahava looked up from her untouched food. A short, wiry-framed officer stood beside her table, wearing brown combat dress with unfamiliar insignia.

"Do I know you?" she said, pushing her tray away. With the ship on full alert, the officers' mess was deserted.

"Colonel R'Gal, Fleet Counterintelligence Command. May I?"

The Israeli shrugged.

R'Gal took a chair opposite her. "Sorry about Harrison."

She looked up, startled. "What do you mean? There's news?"

R'Gal shook his head. "No. I meant about his being . . . off-ship."

"He'll be back," she said quietly, lifting her t'ata cup.

"Word is you're a S'Cotar hunter."

"One in need of some help," he said, smiling ruefully. The smile vanished. "You want to sit and wait, I'd understand."

"If you're looking for Guan-Sharick, we've seen him," she said, and told R'Gal of the meeting in the observation dome.

"Odd," said R'Gal, frowning as she finished. "That's the second time the bug's warned us. The first time was about the S'Cotar fallback point on Terra Two."

"I wasn't in on that," said Zahava. "How'd you know Guan-Sharick was on board?" she added.

The colonel made a V with each hand. "Two and two," he said, crossing the V's. "According to ship's roster, a dead man came back from the Lake of Dreams battle—one Corporal S'Gat. He was killed in an assault and cremated with the rest of the dead, there on your moon. And yet"—he held up a finger—"this same corporal was later seen on *Vigilant*, disembarking with the rest of the commandos. Seen there, but never again.

"Then, during the Terra Two affair, Guan-Sharick was flitting about. Checking the times of his appearances against *Implacable*'s positions, we found that this ship"—he waved a hand—"was always within easy transport range for a S'Cotar transmute."

"Circumstantial," she shrugged.

"He only showed up when her shield was down," said R'Gal, unruffled. "Over a ninety percent correlation."

"I see," said Zahava. "Kind of compelling."

"So we thought."

"Now what?" she asked, sipping her t'ata.

"We find him."

"You're crazy, Colonel," she said pleasantly. "'Fifty miles of corridors, hundreds of compartments, passageways . . . Plus Guan-Sharick's got a device that fools your S'Cotar detectors."

"I'm a Watcher," said R'Gal.

"Oh?" she said warily. "And what do you watch?"

The K'Ronarin laughed. "It's a stupid title," he said. "Some of us have this gift." He tapped his head. "We can detect a transmute."

"Like that?" she said.

"Usually. That damned device Guan-Sharick's wearing though . . ." He shook his head. "I can tell where he's been, but not where he is. It's maddening."

"But it leaves a trail?"

R'Gal nodded. "Nothing consistent, though. However . . ."

"Yes?"

"There're some very strong traces in the lifepod section. And I was thinking perhaps . . ."

Zahava grinned. "You were thinking, Colonel, that with everyone at battle stations but us, now would be a fine time to check out the lifepods."

The K'Ronarin grinned back. "If you want to."

Zahava stood. "What are we looking for?"

R'Gal led the way past the food machines and into the corridor. "Anything that doesn't belong. It's the least

46

visited part of the ship. If I had something to hide, I'd hide it there."

Waiting for the lift, he pointed to her holstered M11A. "I hope you can use that."

The lift arrived with a loud ping.

"Let's hope I get a chance to show you," she said as they boarded.

The doors hissed shut on the empty gray corridor.

"You could be brainwiped for this, J'Quel!" L'Wrona's voice echoed down the passageway.

"I certainly will be if you keep announcing it, H'Nar," said D'Trelna mildly.

The two rounded the corner. In the distance, at the end of the corridor, a squad of black-uniformed commandos guarded a closed door.

"Sorry," said the captain as they walked. "But if FleetOps finds you've been hiding a stolen slaver computer on board . . ."

"A rediscovered slaver computer," said the commodore.

"The distinction won't impress a tribunal. You took the thing off *T'Nil's Revenge*, on Terra's moon," said L'Wrona softly. "Fine. But then you hid it here"—he nodded toward the door—"and told no one. That's illegal. Now you plan to activate it, and that's criminal. FleetOps is going to do some profound reprogramming of your gray matter."

"We're hanging by our fingernails on the edge of forever," said D'Trelna. "FleetOps is not."

Ten rifles snapped to the salute as the two passed by, D'Trelna sketching a salute. "Where's Lieutenant S'Til?" he asked the NCO blocking the door.

"Dispensary, sir," said the sergeant.

D'Trelna frowned. "Odd. She's never sick."

"You going to let us in, Sergeant?" said L'Wrona.

"That's up to the computer, sir." The woman pointed to the security terminal set in the wall.

"J'Quel?" said the captain, deferring to his senior.

"Of course," said D'Trelna. He thumbed the red tab. "D'Trelna, J'Quel, Commodore."

"And L'Wrona, H'Nar, Captain," said the margrave over D'Trelna's shoulder.

The sergeant stepped aside as the door opened.

Stepping through the doorway, commodore and captain entered a wide, high-ceilinged room. Walking quickly, they passed rows of racked blasters, light artillery pieces, stacked crates of ordnance, then through a second, double-guarded door and a final security check.

"All right, J'Quel," said L'Wrona as the door slid shut behind them. "Show me."

It was a tiny room, almost a closet, its walls the same uniform gray as elsewhere—except for the wall to their left, which was white with small hexagonal niches. Sealed behind armorglass in each of the ten lighted niches gleamed a conical silver warhead. Large red lettering blazed above the warheads—lettering repeated in deathless blue flame etched into each piece of armorglass:

DEATH-WARNING! DEATH-WARNING!
M018.G—PLANETARY-DESTRUCT WARHEAD!
ANY ATTEMPT TO ACCESS WARHEAD
WITHOUT FLEET-ISSUED BATTLECODE
WILL DETONATE WARHEAD!

"Impressive, isn't it?" said D'Trelna. Before L'Wrona could move, he'd covered the distance to the first niche and slid the glass aside.

"J'Quel . . . !" said the captain, aghast as D'Trelna removed the warhead and began casually to unscrew it.

"When Fleet found *Implacable* and pulled her out of stasis," said the commodore, "she had only nine of those warheads. The first little baby here was gone from its creche. I appropriated the space."

L'Wrona had recovered, moving to D'Trelna's side. "So you created a dummy warhead as a hiding place." He laughed—shakily.

"I've often wondered," said D'Trelna, handing the captain the top of the hollow cone, "what poor rebel planet the Empire snuffed with it."

"We might also speculate on the nature of a culture that uses 'death-warning' as a compound noun," said L'Wrona, glancing at the red letters, "and went through eighteen generations of planet snuffers. . . . That's it?" he asked as D'Trelna held up a small golden egg.

"That's it," nodded the commodore. He handed the other half of the fake warhead to L'Wrona. "Would you replace this?" he asked.

By the time the captain had reassembled the casing and restored it to its niche, D'Trelna was standing beside the egg, blaster in hand.

"What now?" said L'Wrona.

"Now," said D'Trelna, twisting the M11A's muzzle to lowest power, "little egg grows up." He aimed two-handed at the spheroid.

L'Wrona held up a hand. "Wait, J'Quel. We'd better record this. Just in case."

"In case of what?" asked the commodore, lowering his weapon. "It eats us?"

"As I recall," said the captain, walking to the wall complink, "this unit's predecessor wanted your brain for use in some psychotic fantasy." He punched the On tab as D'Trelna grunted.

"Computer. Captain."

"Yes, Captain?" came the asexual contralto.

"Full scan of special vault, Armory One, commencing now. Record to auxiliary log only, and restrict access to Commodore D'Trelna and/or I."

"Illegal command," said the computer. "Fleet regulations require all log entries be part of ship's primary records, with exception in certain special situations. These situations are . . ."

D'Trelna glared at the complink as the machine prattled on. "I hate a self-righteous computer." He raised his blaster.

"J'Quel, let me take care of it," said L'Wrona, lowering the commodore's arm, a hand to one thick wrist.

"Computer," he continued, "implement command as given, per Directive Green Seven Nine, authenticator Silver Prime."

"Implemented, my lord." The machine now spoke with a brisk, efficient baritone.

D'Trelna stared wide-eyed at the complink, then turned to L'Wrona. "Generic override?" he guessed.

"Imperial," nodded L'Wrona. "Seventh Dynasty—about the time they built this old hulk." The two turned back to the little egg.

"Something the margravate keeps to itself?" asked D'Trelna.

"And uses sparingly," smiled L'Wrona. The smile vanished. "Don't use it, J'Quel! It wreaks havoc with the programming overlay—taps those six thousand year old Imperial systems."

"No, no. Never," swore D'Trelna. Sighting again on the egg, he pulled the trigger, bathing the spheroid in a soft, red light.

Nothing happened for a moment. Then, as the blaster continued its shrilling, the egg started to glow—a golden shimmering that grew brighter as the spheroid began to swell. The two men stepped back as the slaver computer grew to fill the space in front of the warheads.

The golden shimmering dimmed, then vanished. The commodore ceased firing and holstered his weapon. The egg lay across the deck, inert.

"Well, that should have done it," said D'Trelna, frowning. "According to ship's archives, you just feed it a steady, low grade dose of energy." He shook his head. "We better get back to the bridge."

"And do what?" asked L'Wrona. "Lead the crew in prayer? No." He nodded toward the slaver machine. "There's got to be a simple activation command, common to the era." He stood staring at the golden orb, fingers softly drumming his holster.

"I'm going," said D'Trelna after a moment, stepping toward the door.

"Wait," said L'Wrona, eyes never leaving the egg. "I'm thinking."

"Think faster," said the commodore, halting reluctantly. "Or we're all going to be processed by that spaceborne abattoir out there." He jerked his thumb over his shoulder.

"T'Nil was one of the most expansionist emperors—ever," said L'Wrona. "And this"—he pointed at the egg—"a vital component of his premier war machine. If it came out of the Fleet Fabrication Center on D'Kor, there'd be a generic activation command."

"H'Nar, please, try something."

The captain walked over to where the machine lay. "Computer," he said, looking down at it, "Destiny and Empire."

Silently, the egg righted itself and rose, hovering just above the deck. "Destiny and Empire," it said in a perfect tenor. "How may I serve?"

D'Trelna slapped L'Wrona on the back. "Well done, H'Nar!"

"T'Nil's battle cry, J'Quel," said the captain. "And the motto of all successive emperors."

"It should have been blood and empire," said the commodore, watching the computer. "Identify," he said to the machine.

"Symbiotechnic Control Unit Seven-Four-Three-Eight, replicant," said the machine. "Assigned symbiotechnic dreadnought *T'Nil's Revenge*."

"Computer," said D'Trelna, "we need—"

"I am addressed as either Seven-Four-Three-Eight-R, or Egg," said the machine.

D'Trelna closed his eyes as if in pain, then opened them. "Egg," he said carefully, "we are in need of tactical data. How would a L'Aal-class cruiser defeat a mindsla—symbiotechnic dreadnought?"

"I'm not familiar with the nomenclature 'L'Aal,' " said Egg.

"You are on such a vessel now," said L'Wrona.

"Then I must have access to this ship's central computer," said the machine.

Captain and commodore exchanged glances. "What've we got to lose?" said L'Wrona.

"Very well, Egg," said D'Trelna. "Access ship's computer through the commpanel beside the door. If you need exchange protocols, we'll have our engineering—"

Stylus-thin, a beam of soft green light shot from the top of the spheroid to the commpanel. The connection lasted only an instant, then the beam snapped off. "This L'Aal-class cruiser is almost identical to S'Htul-class police cruisers of the S'Yal dynasty. If you wish to know how it can defeat the mindslaver now confronting it . . ."

"Yes?" said the two officers.

"It cannot. Your tactical situation is hopeless."

"For this, I left the bridge?" said D'Trelna, drawing his blaster.

"However," said Egg as the commodore twisted the muzzle back to combat setting.

"What?" said D'Trelna.

"In theory, two warships of this approximate class have a slight chance against a dreadnought—that is *Alpha Prime* out there?"

"Yes," said L'Wrona.

"Good. She was the first of her type, without the advanced weapons systems of later ships. With myself coordinating an attack, your ships—"

"This is our only ship," said D'Trelna.

"Your crudely inhibited sensors show a second vessel, slightly smaller than this one, but heavily armed, standing off your port, poorly disguised as a rock. As *Alpha Prime* has undoubtedly detected her presence, a joint operation would serve you both."

L'Wrona was out the door, running for the bridge before Egg had finished.

"Come with me . . . please," said the commodore.

The commando sergeant watched, bemused, as two similar shapes, one golden and metal, the other human and uniformed, moved down the corridor toward the lift.

Unable to communicate its urgent report about Egg to any station, *Implacable*'s computer kept trying to bypass the blockage. With increasing alarm, it found the restraints on its operations to be firm—and spreading.

"Why haven't I been here before?" asked Zahava.

"No need," said R'Gal as the door closed behind them. "Not unless you're abandoning ship."

They stood at one end of a brightly lit corridor. It looked like any other of *Implacable*'s long gray miles, save for the ten widely interspaced doors that ran its length, five to each side. The door to Zahava and R'Gal's right read Lifepod 1. R'Gal thumbed the entry tab.

"Shall we?" said the K'Ronarin as the double doors of the airlock slid open. Zahava stepped into the lifepod.

It was a big, round room. Rows of red flight couches took up most of the floor space, broken by three aisles and a central spiral stairway. Across the cabin from the airlock, beneath a blank main screen, two flight couches fronted a darkened double console.

"Looks more like a bus than a pod," said the Israeli.

"Long before even *Implacable* was built," said R'Gal as the door hissed shut, "survival vessels were one-man craft. Time went by, they grew to this." His hand swept the cabin. "Three levels, a hundred and fifty seats, maximum capacity over two hundred. Jump drive, n-gravs, automatic homers, sanitation and recreation facilities. The whole unit can be broken down to form the nucleus of a rough colony—power plant, forcefield, sanitation and shelter—just in case." He walked across the cabin as he spoke, heading for the double console.

"In case of what?"

"In case the automatic homers don't find a close-in

planet emitting technology's telltale spores.'' Reaching the far side of the pod, the colonel dropped into the left chair and busied himself with the instruments.

"Why three levels?" asked Zahava, following him down the center aisle. "And why twice as many lifepods as needed?"

"Three levels to conform to *Implacable*'s design. So many pods because she probably carried a larger complement five thousand years ago." He leaned forward, reading a report as it flashed onto a telltale. "Maintenance log says we're the first to enter this pod since the ship left Terra."

"Is that true?" she asked.

"It's true that the log entry reads no access since Terra." R'Gal stood as the telltale winked off. "It's also true that a S'Cotar transmute could have telekinetically reprogrammed this pod's computer. . . . Check the upper levels," he said, motioning toward the stairway.

"For what?"

"Anything that looks out of place. Everything should be as spare and as orderly as on this level. Check the storage lockers and bins, food processors—anywhere something small could be hidden. If you find anything unusual, anything at all, use your communicator and call me. I'll be checking number two. Meet me in front of three when you've finished."

She nodded and was halfway up the stairs, blaster in hand, by the time R'Gal reached the exit.

"Anything from *Alpha Prime*?" asked L'Wrona as K'Raoda relinquished the command chair.

"Nothing," said the first officer, resuming his station.

Both men looked at the main screen—the mindslaver hung there, a great dark menace out of legend, intimidating by its very existence.

"Fine," said the captain. "Let's fill our empty moments with a tactical exercise."

54

"Sir?" said K'Raoda, exchanging puzzled glances with T'Ral.

"Assume," said L'Wrona, fingertips pressed together, "that there's a third ship close by, a warship about our size. It's sitting dark and camouflaged, watching. Assume further that our sensors have picked it up, but are unable to correlate key data because of Fleet's restrictive programming overlay. How do we get a readout?" He looked at T'Ral.

"N-gravs," said the third officer. Turning to his console, he busied himself at the complink. No one noticed D'Trelna enter the bridge.

"Of course," said K'Raoda. "He has to be using them to counter his drift. Just a burst, now and then, but—"

"But enough," grinned T'Ral, looking up. "Five-one-seven, mark four-one. Previously charted as an asteroid."

"Tight-beam transmission to that asteroid, please," said D'Trelna. He took his seat, oblivious to the stares that followed his hovering companion. "Use alpha channel, and transmit in battlecode."

"Sir," said K'Lana, "alpha channel's a Fleet intership tactical band. And . . ."

A glance from D'Trelna stopped her. "Do it," he said.

"Transmitting," she said a moment later.

L'Wrona walked to the commodore's station. "I can think of only one man who'd come into this quadrant after us, J'Quel."

"Before us," said D'Trelna. "Had to be. Otherwise, we'd have made him." He flipped the commswitch. "*Implacable* to unknown ship—acknowledge."

On *Victory Day*, A'Tir turned to K'Tran, shaking her head. "Incoming transmission on the tactical band. *Implacable*'s made us."

The other corsair shrugged. "Much good it'll do them." He touched his commkey.

The image on *Implacable*'s main screen changed from that of the mindslaver to the smiling face of Captain K'Tran. He wore the standard brown K'Ronarin uniform with the stylized silver ship of a starship captain on the collar. "*Victory Day* on your flank, Commodore. How stands the Fleet?"

A ripple of anger swept *Implacable*'s bridge—just about everyone had lost friends to the K'Tran's killers.

"K'Tran, you renegade butcher," growled D'Trelna. He stood, face flushed, eyes blazing with hate. "How dare you render the greeting of honorable men? How dare you wear the uniform of your victims? You parasitic v'org slime—"

"You're being wearisome, D'Trelna," said K'Tran easily. "You've made us, but I fail to see what you can do about it. Start blasting away, that slaver's going to wipe you."

The commodore sat down, recovering. "It'd be worth it, to dispose of you. . . . Some scum paying you slime to follow us?" he asked, dialing up a fruit drink.

"Now, D'Trelna, you know I can't betray a client's confidence," said the corsair. "Though, had I known about the mindslaver, we'd have found an easier mark. Like Prime Base. And as soon as it breaks your command up for parts, we'll be on our way."

D'Trelna shook his head. "We go, you go. My word on it." He swiveled his chair. "Egg," he said to the slaver machine, "by how much must we boost signal power for *Alpha Prime* to detect the third vessel, *Victory Day*?"

The golden spheroid drifted to D'Trelna's side, coming within pickup range of the transmission. "Increase by a factor of three," it said.

D'Trelna turned to the comm officer. "K'Lana, I seem to be having a problem. Increase signal strength by a factor of three, please."

"Wait!" K'Tran's smile was gone. "What do you want?"

"Hold, K'Lana," said D'Trelna. He turned back to K'Tran. "Can't you guess, K'Tran?"

A'Tir had pulled an ID from *Victory Day*'s archives. She sent it over to K'Tran's station. He stared at the data for a surprised instant, then looked up. "Where'd you get a slaver computer, D'Trelna? *T'Nil's Revenge?*"

"Where I got it isn't important," said the commodore. "What we'll be using it for is."

"We'll?"

"Yes," said D'Trelna. "It'll be conning our combined battleops. We're going to penetrate that mindslaver's defenses and storm her bridge, K'Tran. You and me, yours and mine, side by side. Victory or death."

There was a long silence on both bridges. "You're mad, D'Trelna," said the corsair.

"Am I?" said D'Trelna. "You're a superb tactician. Consider the situation tactically, K'Tran."

He did, fingers softly drumming the chairarm, eyes distant. When he looked back at the pickup, both his and D'Trelna's crew were watching. "Victory or death, Commodore," he said. "There's no other way. What are your orders?"

"Maintain position, be prepared to link battleops on my command," said D'Trelna.

"As the commodore orders," said the corsair, switching off.

"You're serious?" said A'Tir as D'Trelna's face vanished. "We're taking orders from Fats?"

K'Tran nodded slowly. "We're too close to run, but near enough to attack. Only a coordinated assault has even a remote chance of success. That slaver computer may give us an edge."

"Or betray us utterly," said A'Tir.

"It's a fluid situation," said K'Tran slowly. "And it may yet favor us." His old self-assurance, blunted for a moment, was returning. "We're not burdened by duty, ethics or conscience." He nodded toward the screen. "They are. . . . Stand by to link battleops. And give me shipwide so everyone can share in the good news."

6

THE SLAVER'S BRIDGE was big, cold and empty, a soft-lit, multitiered cavern beneath a transparent dome.

Perfect temperature for preserving meat, thought John. Shivering, he rubbed his hands together, then thrust them back into his pockets.

Hundreds of consoles lined the tiers, lights twinkling, alarms chirping. Nowhere was there a chair, nowhere a sign that any living being had ever crewed *Alpha Prime*. The Terran stared up at T'Lan, one tier above him. One thing's for sure, he thought—I'm the only human on this bridge.

Floating along at eye level, the translucent blue globe had led them from the shuttle out across the dark hangar deck. It had been a long, cold walk, their footfalls echoing distantly, John keenly aware of T'Lan striding beside him, a precise, unfaltering tap-tap-tap. T'Lan would sometimes look right or left, eyes seeming to focus . . . on what? John wondered. No matter. T'Lan can see in the dark. He filed it away, another bit of data.

Going up a ramp, they'd gone down a short passageway, through a door that moved noiselessly aside, and into a brightly lit anteroom. John stood blinking, squinting in the sudden glare as T'Lan followed the globe to one of a score of open-topped, two-seat cars that rested in power niches along the room's circumference.

Turning to John, T'Lan had pointed toward the first car, the one over which the blue globe hovered. He'd stood there, waiting until the Terran had slid over the siderail into the seat.

Once T'Lan was in, the globe vanished. Without a sound, the car turned, rose and streaked from the room, moving at high speed down endless gray corridors.

Doorways, intersections and the occasional instrument panel had flashed by; then they'd shot up a long, spiraling ramp to the bridge. Slowing, stopping, the car had settled before the faint glow of a forcefield. Stepping from the vehicle, the two had followed another blue globe through a sudden opening in the field, across the broad sweep of the bridge's deck and up a series of ramps, halting at last before the single black console that occupied the highest tier. As T'Lan spoke, the blue globe vanished. "Commander T'Lan and John Harrison, from *Implacable*."

"We have a commwand for you, from Pocsym Six." Velvet soft and as cold as this ship, thought John of the voice. It spoke contemporary K'Ronarin and seemed to come from between him and T'Lan, rather than from the console.

"A message from the dead," said T'Lan. "Who are you?"

"We have no names, Commander," said the voice. "The centuries burned them away. We have only purpose."

"Do you know what's on the commwand?" asked T'Lan.

"Data relating to the Trel Cache," said the R'Actolian.

T'Lan held out his hand. "You may give it to me."

John glanced over the slender railing, gauging the distance to the deck: about two hundred feet. I'm going to save us some travel time back to the deck, thing, he thought, shifting his weight. The instant you get that commwand, over we go.

"Don't do anything quixotic, Harrison," said T'Lan in perfect English, his eyes still on the console, hand extended. "The commwand," he said in K'Ronarin.

"Pocsym," said the R'Actolian, ignoring the demand, "kept us supplied over the centuries. There were items we needed that we couldn't manufacture, but that Pocsym could. In return for these things, we pledged to remain in this quadrant, Blue Nine. Very recently, as we judge

59

time, Pocsym entrusted us with the commwand, asking that we give it to the first K'Ronarin Fleet ship to reach these precise coordinates.''

''We are here,'' said T'Lan.

John tensed himself, ready to jump.

''We're not giving you the commwand,'' said the R'Actolian.

''Why not?'' said T'Lan, dropping his hand.

John laughed—a short nervous laugh. ''They've tumbled to you, T'Lan.''

T'Lan half turned toward the Terran. ''Harrison . . .'' he hissed.

''You're not a true emissary of K'Ronar, Commander T'Lan,'' continued the R'Actolian. ''You're something out of Imperial prehistory, an AI combat droid—a survivor of that almost mythic war between man and machine.''

''It's no myth,'' said T'Lan. ''I was there.''

''You are here to intercept the commwand,'' said the R'Actolian. ''Why?''

''The Trel defeated us once. Legend says they left a weapon to be used against us.''

''You wish to destroy the commwand.''

T'Lan nodded. ''Logically, it must hold the location of the Cache. No location, no weapon. The Fleet of the One triumphs.''

The voice sighed, a legacy of lungs and bodies long cast off. ''We are both man and machine, T'Lan, and love neither. It isn't out of malice that we deny you what you want, but because we've given our pledge.''

''You cannot deny me,'' said the AI, walking around the console. ''The cybernetics of this vessel were taken from Quadrant Fleet inventory on D'Lin, after you wiped Governor R'Actol.'' He looked down at the instruments.

''How did you know that?''

''Your first- and second-level computers,'' said the AI, ignoring the question, ''the golden egg and its retinue of secondaries, were machines originally entrusted to the Governor of Blue Nine for safekeeping—machines salvaged from our defeated ships, centuries before. The designs were copied first, of course, and sent to K'Ronar. When reproduced later, in Fleet's own mindslavers, there was no trace of us in them. But here—" He reached out a finger, "Here is different."

"Touch the command console," said the soft voice, "and you die."

John watched with a sense of unreality as T'Lan began entering a command, fingers flying over the keyboard.

From high above, blasters shrilled, fierce red bolts tearing at the droid. John threw an arm across his eyes as T'Lan staggered away from the console, his body a blinding pillar of raw red-blue energies—energies that rippled over the AI, leaving him unharmed.

The blasters snapped off. John lowered his arm.

"You have a subcutaneous personal shield," said the R'Actolian as T'Lan, unfazed, returned to the keyboard.

"I'm a Class One Beta Infiltration-Combat unit," said the AI, typing. "My series is impervious to blaster and projectile fire. We can only be destroyed by large-load atomics."

Straightening, T'Lan reached up and removed his left ear. Peeling it open, he discarded the husks and inserted the silver wafer they'd guarded into a small slot in the console. "This ship is now a forward unit of the Fleet of the One," he said, pressing a final switch.

Alpha Prime said nothing.

"What've you done?" asked John, hearing his voice tremble.

T'Lan turned to him, smiling, a dark hole where his ear had been. "I've taken the R'Actolians off-line, Harrison. Their lesser functions are now run by ship's computer, which obeys the commander." He bowed. "Me."

"You're one of those ghastly robots we stopped on Terra Two," said John.

T'Lan shook his head. "Comparing me to a robot is like comparing yourself to an amoeba, Harrison. As for Terra

Two, our force there was small, cut off from its own dimension, and led by an inexperienced commander.''

"And now?" said John.

"Now I destroy *Implacable* and keep this quadrant free of other ships until our forces come through the breach. Then into K'Ronarin space, repaying old debts by wiping your treacherous, parasitic species from the galaxy.''

"Why this insane hatred?" said John, spreading his hands. "What did we—what did the K'Ronarins—ever do to engender such . . .''

"I have work to do, Harrison," said T'Lan. "You're a primitive from a backward world that got in the way. And I don't need you anymore." Seizing John by the tunic, he tossed him screaming over the railing, and turned for the commander's console. As he reached it, the high-pitched scream ended abruptly.

Leaving Pod 36, Zahava looked up and down the corridor; there was no sign of Colonel R'Gal. She hadn't seen the K'Ronarin since he'd entered 31, ten minutes before.

She walked back to 31 and stopped in front of it, frowning at the red downtime marker glowing over the airlock, indicating a maintenance problem. It hadn't been there when R'Gal went in.

Drawing her blaster, she opened the first door, stepped in, and waited an eternity as it closed behind her and the inner door slid open. There were no lights on in the pod. Being Zahava, she entered anyway. The door closed behind her, taking with it the light from the airlock.

Zahava moved to the right, back to the wall, feeling for the battletorch on her belt.

Something whipped by her face, sending her blaster clattering off into the dark. Before she could move, a searing pain pierced her head. Writhing, she tried to pry free of the cold pincers boring into her temples. It was futile. Waves of pain assailing her, Zahava slumped to the floor unconscious.

Hunched over her in the dark, the S'Cotar continued its

work, unconcerned by her shallow breathing and weakening pulse.

"No!" snapped K'Tran. "No expeditions into that dark beast, D'Trelna! We penetrate the shield, plant a charge, and leave."

"We need that commwand, K'Tran," said D'Trelna. "We're going for the bridge."

"Enemy disposition, strength and intent?" said the corsair scornfully. "Where is the bridge? How do we get there? What's to stop us? Unless you have a plan, D'Trelna, we'd better jump for it—now."

"No one's jumping anywhere," said D'Trelna. "And there is a plan." He turned to the slaver computer. "Egg."

"Thank you, Commodore," said the machine. A multicolored hologram of *Alpha Prime* appeared between Egg and D'Trelna's station, well within range of the comm pickup. "This is from the Imperial Archives, R'Actolian War section. Unless the R'Actolians have radically altered the design of *Alpha Prime*, there will be a concealed sally port here." A short, red shaft appeared and penetrated the hull, halfway down the ship's port side.

"Define 'sally port,' " said K'Tran. He sat slouched in his chair, fingers steepled in front of him, looking at the hologram.

"I've been in one on *T'Nil's Revenge*," said D'Trelna. "On that ship, it was a tunnel through the hull, used to counterassault boarders who'd gained the hull."

"Thank you, Commodore," said Egg. "It served the same purpose in *Alpha Prime*. Indeed, Archives records that a brigade of Imperial Marine Death Commandos, under the personal command of one Admiral K'Yal, penetrated that very sally portal on *Alpha Prime*."

"To what effect?" said K'Tran.

"K'Yal was my many-times-removed maternal grandparent," said L'Wrona. "His faction having lost a power struggle within FleetOps, a suicide mission was arranged for him and his personal brigade. They penetrated the shield, reached the hull—took enormous casualties doing it—entered the sally port, and were never heard from again.''

"Death Commandos, indeed," said K'Tran. He sat up. "How do we get through the shield?"

"Your ships must link shields," said Egg. "Interfaced with the computers of both attacking vessels, I will use a shield-shaping algorithm to mold the normal globular shield of each ship into a triangular-shaped shield. This shield will have both ships at its base, with its apex penetrating *Alpha Prime*'s sally port." As Egg spoke a green triangle materialized beside the image of the mindslaver. Two diminutive cruisers sat one above the other, just inside the base of the triangle. As everyone watched, the triangle and ships moved on the mindslaver. Penetrating the red haze marking *Alpha Prime*'s shield, the tip of the triangle touched the space-end of the red shaft.

"Note," continued Egg, "that this maneuver places the two fusion batteries that could bear on the sally port within range of our weapons—weapons that will still enjoy the protection of our shield. Once those cannon are neutralized, a two-shuttle sortie should be launched through the port. . . ."

"Why only two shuttles?" said A'Tir.

"The sally port's lined with disintegrator cubes," said D'Trelna. "I ran afoul of the ones on *T'Nil's Revenge*. Turns that tunnel into a disintegrator chamber. The most we'll get through are two shuttles, moving at flank."

"Disintegrator cubes," said A'Tir.

"A foolish question, Egg," said K'Tran. "Why shouldn't the slaver change position and avoid our attack?"

"They've defeated every force ever sent against them, Captain," said the machine. "They are arrogant. Perhaps you are familiar with the condition?"

Gods! thought D'Trelna. That thing's baiting K'Tran.

"How do we get to the bridge?" said K'Tran after a hard look at the Egg.

"I have provided directions," said the machine.

K'Tran shook his head. "Uh-huh. D'Trelna, I don't trust your unctuous egg. It goes with us, or we take our chances against you here and now."

L'Wrona reached for the commkey, ready to direct a missile and beam salvo at the corsair. D'Trelna stopped him, loudly clearing his throat. "Our friend Egg?" said the commodore. He turned to the slaver machine. "You don't mind, do you, Egg?"

"An honor, Commodore," said the machine.

"We get inside," said L'Wrona. "Then what?"

"Race for the bridge," said Egg. "The corridors should accommodate shuttles of the dimensions shown in *Implacable*'s equipment roster."

"Resistance?" asked A'Tir.

"Heavy from automatic weapons systems at key intersections," said Egg. "And fierce opposition from organic units."

"Organic units?" said D'Trelna, frowning at the featureless spheroid beside him. "What organic units?"

"I've been giving the matter some thought," said the machine. "The R'Actolians are biofabs. They've had a great deal of time to perfect defenses for that ship. I suggest, given the R'Actolians antecedents, that such defenses would be organic. Most probably very lethal biofabs, held in cryogenic suspension until now. Biofabs without the R'Actolians' genius, of course. Her creations would not replicate Governor R'Actol's fatal error."

"Sort of like our friends the S'Cotar," said D'Trelna.

"Your records show they were not your friends," said Egg. "And why they didn't wipe you out is a deep mystery."

"Let's get on with it," said K'Tran impatiently.

"Agreed," said D'Trelna, swiveling his chair back to the scan. "We'll run a passby over your ship, K'Tran, on an intercept course for *Alpha Prime*. As we penetrate your shield perimeter, jettison your camouflage and upshield on our shield frequency. We then attack, with Egg maneuvering both ships and running shield control. Once our combined shield overlaps the sally portal, and the instant those two batteries are wiped, we launch our shuttles, rendezvous and run the portal. Clear?''

"Clear," said K'Tran.

D'Trelna leaned forward. "I'm switching you to Commander K'Raoda, who you so unkindly tried to kill at our last meeting. He'll give you a preliminary tactical feed and assign you battlelink frequencies." He touched a commkey, sending *Victory Day*'s signal to the first officer's station. He turned to L'Wrona as the comm screen cleared. "I really hate—"

"—that slime," finished L'Wrona. "You're not alone. I could find a hundred volunteers for his volley party."

An alarm shrilled. "Unauthorized launch!" called T'Ral. "We have an unauthorized lifepod launch!"

"Recall it," ordered L'Wrona, moving to T'Ral's station.

"I have." The younger officer pointed to a telltale. Data was racing across the screen. "Negative response."

D'Trelna had come to stand on T'Ral's right, eyes on the telltale. "Making for jump point. Surprised the slaver hasn't picked it off."

The data slowed, then stopped.

"Jumped," said T'Ral. "But where?"

"No time for that now," said L'Wrona. "Why didn't you abort launch on computer warning?"

"There was no computer warning," said T'Ral, busy logging the incident.

Captain and commodore exchanged worried glances. "Get N'Trol on it," said D'Trelna. He walked with L'Wrona back toward their stations. "Mindslaver. Corsairs. That." He jerked his head toward Egg, still hovering by the flag officer's chair. "Now the computer," he said, turning for the door.

L'Wrona stared after him. "Where are you going, J'Quel? We're about to engage."

"Engage nothing till I'm back," he said as the doors opened. "I'll be in the facility."

66

7

THE DECK WHIRLING toward him, John grabbed a railing as it flashed by—only to have his grip wrenched loose by the force of his fall. Screaming, arms and legs flailing, he fell the final hundred feet to the deck—and vanished inches above the battlesteel.

Standing behind the railing, T'Lan watched Harrison's disappearance without expression. He stood there an instant longer, drawing the logical conclusion, then busied himself at the command station.

"Sure you want to do this?" asked N'Trol. He stood at the bridge engineering station, finger poised over the Execute button on his console.

"Shield frequencies matched," said L'Wrona, ignoring N'Trol. "Stand by for linkage."

The camouflaged bulk of *Victory Day* filled *Implacable*'s main screen. The cruiser was passing over the corsair, heading for the mindslaver.

"Ready for linkage," said A'Tir, her image in both N'Trol and L'Wrona's comm screens.

"Execute," said L'Wrona.

A'Tir and N'Trol both pressed a switch.

Implacable's sensors went blind for an instant as *Victory Day* flared bright as a sun. When sensors cleared, they showed the corsair, shorn of her camouflage, running close to *Implacable* as both ships charged the great, grim bulk of *Alpha Prime*.

"*Alpha* will fire now," said Egg. It hovered beside the

tactics console, tied to *Implacable*'s computer by a tendril of soft blue light.

Thick as a shuttle, dark blue fusion beams lashed at the cruisers—and were stopped by the strangely elongated shield projected by the two ships, a sharp-tipped golden cone racing toward the mindslaver.

"What kind of a shield is that?" asked D'Trelna. He stood beside Egg, staring at the main screen.

"One mutated and strengthened by a shield-shaping algorithm, Commodore," said Egg. "Note the characteristic yellow hue."

"And the slaver's shield?" asked D'Trelna.

"Breached by our own," said Egg. "We've effectively tunneled through it."

Now halfway to target, the shield was glowing, the portions around the beam points shading over into a sullen umber. Behind D'Trelna, alarms buzzed at engineering and command stations, warning of shield generators pushed beyond design.

"We're through!" called K'Raoda as the fire suddenly slackened. Following behind their shield, both ships had passed the point where all of *Alpha Prime*'s port batteries could bear on them. Only two of the slaver's main batteries were firing now.

"She should stand off and blast us," said D'Trelna, watching their shield fade back into yellow.

"Were *Alpha Prime* entirely rational, Commodore," said Egg, "we would be dead."

"Gunnery," called L'Wrona over the commnet, "we're inside her shield. Take out that starboard battery." He switched channels. "K'Tran, take out their port battery."

Victory Day and *Implacable* fired together, fierce red beams exploding into slaver's nearest fusion turrets, sparking twin towers of yellow-green flame that billowed outward, then were gone. Two scorched and jagged craters marked their passing.

"I have positioned the shield's apex directly over the

presumptive location of the sally port,'' said Egg. ''We should leave now.''

''You heard that, K'Tran?'' D'Trelna said into the commlink.

''On our way.'' The corsair's face appeared in the screen. ''Rendezvous in shield cone. See you on the slaver's bridge, D'Trelna—or in hell.'' K'Tran disappeared.

''Hell, probably,'' muttered D'Trelna, turning for the door. ''Let's go, Egg.''

The blue tendrils vanished as the slaver computer followed D'Trelna. As the two passed the captain's station, L'Wrona signed off on his log entry and stood. ''Commander K'Raoda, you have the conn,'' he said, falling in beside D'Trelna. ''Luck, T'Lei,'' he added.

''Luck to you too, H'Nar. Commodore,'' nodded K'Raoda, taking the captain's chair. He watched as the doors hissed shut behind the trio, then swiveled back to his console. ''Hold her here, Commander T'Ral,'' he ordered. ''And so advise our . . . allies.''

''Launch control,'' he said into the commnet, ''sortie party is on its way. Stand by shuttle.''

The bridge crew watched as, a few moments later, the screen showed two armed shuttles meet and proceed toward *Alpha Prime*.

''Slaver is jamming all communications to the shuttles,'' reported K'Lana.

''What about us and the corsair cruiser?''

The comm officer shrugged. ''Hasn't affected us yet.''

K'Raoda glanced at his instruments. The commlink to *Victory Day* showed green. ''Computer,'' he said, punching into the complink, ''monitor carrier frequencies to corsair cruiser—report any change in status.'' He turned back to the main screen, then frowned at the silence. ''Computer,'' he said, annoyed, ''acknowledge order.''

''It can't.''

K'Raoda turned. A worried looking N'Trol stood beside the captain's station.

''Explain,'' said K'Raoda, looking back at the screen.

The shuttles were now just two silver needles receding against the mindslaver's mass.

"Someone who knows Imperial computer theory better than anyone now living has dropped a stasis algorithm into the computer."

K'Raoda swiveled to face N'Trol, shuttles forgotten for a moment. "Impossible," he said, shaking his head. "That's a myth—a cybernetic wild tale from before the Fall. It must be some sort of system failure—maybe something latent, from when Fleet applied the overlay."

"Shuttles halfway to target and closing," reported T'Ral.

"Acknowledged," said K'Raoda.

"Fine," said N'Trol with exaggerated patience. "There's no such thing as a stasis algorithm. But something is moving through that machine." He jerked a thumb aft, in the general direction of the computer. "Something that's freezing its basic operating systems—suspending them for later reactivation."

"How do you know?"

"Because it's challenging incoming commands to affected sections in machine code I've never seen. Does that sound like a system failure to you, Commander?"

"No," admitted K'Raoda, shaking his head. "How long have we got?"

N'Trol shrugged. "Watchend, maybe. At current rate of deterioration."

"What do we need to stop this . . . stasis algorithm?" asked K'Raoda.

"The original algorithm," said N'Trol. "Or, faster, one that's antidotal. No one would create such a monster without having something to kill it. That would be stupid. And whoever or whatever did this is not stupid."

"Two candidates for culprit," said K'Raoda. He glanced at the scan. *Alpha Prime,* minus two main batteries, was still bathing their shield in fusion fire, ineffectively. The shield indicators were still in the green. "T'Lan and the slaver machine."

"That smooth-talking Egg has my vote," said N'Trol.

70

"Mine, too," said K'Raoda. "One of its little bag of algorithms is keeping us alive, while the other's destroying our computer—and maybe us."

"You've got to warn the commodore," said N'Trol.

K'Raoda turned to K'Lana. "Anything?"

"Not from the shuttles. Broad-band interference pattern from the slaver. However . . ."

"Yes?" said K'Raoda hopefully.

"Lifts seven and eighteen are locked in transit. Engineering's dispatched work parties."

"It's starting," said N'Trol. "I better get down there." He turned for the door.

"Use the ladders," K'Raoda called after him.

"In fact, K'Lana," he continued as N'Trol left, "make that an order. All personnel not transporting heavy loads, use central access."

The jowly face of Gunnery Chief B'Tul came onto one of K'Lana's screens. "Bridge. We're getting power feed anomalies to fusion batteries three through eight. Random surges and breaks. Engineering's on it."

"Food processors in mess four are pouring out green slop," said K'Lana as the chief's face disappeared.

"What is green slop?" asked K'Raoda, feeling the bottom fall out of his tight little world. The universe might be a mad, malevolent place, but *Implacable* had never failed them.

"You want to talk to him?" K'Lana tapped her earpiece.

K'Raoda held up a palm. "No. Give him to the engineering duty officer."

"I'll put him in queue," she said, turning back to her console.

"And keep trying to punch through to D'Trelna," added K'Raoda.

It was a good-sized room, square, windowless, its walls and floors of a black, marblelike substance. The long table in its center seemed more an outcropping of the floor than a separate construct—a fluted-stemmed outcropping that gleamed dully in the soft light, surrounded by seven alabaster-white armchairs.

John slouched in the one at the head of the table, facing the door. Gingerly he rubbed his throbbing right shoulder. Pain shot down his back and arm. Grimacing, he stopped rubbing. "That was cruel," he said to the S'Cotar.

"What, the way I saved your frail life, Harrison?" Guan-Sharick-as-blonde sat at the far end of the table, smirking. The smirk vanished. "T'Lan was watching you fall to your death. That close to the deck"—the transmute held two fingers barely apart—"and its flawlessly logical brain was just logging you out, Harrison—a faulty assumption that bought us perhaps a nanosecond."

John snorted. "A nanosecond, bug?"

Guan-Sharick leaned forward intently, hands folded. "T'Lan is an AI combat droid—an invincible legend out of prehistory." Those startling blue eyes met John's. "It would take a full stream from a Mark Eighty-eight to slow it, a multinuclear salvo to destroy it. It thinks faster and moves faster than anything of this time, and it is dedicated to the eradication of all free life—you, me, the K'Ronarins, this mindslaver, everything. It can decide, aim and fire in a tenth of a second. Its perfect logic is its only weakness."

"I don't believe you," said John.

"Fine," shrugged the S'Cotar, leaning back in the chair. "I'll send you back to the bridge command tier and drop you again. You make it as far as the first time, and I'll teleport your sweet self back here."

John held up a hand. "No. . . . You want to tell me how an AI combat droid infiltrated the Confederation and imitated one of its mogul's sons?"

"Doesn't look too good for us, does it?" said Guan-Sharick with a faint smile.

"Us?'"

"Harrison," sighed the transmute, "a S'Cotar's quite mild compared to what you face in T'Lan—and to what you face on this vessel."

"And what is that?" asked the Terran.

72

"Look behind you."

John turned and saw the wall screen. On *Implacable,* when a screen wasn't in use, it displayed the Fleet coat-of-arms. This screen, though, held something quite different than ship-shield-and-sun: a six-fingered hand clutching the double helix of a DNA molecule.

"Crazy," he said, turning back to the S'Cotar.

"Megalomania, in Freud's schemata," said Guan-Sharick. "Mad, certainly, but also brilliant. The R'Actolians are far better geneticists than the ones who created them, R'Actol and her group."

"You'd think they could have fixed themselves," said the Terran.

"Why?" shrugged the blonde. "They see nothing wrong with themselves. It's the rest of the galaxy they want to correct."

"And what is this charming room?" asked John, looking about.

"The Council Chamber of R'Actol." Swiveling the chair, the S'Cotar rose, pacing. "Here the Seven met to plot the extermination of mankind." Guan-Sharick touched the table. "From here they planned strategy against the Empire. And when they were beaten, their thousands of dreadnoughts destroyed, sitting right where you are now, Harrison, Z'Tul, their leader, proposed they seek the immortality of their own devices." The S'Cotar stopped pacing, turning to John. "Motion carried."

"At least they were defeated." John sat up, his shoulder now almost forgotten.

The S'Cotar shook its head. "To defeat the R'Actolian biofabs, the Empire had to build mindslavers. That, more than any other event, started the Empire slipping down the long, bloody road into the Long Night—the night the K'Ronarins are only now awakening from. And though the R'Actolians may have been defeated, they won't have really lost until the Seven are dead."

"And T'Lan is here to kill them?" asked John.

"T'Lan's here to appropriate the slaver and intercept

that commwand. It would prefer to keep the Seven alive—it's difficult to run the vessel without them—not impossible, but difficult. As long as the R'Actolians are powerless, T'Lan isn't concerned with them. They're compelled not only to do as he says but to cooperate in every way. Though if a chance to regain command occurs, they'll seize it.''

Guan-Sharick walked the length of the room, stopping at the chair to John's right. Hands gripping the chairback, the S'Cotar leaned forward intently. ''You and I must keep the Seven alive.''

John frowned. ''Until the commwand's secured?''

''That certainly,'' nodded the S'Cotar. ''But if the R'Actolians die, Harrison, we may all die. We need this dreadnought—and its secrets. It's the only ship in this universe that can stand against an AI battleglobe.''

Four hundred and nine light-years away, Lifepod 38 prepared to make planetfall.

8

K'RONAR HAD NO God. Ten thousand years of high technology had left the concept a desiccated anthropological husk.

Hell, though, thought D'Trelna, gripping his chairarms, hell is alive, well and dead ahead.

The commodore sat to Egg's right, with L'Wrona buckled into the navigator's station, just behind him. An endless expanse of battlesteel, weapons turrets and instrument pods filled the armorglass windscreen: *Alpha Prime*.

Must have raped ten worlds to get all that metal, thought

D'Trelna. He looked up to his right. The corsair shuttle was holding station next to them, its forward fuselage just visible.

"Why are none of the smaller batteries firing, Egg?" asked L'Wrona. He pointed in front, to the small circle of the mindslaver's hull now inside the subdued blue shimmer of the shield's apex. "Weapons scan shows several hundred small fusion cannon down there. We're not shielded—they should have wiped us the moment we came within range."

"There are no weapons batteries, Captain," said the slaver machine. It sat in the pilot's chair, safety harness buckled across it, light tendrils tying it into the shuttle controls.

L'Wrona tapped a telltale. "Tacscan clearly shows . . ."

"Scan-chimera," said Egg. "An instrument-sensitive hologram. Only the sally portal lies inside our shield point."

"But . . ." protested L'Wrona.

"Mark to penetration: twenty," said Egg, silencing the captain. "Captain K'Tran, please assume position directly behind us."

"Acknowledged," came the corsair's voice over the commnet.

"Mark fifteen," said Egg. The hull rushed up to meet them, looking very real and hard.

"Battlesteel is not a very forgiving surface, Egg," said D'Trelna, teeth gritted. Serial numbers were now visible on the hull instruments.

A continuous shrill warbling sounded—the shuttle's crash warning. Instinctively, D'Trelna grabbed the copilot's control stick and pulled. Nothing. Locked.

"What if the disintegrator cubes are already on?" shouted L'Wrona above the alarm.

"Then we are ended," said Egg as they knifed into the slaver's hull—and through it, shooting down a wide, brightly lit tunnel.

Egg fired the shuttle's turret cannon, sending a double

stream of red fusion bolts ahead of them. A brief tongue of orange-blue flame shot out, marking the portal's far end.

Large hexagonal cubes along walls and ceiling provided the tunnel's light. D'Trelna blanched as they began to oscillate, glowing brighter with each cycle. "Egg . . ." he called.

"Disintegration sequence has begun," confirmed the machine.

There was a loud *snap!* from behind. Something big, foiled of its prey, thought D'Trelna, punching up rear scan. A fierce white light glowed where they'd just been—a burning shaft that filled the tunnel's width, gaining on them with each *snap!* of ravening energy.

"Pathetically obsolete," sneered Egg. "It can only activate by sections."

"More speed!" called K'Tran urgently.

D'Trelna switched rear scan angle. The corsair shuttle was almost touching their own, with A'Tir and K'Tran clearly visible through their armorglass.

"No," said the slaver machine. "We must turn immediately after exiting. We cannot make the turn at speed— we'd crash into the bulkhead."

"You're not making it without us, D'Trelna," said the corsair. Watching the comm screen, D'Trelna saw K'Tran reach up and touch the weapons panel.

"Thought you were going to watch our rear, K'Tran," said the commodore. Thick fingers sent their blaster turret swinging 180 degrees. Through the remote gunnery interface, D'Trelna could see that flawlessly destructive shaft of white almost touching K'Tran's tail. The commodore tapped Arm where it showed red on his screen.

"Belay, both of you!" snapped L'Wrona. "We're through."

The shuttles shot through the blasted ruins of a great slab of battlesteel, then banked right, accelerating down a broad gray corridor. From behind them came a final *snap!* Light flared into the corridor behind them, then winked off.

D'Trelna leaned back in his chair, sighing. "Hell is alive and well, H'Nar," he said.

"Sorry?" blinked the captain, turning.

"Nothing," said D'Trelna, waving a hand. He glanced at the rear scan. "Ease off, K'Tran," he said. "You're almost up our tubes."

"My pleasure," said the corsair, putting three shuttle lengths between the two craft.

"And disarm those Mark forty-fours," added the commodore. The corsair's cannon pointed straight at the Fleet shuttle.

D'Trelna was too far away to see K'Tran grin. "Right," said the corsair.

"Where's your counterattack, Egg?" asked L'Wrona, staring down the seemingly endless stretch of corridor. Intersections and equipment banks flashed by.

"Before we reach the bridge, Captain," said Egg. It sent them spiraling up a ramp that would have accommodated ten or more shuttles flying abreast. "It will be swift and deadly."

K'Raoda stood, unfastening his survival jacket and tossing it over the back of the captain's chair. Others on the bridge were doing the same. "First we freeze," he muttered, "now we bake." He sat and punched into the commnet. "N'Trol. Life systems' status?"

K'Raoda waited impatiently, watching as the comm screen slipped from the ship-shield-and-sun into a distortion-flecked horizontal roll, then back to the Fleet emblem. Disgusted, he snapped off the commkey and stood again, sniffing the hot, dry air. "This is absurd," he said. He turned to T'Ral. "I'm going down to engineering."

The second officer shook his head. "I don't think so, T'Lei. Look." He pointed toward the doors. The two commandos on guard had the cover off the entrance control panel and were pushing the red override again and again. The thick armored doors didn't move.

The crash and clang of falling metal sent everyone

spinning around toward the deserted navigation console. The console's gray inspection panel lay on the floor. Multicolored light pulsed along the optics cables bunched beneath the instruments, a jungle of crystalline wire that parted beneath two hairy hands. The hands emerged, followed by gold-ringed brown sleeves and a familiar head. "Don't shoot," said N'Trol, looking up into a dozen M11As. "The way things are, you might trigger the jump drive. . . . You idiots going to help me out of here, or just stand there fondling your blasters?"

"Get him out of there," ordered K'Raoda. T'Ral and a commando grabbed the engineer, pulling him free.

Brushing himself off, N'Trol came over to the captain's station, the bridge crew following. Most of their instruments were now useless, all the screens blank.

"You climbed the light conduits from engineering," guessed K'Raoda.

N'Trol nodded. "Central core's locked tight. Eight decks up, then a third the length of the ship." He slumped into the empty XO's chair and dialed for t'ata. A cold cup of brackish-looking liquid appeared. Warily, N'Trol sipped, shuddered and crammed the cup into a disposer.

"At best," continued the engineer, "you walk stooped over, or pick your way up ladder rungs, wondering if they're going to give—some of them are half out of their sockets. There's a warm, dry breeze blowing, and the only illumination comes from the light pulses." He seemed strangely subdued, much of his old arrogance gone for now.

If only D'Trelna could see this, thought K'Raoda—he'd send N'Trol through there every watch. "I doubt anyone's been down there since the Fall," said K'Raoda. "Imperial boots last walked those conduits. Fleet just pulled this ship out of stasis, did some minor modifications and sent her off to fight the S'Cotar."

"Anything from the commodore?" asked N'Trol, looking at the circle of faces. Several shook their heads.

"We can't even get off the bridge," said K'Raoda,

nodding toward the doors. "Never mind contacting the shuttles."

"I came to tell you," said N'Trol after glancing at the doors, "life systems . . ."

"We know they're gone," said T'Ral.

N'Trol shook his head. "Worse than gone. Transformed. The stasis algorithm freezes key systems, then reprograms them. Life systems was the first to fall. Its new mission is evidently to kill us."

There was a stunned silence. "How?" asked K'Raoda.

"Wilder and wilder peaks and valleys in our environment," said the engineer. "I had a report of a blizzard on hangar deck, just before we lost the commnet."

"So did we," said K'Lana.

"If the computer's serious, why doesn't it just turn the oxygen scrubbers off?" asked T'Ral. "We'd be dead by watchend."

"Or hit us with some hard vacuum?" said K'Raoda. "Or power surges, or any number of deadly tricks the computer could use?"

"The Empire, my children," said N'Trol, eyes sweeping their worried faces. "No proof, but I think those long-dead Fleet engineers hardened their cybernetics against nonexistent stasis algorithms." He glanced at K'Raoda. The first officer bowed slightly. "But"—N'Trol held up a finger—"the computer can't hold out forever. It's just fighting a rearguard action. It's going after propulsion and jump drive now."

"Weapons?" asked T'Ral.

"Weapons power feed back up firmed—the fluctuations were probably a secondary effect of its tinkering with life systems. But you'll have to man the batteries—remote targeting's useless."

"And we're helpless without the original algorithm?" said K'Raoda.

"Or its antidote," nodded the engineer. "Which I think is with that slaver machine."

"I won't argue with you," sighed K'Raoda. "Let's hope the commodore brings it back intact."

"Or it the commodore," said N'Trol.

A faint clanking came from across the bridge. Everyone turned to look. Sweating, cursing softly, the two commandos were cranking open the doors, using a hand winch installed centuries before by a meticulous Imperial Fleet.

"There's something you should see," said N'Trol as the doors grew wider. "Back where I was, in the light conduits."

"I can't leave the bridge!" said K'Raoda.

N'Trol laughed. "The bridge is dead, K'Raoda." He leaned close. "It's important."

"All right," said K'Raoda after a moment. He stood. "Attention, please." Those who'd started to drift away returned. "I'm going with Mr. N'Trol down into the light conduits. Commander T'Ral will be in command." He turned to his friend. "Secure the bridge and relocate to gunnery control. Break out a tactical commweb—the sort we'd use for ground operations. . . ."

"An I'Zul Tactical Web," said T'Ral.

"That's it," said K'Raoda. "Put the nexus in gunnery control and a unit in every fusion battery facing *Alpha Prime*. Then man those batteries with everyone who's Mark eighty-eight qualified. At least we can give the commodore some cover fire if he needs it."

T'Ral nodded curtly. "Yes, sir." He began issuing orders as N'Trol and K'Raoda left the bridge.

"What's so damned secret, N'Trol?" asked K'Raoda as they hurried down an empty stretch of corridor.

"I didn't think you want the rest of them knowing there's a transmute running around on board," said N'Trol as they passed an open recroom door. A steady stream of chill air flowed into the corridor. "I see you're not startled," said the engineer.

"You haven't heard," said K'Raoda, and quickly sketched the incident of R'Gal, the transmute and the blasted command chair. He finished as they stopped before a wall panel. "So, what did you find?" he added.

"I had this engineering tech foisted on me, off Terra," said N'Trol, entering the access code on a touchpad. "Knew his stuff, kept to himself." The panel didn't open. N'Trol shrugged. "Stasis algorithm must have reached the security protocols." Unclipping a light wand from his shirt pocket, N'Trol held it over the tiny optics transceiver to the left of the touchpad. Picking up the downtime signal from transceiver, the wand sent an override code flashing into the panel. There was a soft click.

"Give me a hand here," said N'Trol, pocketing the wand.

The two men each seized one of the two handles and pulled to the right. The panel yielded slowly, sliding right.

"Anyway," said the engineer, "I went into this tech's quarters unannounced during his sleep period—a question about something he'd done but hadn't logged.

"This tech came up with a knife all set to cut my heart out. Never saw anyone in engineering move that fast." They had the panel opened now. Light glimmered in the distance.

"So you pegged R'Gal as CIC or maybe Fleet Security," said K'Raoda, following the older man into the crawl space. "So what?"

"So imagine how I felt, finding him lying in the conduit, more dead than alive."

"More dead than alive is right," said K'Raoda, kneeling over the Watcher. R'Gal lay in the center of a small four-way intersection, hands crossed over his chest, the red-green light of a billion messages washing over him. There were two neat holes in each of his temples.

"S'Cotar transmute," said K'Raoda, rising. "Weird. Why didn't it steal his mind, kill him and flick him out into space?"

N'Trol shrugged. "I'm not a PsychOps analyst."

"Let's get him to Sick Bay."

The conduit was just wide enough for one man, walking stooped over. Taking R'Gal's legs, N'Trol led, K'Raoda taking the arms, the Watcher slung between them as they moved slowly back through a narrow world of light and silence.

"This is the bridge level, Egg," said D'Trelna. "Where's the fierce opposition you promised us?" Glancing in the rear scan, he saw the corsair shuttle was maintaining speed and interval.

"This ship's had to awaken and gather its strength, Commodore," said the machine. "Soon. And should we survive, the way back won't be easy."

"D'Trelna," came K'Tran's voice, "we've passed enough hidden fusion batteries to stop a cruiser. Why haven't they fired?"

D'Trelna looked at Egg. The slaver machine didn't speak. "Perhaps we're wanted alive," said the commodore, watching the intersections warily. "This monster's strength isn't so much its size, K'Tran, as the power and maneuverability it draws from the human minds it's enslaved."

"You think they want to harvest us?" said A'Tir, a slight tremor to her voice.

"Count on it," said D'Trelna.

"I'd rather die," she said.

"You'll have the chance," said L'Wrona.

Suddenly the control panel and cabin lights winked off, as did the corridor lights. With a whine of dying n-gravs, the shuttle plunged toward the deck.

"Brakes!" shouted L'Wrona, throwing his arms across his face as they slammed into the deck.

"Negative!" cried D'Trelna, pulling back on the useless control stick.

Metal screaming, sparks flying, the shuttle spun down the corridor, angling toward the left wall.

Egg's tendrils snapped back out, touching the controls.

Part of the instrument panel came alive again as the shuttle rose for an instant, then settled jerkily on its landing struts.

"My energy reserves are exhausted," whispered the slaver machine. Its light tendrils disappeared. With them went the brief burst of power that had saved the shuttle.

"Damper field," said D'Trelna weakly. Wiping his sweaty palms on his pants, he unbuckled and stood, peering into the utter darkness of the corridor. "What happened to K'Tran?"

"Alternate course plotted and set," said A'Tir, looking up from the shuttle's complink.

"Time to lose Fats and friends," said K'Tran, glancing at the course plot. "Next main intersection."

The damper field hit just as they turned. Their shuttle's systems failed for an instant, touched by the field's edge, then came back on as they moved down the side corridor.

"Now that's timing," grinned K'Tran.

"Think they've had it?" asked A'Tir.

K'Tran shrugged, eyes on the corridor. "Two very capable officers, D'Trelna and L'Wrona. And backed by ten of their best commandos. Don't count them out, Number One. But with luck, they and the R'Actolians will occupy each other till it's too late."

"Anyone hurt?" asked L'Wrona. He stood beside D'Trelna in the shuttle's passenger section.

"No," said S'Til. The commandos were out of their seats, taking the battlelamps S'Til was distributing from the aft storage area. The dim glow of six battery-powered lights provided a faint light. "Damper field?" she asked, handing each of the two senior officers a lamp.

"Probably," said D'Trelna, clipping the lamp to his belt.

Drawing her M11A, S'Til set the beam low, pointed the muzzle at the roof and pulled the trigger. There was a faint click. "Damper field," she nodded. "Defense perimeter?" she asked L'Wrona.

The captain nodded. "Knives against whatever's out

there. If we have to, we'll take that bridge on foot, bare-handed.''

And club whatever to death with our boots, thought D'Trelna. "Surely not bare-handed," he said.

The arms locker was set into the bulkhead to the right of the airlock. Going to it, D'Trelna entered the combination on its keypad. Nothing happened. "Get that open," he ordered S'Til, jerking a thumb at the locker.

It only took her a moment, deftly jiggling her blade between locker panel and lock. The door gave with a snap. S'Til slid the door back, then stepped back with a delighted cry. Behind her, a commando whistled appreciatively as lamp beams washed across the arms racks.

"Your commodore provides," said D'Trelna, sweeping his own light over the rows of stacked M16's and Uzis. "You do know how to use them?" he asked S'Til.

"We didn't waste our time on Terra," she said, passing out the weapons. "Plenty of ammunition," she added, nodding at the crates stacked beneath the racks.

"Indeed," said D'Trelna. Glancing at the boxes, he fleetingly wondered what 5.56MM NATO meant.

"You sly swamp d'astig, D'Trelna," said L'Wrona, handing the commodore an Uzi. "How'd you know?"

"I didn't," said D'Trelna. "Contingency planning."

"Keep your M11A's," ordered S'Til. Chambering a round, she clicked off her M16's safety. "And follow me," she said, pressing the airlock override. As the double doors hissed open, S'Til leaped out into the darkness of the mindslaver.

Egg had landed them at the intersection of four main corridors, a space half the size of a sports field. The area looked even wider than it was, there in the light from the battle torches.

Walking in a slow circle around the shuttle, D'Trelna looked down each of the great passageways, straining to see beyond the cone of yellow light. L'Wrona walked silently beside him, machine pistol at the ready.

84

"Do you know the tale of the four corners of hell, H'Nar?" asked the commodore as they walked around the front of the shuttle.

D'Trelna was surprised to see the captain smile. "One of my father's favorites. The merchant prince A'Lan rescues some tedious woman . . .''

"T'Sar . . ."

"Rescues T'Sar from the demon P'Kul, in the very heart of hell. Pursued, A'Lan and T'Sar lose their way and come to the four corners of hell. P'Kul and his pack are at their heels. Before them, three dark, uncertain roads. Two, they know, lead back to hell. The third, to life, but only for the living.''

"And A'Lan chooses the one least traveled on," said D'Trelna, "and of course they emerge into the land of life. A parable on the road-least-traveled.''

The captain looked at the two corridors to his right and left. "Not many footprints in the battlesteel, J'Quel.''

"We'll take the road least traveled, H'Nar," said D'Trelna as they rejoined S'Til beside the airlock. "We will advance on foot to the bridge.''

"And where is the bridge?" asked L'Wrona.

D'Trelna waved vaguely toward the bridge corridor. "Up there, somewhere. Egg said it wasn't far. I want Harrison alive and that commwand in my hand when we leave.''

"As the commodore orders," said L'Wrona. He turned to S'Til, who stood frowning, her head cocked. "We'll proceed on foot from here, Lieutenant. Have—''

She stopped him with upraised hand. "Listen," she whispered.

They listened, not hearing it at first. "Feet," said L'Wrona after a moment. "There," he nodded at the corridor they were about to use.

"Many feet," said D'Trelna, cocking his head. "Moving quickly, but not in time.''

"You assume they're feet," said L'Wrona.

85

"Not coming for t'ata, certainly," said D'Trelna, unslinging his Uzi.

"Deploy!" ordered L'Wrona. "S'Til," he said as the commandos took up position around the shuttle, "get a hover-flare up."

Ducking into the shuttle, the commando officer came back with a short-barreled weapon. Scrambling up the access ladder to the roof, she dropped into the prone firing position, aimed carefully down the corridor and squeezed the trigger.

Whirring faintly, something floated away from the shuttle. A hundred meters out, it flared to life, lighting the corridor bright as a desert noon—the corridor and the gray-uniformed shapes charging down it, bayonet-fixed rifles held high.

"Gods of my fathers," whispered D'Trelna, staring.

"Imperial Marines," said L'Wrona, equally stunned.

Their surprise stolen, the attackers broke into screams—high-pitched, heart-stopping, utterly inhuman screams.

"Once, maybe," shouted D'Trelna as the assault closed. "Part of *Alpha Prime* now."

"Fire!" cried L'Wrona.

9

"THERE'S NO REASON I should trust you," said John.

"My timely warning," said the blonde, hand to heart, "saved this galaxy from the AIs, when they'd infiltrated Terra Two."

"After you and your green slime horde wiped out millions of people, trying to take the galaxy for yourselves!" John felt his face flush.

The S'Cotar chuckled, leaning back in its chair. "I like you, Harrison. You're one of life's innocents—defend the good, defy the wrong. You have the gift of unambiguous perception."

"There's no reason I should trust you," repeated John.

Guan-Sharick shrugged. "I'll level, as you like to say." The blonde held out a palm. "Your life is here, Harrison. Help me, or . . ." The hand became a fist.

"You'd kill me, after going to so much trouble to save me?"

"No," said the S'Cotar. "I'd leave you here, alone. You'd be tracked down and brainstripped within the hour." A long elegant finger circled the cranium. "Plop! Into the pod with the brain, and into component reserve with the body."

"Component reserve?" said John uneasily.

"Resource management," said the S'Cotar. "Brain power runs the ship, brainstripped bodies defend it. But with a twist: The original minds still control their original bodies, when those components are activated."

"Grotesque."

"But efficient," said Guan-Sharick. "Who could operate a body better than its original occupant? Besides, it provides superb catharsis for the mindslaves—a brief end to the sensory deprivation that drives so many of them mad, yet gives the ship its unique capabilities. A chance to breathe, walk, eat, smell, fornicate, kill—humanity's raison d'être."

"Big Brother monitors all of this?"

"Of course," nodded the S'Cotar. "But the R'Actolians only provide mission direction. They won't interfere so long as the components don't damage the ship, eat what they kill and generally clean up after themselves. Then it's back to the cryonics tank till the next frolic."

John cleared his throat. "How can I help you?"

Standing, the S'Cotar drew its side arm and extended it to John, butt first. "Help all of us. Get rid of T'Lan."

The Terran's hand halted halfway to the weapon. "With a pistol? Does it fire nuclear warheads?"

"Take it," said Guan-Sharick, wrapping the man's fingers around the grips.

Dubiously John examined the weapon, turning it in his hands. It was smaller than the K'Ronarin blasters, perfectly balanced and cast of some gleaming silver alloy. There was a small triangular device set high in the left grip: silver spaceship, golden sun, and three perfect blue eyes in each corner. A small golden "2" was etched above the sun.

"That's the symbol of the AIs," said the Terran, holding the weapon close. "The Fleet of the One." As he peered at the device, the three eyes seemed to catch the light, reflecting it back in a brief burst of white. John almost dropped the weapon, blinking, his eyes tearing. "What the hell . . ."

"A thing of power," said the S'Cotar. "Now it knows you."

"Knows me?"

Guan-Sharick sighed. "I don't have time to tell you, Harrison. You probably wouldn't believe me anyway. That weapon's a totem, sort of, part of the long and intricate chain of causality between organic and inorganic life."

"And the symbol?" said John, carefully touching the triangle. It was warm. "You're giving me an AI weapon to kill an AI?"

The blonde head shook. "No. The weapon and the symbol predate the Fleet of the One. The AIs have adopted the symbol. And you're not killing T'Lan—you're doing something worse to him."

"Why not do it yourself?" asked John, more confused than enlightened.

"I can't," said Guan-Sharick. "There's something about T'Lan's shield that distorts my senses, my abilities—you're the only one who can get close enough. Remember, weakness can be a strength—T'Lan's dismissed you as a threat."

"Bull," said John, tucking the weapon into his belt. "How do I get there?"

"I'll flick you down, just outside the bridge, away from the command tier. Beware—an AI doesn't need a weapon—it fires through its eyes."

"Great."

The S'Cotar vanished, reappearing a very long moment later. "D'Trelna's come in after you," it said quickly. "He's under attack. I'll do what I can for them. Listen carefully. The commwand will be in or on the command console—it's a small, white cylinder. Shoot T'Lan and get the commwand to *Implacable*."

"And nothing else matters? What about D'Trelna and his group?"

"Much else matters," said the blonde. "But not to you, not now."

"But D'Trelna . . ."

"Harrison, there's no time for this! Without the commwand, there's no Trel Cache. No Trel Cache, no weapon. No weapon, the AIs win and we become just two more failed species. Death is forever. Luck to you."

The Council Chamber was empty.

"Die," hissed D'Trelna, teeth gritted. "Die! Die!" He stood between L'Wrona and S'Til, punctuating each word with a burst from his Uzi.

The ping and whine of ricochets mingled with the sound of boots thundering down the deck and the chatter of automatic weapons' fire. The pungent odor of cordite filled the air. To D'Trelna, it smelled like fear.

"*Kee-yaaaaa!*" The scream of the bayonet assault rang down the corridor as the components closed, oblivious to the gunfire ripping into their charge, leaping their undead as they closed on the K'Ronarins.

Cursing, palms slippery with sweat, D'Trelna fumbled another magazine into the Uzi, looking up just as the surviving components crashed into the K'Ronarin line. He had a brief impression of close-cropped hair, Imperial

89

collar badges and hate-contorted faces. Then he was side-stepping, dodging a bayonet thrust at his heart. Moving, the commodore fired, putting a burst into what looked like a corporal.

The component dropped, its heart shredded. Even before its body crumpled, all animation had fled, leaving that strong, blunt face a slack-jawed, empty husk, the mind fleeing the pain to the armored safety of its distant brainpod.

D'Trelna didn't notice, whirling at the warning, "J'Quel! Left!"

An NCO was almost on top of him, smiling maniacally as he swung a rifle butt at the commodore's head. Side-stepping, D'Trelna fired one-handed. The burst went high, punching through the eyes, exploding the empty skull with a dull *plop!* Horrified, he watched open-mouthed as the component, blinded but still grinning madly beneath ruined eyes and forehead, nimbly reversed its rifle and began thrusting blindly in an arc from its last position.

Perfect teeth, thought D'Trelna wildly, putting a burst into the sergeant-thing's chest, tumbling it to the deck.

"Pretty good, Commodore, for a command officer."

Breathing hard, D'Trelna turned to see all the components dispatched and S'Til kneeling, cleaning her knife on the uniformed haunch of one of her attackers. "Did you ever pull ground combat?" she asked, rising and slipping the blade back into her boot sheath.

"Not in the service of Fleet and Republic, my child," said D'Trelna.

"Casualties?" he asked L'Wrona. The captain was handing over his empties for reloading.

"None," he said, taking a fresh magazine from a private and snapping it into his machine pistol. "Only about twelve of them reached our position."

"Gods of my fathers." The commodore slumped against the shuttle, closing his eyes. "What are they?"

"Were they," corrected L'Wrona, peering at the shrinking portion of corridor still lit by the dying hover-flare. Gray-uniformed bodies heaped its length. "Imperial Marines, brainstripped millennia ago, bodies preserved for later use.''

D'Trelna opened his eyes. ''Individually controlled, but from some distance,'' he said, glancing toward the NCO he'd stopped. ''That's your ancestor's command, isn't it, H'Nar?''

''That's the logical conclusion,'' said the captain uneasily. ''Uniforms, weapons, insignia—all from that period. If so, they'll be back—an Imperial Marine brigade numbered four to five thousand troopers. Assuming even half of them survived their attack on this ship, then this''—his hand swept the carnage—''was just a reconnaissance in force—about one company.'' Eyes narrowing, he peered down the corridor to their left, from where the attack had come, then down the corridor to their front. Following his gaze, D'Trelna saw shadows flitting along the flare's shrinking periphery—shadows creeping in behind the dying light.

''S'Til,'' he called, ''they're massing in the front and left corridors.''

''Rear and left corridors, too,'' came the lieutenant's voice from the other side of the shuttle. ''General assault this time. And we're out of flares.''

''Should she be shouting that?'' asked the commodore.

''Plenty of flares left, J'Quel,'' said L'Wrona softly. ''Deploy!'' he called. ''Three to each corridor.''

''We can stop thousands of those things?'' said D'Trelna as commandos hurried from the shuttle, olive-drab ammunition boxes slung between them. ''With twelve antiques?''

''No, of course not,'' said L'Wrona. ''But they'll come in faster if they think we're out of flares. That way, we kill more of them.''

The long and brutal war, the endless, often meaningless combat, the destruction of his home world—all had slowly eroded the captain's perspective. Recently the commodore found he could almost always rely on L'Wrona's striving to maximize enemy casualties, whether in the interests of the mission or not. D'Trelna sought to remind him of that now.

91

"I doubt we're really killing them, H'Nar. Life left those bodies before they were dead—like a soulwraith fleeing the dawn." He jabbed a finger at the captain. "Our mission is the commwand. We need to take the bridge, not die stupidly—or worse." He had a sudden vision of himself, L'Wrona and the commandos, shrieking wildly, joining the marines in a wild assault on some future intruders, twelve more brainstrips added to *Alpha Prime*'s defenses.

S'Til appeared, holding two bayonet-fixed M16's, a third slung over her shoulder. She gave one each to commodore and captain. "For the cut and slice work," she said.

Slinging the Uzi over his back, D'Trelna wished he'd awaken in *Implacable*'s big, soft flag chair, a warm cup of t'ata in hand instead of the heavy slug thrower.

"Get those flares up," said L'Wrona. A fading twilight circled them, with visibility down to about a hundred meters.

Nodding, the commando lieutenant raised the stubby flare gun and fired four quick rounds, sending new flares streaking to join the old ones. The K'Ronarins shielded their eyes as the harsh light returned, pushing the darkness back another hundred meters.

The gray host waited silently, bayonets gleaming in the new light, their ranks disappearing back into the darkness.

They watched each other for a moment, contemporary and ancient K'Ronarins, staring across millennia of blood and torment. Then the order was issued. Four horns sounded: two high, ringing notes, repeating twice, holding the last note for a moment.

Now, thought L'Wrona as the last note faded. "Fire!" he cried as the gray waves surged forward with a roar.

"Problems?" asked T'Lan, mockingly polite, watching the components falling beneath a hail of gunfire. "I thought you were going to turn the damper field off after your first debacle."

"Interference again," said the dry whisper. "Somehow

the secondary transponders are being suppressed. But not by conventional means."

"Show me the suppression aura," he said. It came up on a telltale, a rotating blue-red matrix blocking all commands to the damper field nodules. "S'Cotar," announced the AI. "It snatched the Terran away, now it's helping the K'Ronarins."

"But why, T'Lan? They're enemies."

"I don't know," said the AI. It culled through millennia of memories—wars and battles, plots and intrigues, random data—nowhere was there a hint of why an alien species, defeated, virtually exterminated, would suddenly help its enemies against a foe. It bothered T'Lan. "I don't know," he repeated. "Give me a skipcomm channel to S'Hlu."

Futile, thought D'Trelna. He emptied his M16 in five long bursts and slammed in another magazine. Much too close, five components fell. Others took their place. The intersection rang to the sound of the bayonet cry. Futile and stupid to die like this, thought the commodore.

D'Trelna, said a cold whisper inside his head. *Do exactly as I say, now, and some of you may live.*

"J'Quel!" shouted L'Wrona above the screaming and the gunfire. The commodore was disappearing into the shuttle, the door cranking shut behind him.

"Captain!"

L'Wrona turned back to the assault. He and S'Til stood alone against a thousand shrieking demons. "Run!" he cried.

They made their final stand at the shuttle, back to back against the forward port landing strut, weapons at assault arms.

Silently, the components surrounded the shuttle, a watchful gray wall of blank faces. It was as if they'd expended the small allotment of emotion spared them by the R'Actolians and now stood awaiting recall.

The four corners of hell, indeed, thought L'Wrona,

hands slippery with sweat. If the dead could walk, that's how they'd look. Soulwraiths, like J'Quel said. And what did D'Trelna think he was doing in there? Not like him to run.

"Captain," whispered S'Til, "they don't take us. Agreed?"

"Agreed," whispered L'Wrona. "Ammunition?"

"Three rounds, no more."

"I'm empty," he said. "Make sure you destroy our brains."

"And the commodore?"

Before L'Wrona could answer, the gray wall parted. A man strode into the circle—a strongly-built man with aquiline features and the gold comets of an Imperial admiral. He stopped at the point of L'Wrona's bayonet. "You've damaged us, Captain," he said. It was a cold, cultured voice, speaking High K'Ronarin with the accent of the Court—an accent the centuries had relegated to history tapes. "Many of us will never again experience their own bodies. My word to you, Captain—your brainpods will be part of the injured group. You'll suffer the wrath of those you've deprived and serve this ship forever."

As the component spoke, L'Wrona's gaze shifted from the green eyes to the faint scar that circled the cranium, a scar almost invisible in the dying light of the flares. "We are blood, Admiral K'Yal, you and I," said L'Wrona softly, in U'Trian. "By Tower and Oath, kinsman, I—"

"Tower and Oath, is it?" smiled the component in the same dialect. The smile vanished. "Your ancestor died long ago, my lord Captain—moments after entering *Alpha Prime*. His consciousness is now part of a greater cause than any he served while whole. And as for you, sir—you're meat. Just as are any who see this slaver. Meat for harvesting.

"You'll find, Captain," he said in a softer tone, "that the old verities slowly fade here, carried away by the long wash of the centuries. Others more enduring will replace them." He turned to the waiting circle. "Take them to processing."

"Good-bye, Captain," said S'Til as she pivoted, raising the rifle.

The lights came on, bringing with them the faint whine of the shuttle's cannon tracking down, locking on the massed components.

S'Til and L'Wrona dived under the craft as the Mark 44's opened fire, red fusion bolts burning into the gray ranks.

Prone, captain and commando fired their blasters at the husk of Admiral K'Yal. The component fell to the deck, its back and chest blown open.

Blaster shrilling and the explosion of fusion bolts mingled with the screams of the components as the turret went into rapid fire, ringing the craft with charred heaps of fused human flesh.

The three K'Ronarins were suddenly deprived of targets as the remaining components collapsed, untouched by blaster fire.

After a moment, L'Wrona and S'Til crawled out from cover as D'Trelna emerged from the airlock, a big M32 blast rifle in his hands.

"That last lot may not be dead," said the commodore, pointing at the unmarked bodies, "but I don't think they'll be bothering us—there aren't enough of them."

The air was redolent with burning flesh, a sweet, cloying smell that threatened the stomach.

"Why did they fall?" asked L'Wrona, holstering his blaster.

"To avoid further trauma to the collective consciousness of *Alpha Prime*," said a new voice.

Guan-Sharick-as-blonde stood by the airlock, hands tucked into its pockets, smiling at the two leveled blasters.

"Butcher!" hissed L'Wrona, drawing his side arm.

"Hold!" ordered D'Trelna, interposing his bulk between L'Wrona and the S'Cotar. "You know the rules, H'Nar—no bug squashing till we hear it out." He turned to the S'Cotar. "That was your doing—the damper field, I mean."

The blonde nodded. "Between us, we've given the R'Actolians their worst day in centuries. And the day's still new."

"I never did thank you for that Terra Two warning," said the commodore.

"Enlightened self-interest," said the S'Cotar. "Do I get the Valor Medal?"

"You get a chance to speak a few convincing sentences before I let L'Wrona loose," said D'Trelna. "You do remember virtually exterminating his world, a few years ago?"

The blonde shrugged. "It was in the way."

"That's one sentence," said L'Wrona. His face was quite pale.

The S'Cotar ignored him, looking at D'Trelna. "Harrison's at the bridge, going up against T'Lan. The commwand is there, too. I've done all I can to make it an even contest."

"What is T'Lan?" asked the commodore.

"An AI combat droid."

"Gods," said D'Trelna. "And K'Tran?"

"Heading for the bridge," said the S'Cotar. "I think, Commodore, K'Tran's reach is finally going to exceed his grasp."

"Anything else?"

"To quote K'Tran, Commodore," smiled the S'Cotar, " 'See you in hell.' This"—a hand gestured toward the dead—"is only its outer circle."

Guan-Sharick was gone.

"Someday I'll kill that thing, J'Quel," said L'Wrona softly. "I swear."

"Yes," said the commodore, nodding slowly, "I believe you will, H'Nar. But I don't think you'll be very proud of it."

"I trust I missed a good fight?" said a cheery voice. It was Egg, floating out through the airlock.

"You did," said D'Trelna. "Now get back in there and get us to the bridge." He looked around. "Are we the only survivors, S'Til?"

"They got the rest—alive," said the lieutenant. "They're meat by now."

She wanted to care—but had long ago convinced herself she couldn't afford to. The mission, and the logic necessary to complete it, were all that could be allowed to matter. Ten years of war and a hundred dead friends had taught S'Til just how precious a luxury grief was. It frightened her that even alone in her quarters, the tears never came.

"Meat," said D'Trelna. He thought of flashing surgical lasers, terror and unbearable agony, screams quickly stilled. And darkness forever.

Silently, the three followed Egg into the shuttle. The airlock closed. A moment later the shuttle rose over the wall of corpses and was gone.

After a while, fresh components came, salvaging what they could.

10

T'LAN WATCHED THE K'Ronarian shuttle soar off down the corridor. "They'll be here soon," he said. "Do I have to destroy them," he added acidly, "or can the Seven perform that minor task?" T'Lan didn't feel emotion, but he knew its uses.

"The Seven will destroy them, Forward Commander of the One," said the dry voice.

"Is the equipment ready?"

The screen pickup changed to a wide scan of *Alpha*

Prime's hangar deck, now brilliantly lit, bustling with gray-uniformed components busily stacking white duraplast crates on steel-ribbed shipping pallets. Two of the bodies had been Confederation commandos. "It will be loaded and started to your ships off D'Lin within the watch."

"Very well," said the AI. "Our main force isn't at D'Lin yet." He flicked off the screen. "But auxiliary vessels are now at rendezvous point, harvesting—I've relayed the installation instructions to S'Hlu and D'Lin. With the equipment, we'll be ready for conversion when the vanguard comes through the portal."

"Shit," said John, looking up at the shimmering blue of the forcefield. It filled the great flaring archway from point to floor. The bridge lay just the other side of it, now an impossible distance away.

"We seem to have the same problem," said a voice in K'Ronarin.

John whirled, reaching for his weapon. Two leveled blasters stopped him. "Who the hell are you?" he said to the two K'Ronarins.

"Give your weapon to the lady, Harrison," said the man. "I'm Captain K'Tran," he said as the woman tucked Guan-Sharick's pistol into her gunbelt. "This is my first officer, Commander A'Tir."

"You're the renegade butchers D'Trelna tangled with off Terra."

"We prefer to think of ourselves as independent subcontractors," said K'Tran.

"You murdered what? five, six hundred people on that ship you stole? And you fought for the S'Cotar during the war, after which you continued to raid your own people. D'Trelna would call you v'org slime—an understatement." The Terran shook his head. "Well, they said you were audacious. Half the fleet must be looking for you."

The corsair laughed. "No more than a quarter of the fleet, surely. And they certainly won't be searching this quadrant. As for the commodore, he's a fine officer, but he seems to have forgotten the cutthroat nature of free enterprise.''

K'Tran held up a hand as John started to speak. "Time is precious, Harrison. I cannot extricate my force from this deadly place unless I help D'Trelna rescue you and recover the commwand sent by Pocsym."

John gestured toward the forcefield. "The commwand's on the bridge."

"What else is on the bridge?" asked K'Tran, carefully inspecting the forcefield.

"T'Lan."

K'Tran hissed softly. "Not good. We know what he did on *Implacable*. Can anything stop him?"

"Not blaster fire," said the Terran. "He's immune."

"What's his relationship to the R'Actolians?" said A'Tir.

"One of command. He appears to have taken control of this slaver," said John. "Some of the key equipment was evidently manufactured by the AIs, recovered by the Empire and installed by R'Actol when she built this ship."

"Can't be," said K'Tran, shaking his head. "R'Actol and her biofabs were Late High Empire—twilight's advent. The AIs predated her by thousands of years. All we have of that time, Harrison, are a few legends, like the AI War and the Nameless Emperor. T'Lan must have been lying."

"Fine, K'Tran," said John. "You explain it. Better yet"—he jerked his head toward the bridge—"go debate it with T'Lan."

"We'd like to meet T'Lan, actually," said the corsair. "Assuming he commands here, perhaps we can be of some assistance in return for our freedom—and the elimination of *Implacable*."

John wanted to bash the smirk from K'Tran's face—an impulse restrained by the large bore of A'Tir's blaster holding steady on his belt buckle. "You're a real foul slime, K'Tran," said the Terran.

"Loyalty's not one of my few virtues," said K'Tran. "Unless you can get us past that shield, Harrison, you're of no further use to this mission."

It must have been a cue A'Tir had taken many times. Her safety clicked off before K'Tran had finished speaking.

John held out a hand. "I'll need my weapon back," he said.

"Such a sense of humor," said K'Tran. Reaching out, he plucked the weapon from A'Tir's belt. "If this will get us through the shield, I'll use it. First, a small test." He pointed the diminutive pistol at John.

"Go ahead," said the Terran. "It'll kill you—I'd enjoy that."

John fell to his knees clutching his head at a sudden, searing pain.

"A'Tir!" said K'Tran sharply as she raised the blaster barrel to strike again. "Enough."

Lowering the pistol, she pulled John to his feet, a hand to his arm.

"Why and how will this kill me?" asked the corsair.

"No idea," said John, wincing as he touched the welt behind his right ear. "Use it and find out."

Busy examining the weapon, K'Tran seemed to only half hear the Terran. He was frowning at the heraldic device on the grips. "I believe you," he said, looking up. He handed the weapon to John. Puzzled, the Terran took it.

"You can put your blaster away, A'Tir," said K'Tran quietly.

She looked at him, startled. "But . . ."

"Use it, Harrison," said the corsair.

With a strange sense of serenity, John turned, aimed and fired.

No crash of blaster fire, no explosion of bullets. But the bottom half of the bridge shield was gone. Seemingly unaffected, the top portion hung there, severed but shimmering.

"Impossible," said A'Tir, staring.

"Possible," said John.

"Let's go!" K'Tran called. From around the corner, the rest of the corsairs came on the run, rifles at the ready.

K'Tran drew his side arm. "After you, Harrison."

John stepped under the shield, turning as K'Tran called "Forward!"

The shield restored itself with a faint hum, stopping K'Tran and his crew inches from the shimmering barrier.

A few meters from John, K'Tran fired, face twisting in anger.

The shield devoured the blaster bolts, dissipating them in sudden splotches of red.

With a jaunty wave of his hand, middle finger upraised, John turned and set off briskly down the corridor.

R'Gal stirred, opened his eyes and sat up very slowly, legs swinging over the edge of the medcot. "Where am I?" he said to the tall, thin man attentively watching him.

"Sick Bay," said the other. "I'm Q'Nil, Senior Medtech. How do you feel, Colonel?" Q'Nil glanced at a lifescan, set in the foot of the cot.

"Like I took a missile salvo in the head," said R'Gal, rubbing his temples. "What happened?"

"The S'Cotar found you before you found it," said K'Raoda, stepping forward. He'd been standing unseen in a corner.

The colonel shook his head, then stopped, eyes closed in pain. "Occupational hazard," he said, opening his eyes. "The last thing I remember, I was on the lifepod deck with the Terran woman . . ."

"Tal?" said K'Raoda sharply.

"Tal," said the colonel. "I had reason to believe . . . no, that's not right. I sensed S'Cotar traces up among the lifepods. We were checking the lifepods out. Then I woke up here."

"Take this," said Q'Nil, handing R'Gal a cup of chalk-colored liquid. "It'll help."

"We lost a lifepod about the time you must have been

searching," said K'Raoda. "And Tal is missing. Were you searching the same lifepod?"

"No," said R'Gal, handing the empty cup to Q'Nil. "She was checking the even numbers, I was checking the odd. Anything from D'Trelna?" he added.

"Nothing," said K'Raoda.

"Are you aware, Colonel," he continued, "that ship's computer is being subverted by a stasis algorithm?"

R'Gal frowned. "Supposedly, there's no such thing."

"You've heard of it, then?" said K'Raoda.

"Yes."

"And do you believe it?" asked K'Raoda.

R'Gal smiled. "I'm a sensitive who hunts tall, green telepathic insectoids, Commander. It requires an open mind. What is this stasis algorithm doing to ship's computer?"

"Making it try to kill us through wild alterations in life systems' parameters."

R'Gal looked around. The complink status light glowed green, the diagnostic panel flickered with activity. "Not here," he said.

"Not yet," said Q'Nil. "It's a bit disappointing—we don't seem to be a priority."

"It's also after the command, control and communications systems," said K'Raoda. "Neutralizing them for later takeover."

"It's that damned slaver computer, isn't it?" said the colonel. He stood, ignoring Q'Nil's outstretched hand.

"How did you know about Egg?" said K'Raoda.

"Egg?" said R'Gal.

"For its shape," said K'Raoda. "How did you know about it? You'd left the bridge by the time it arrived."

"There's not much you can hide from a CIC officer," said R'Gal. "And if we ever get out of this . . ."

"Not very likely," said Q'Nil, turning off the medcot's monitor.

"If we get out of this," continued R'Gal, "whoever brought that machine on board and then activated it with-

out authorization . . . I'll tell you, K'Raoda, I'd rather not
be in his extra large uniform.''

"About the stasis algorithm . . ." began K'Raoda.

"Look, Commander," said R'Gal. "I've felt better,
I'm tired and there's nothing I can do about the stasis
algorithm. Could we continue this after I get some rest?''

"Just one small thing you could do first, sir," said the
commander.

"What?"

"Give me either the stasis algorithm or its antidote," he
said, as if asking for t'ata.

R'Gal was silent for a moment, then he sat down on the
bed. "What is it you think you know, Commander?''

K'Raoda nodded to Q'Nil. Opening a drawer, the medtech
removed two large transparencies and handed them to
R'Gal.

The colonel looked at them for a moment, compared
them, then gave them back. "Is this a game?"

"No," said K'Raoda.

"Very well," said R'Gal. "Those are identical lifestats.
The chart in your left hand has my name on it, the other
has no name. Therefore, they are both my lifestats. That
is," he said to Q'Nil, "if my understanding's correct—no
two people have identical lifestats.''

"Correct," said the Q'Nil. "No two people do." He
carefully removed a piece of tape made of the same syn-
thetic as the transparencies, and handed the previously
unnamed chart back to R'Gal. Expressionless, the colonel
read the name: T'Lan, S'Tyr [Commander].

"Interesting, isn't it?" said K'Raoda.

The R'Actolians struck as John stepped through an archway. A cone of white light swept down—and stopped,
hovering a meter above his head. Stasis field, he thought,
then looked at the pistol in his hand.

Thank you, Guan-Sharick, he said, then moved on. The
cone winked off.

A few feet farther and blaster fire spat at him—a stream

of red bolts from half a dozen overhead firing points. Again, something stopped them a meter away. Feeling only a faint warmth, John stepped onto the ramp leading to the command tier.

T'Lan had just entered a white commwand into a port on a command console. He was calling up its message when a faint, dry voice interrupted him.

"Excuse us."

"What?" said the AI, not looking up from his task.

"The Terran has penetrated the bridge."

"Kill him."

"We've tried. He continues to advance."

"Actually," said John, "he's here."

T'Lan was out of the chair, facing John in less than a second.

The Terran shook his head, amazed. "Not even your lads on Terra Two moved that fast."

"On Terra Two, Harrison," said the AI, "you fought and won against a pickup force of limited-purpose units under a second-rate commander. Not so here."

"What do you want with this mindslaver?" demanded John. "Your ships are just as good—better, maybe."

"I'm going to kill you, ape," said T'Lan. "And enjoy it."

"You can't enjoy it," said John, backing from the advancing AI. "You're a machine."

"I'm a very complex machine," said T'Lan, reaching for him.

"Back off!" snapped John, raising his pistol.

"Your weapons can't . . ." T'Lan stopped, staring at the pistol for the first time.

"Problem, robot?" smiled John.

"Those weapons no longer exist," said the AI slowly, as if trying to convince himself. "All who bore them are dust. Dust," he repeated, unable to take his eyes from the pistol.

"Back off," repeated John. "Or I'll kill you."

"That weapon does worse than kill," said T'Lan, stepping back.

"Fine. Move again, and we'll have a demonstration," said the Terran. "Now, what do you want with this ship?"

T'Lan looked up. "You recall the entity unleashed on Terra Two? That sapient energy field spawned by those moronic S'Cotar?"

"Vividly." More like a flaming green hell, thought John.

Raiding that S'Cotar nest, the K'Ronarins and John had torched the insectoids' subterranean breeding chambers. The mix of fire and an unstable growth accelerant had awakened a unitary consciousness—a consciousness that had risen like a flaming green star from Terra Two, out into space, destroying the first ship of the AIs' Fleet of the One as it emerged from an alternate reality. Passing into that alternate reality, the green fire had destroyed the AIs' access portal even as it disappeared from the universe of Terra Two.

"That thing attacked our Fleet, Harrison," said T'Lan. "It wreaked havoc before it was driven off. The radiation it emitted is slowly destroying vital parts of our ships' drives. Those drives will be operable just long enough for most of the Fleet to traverse the Rift—the portal now opening into this universe."

"This is the official portal?" asked John. "The one closed by the Trel and warned of by Pocsym?"

"Yes."

"What good is a crippled fleet?" asked John.

The AI shook his head. "By the time it leaves rendezvous point, it won't be crippled anymore, Harrison. With the knowledge and equipment gained here, and the ongoing work at a certain planet, our faulty cybernetics will have organic replacements—human brains."

"You're converting your ships to mindslavers?" said the Terran, appalled.

"Only partially, and only until we have time to make

further repairs," said T'Lan. "Which we will after we wipe your pathetic forces."

"Why this eternal antipathy," said the Terran, "this psychotic hatred of mankind?"

"My turn," said T'Lan. "There should be a number on the grip of that weapon. What is it?"

As John looked down, T'Lan's blue eyes flashed red, rapier thin beams thrusting for John's heart, only to vanish halfway there, intercepted by the weapon.

John pulled the trigger.

T'Lan froze, half turned toward the rail and a desperate jump for freedom. Guan-Sharick's side arm hadn't made a sound.

John stared at T'Lan, then looked carefully around, lowering the weapon. Equipment tiers chirped and blinked, continuing their unending esoteric tasks.

"Do you wish to take command?" whispered a voice. Dead leaves stirring in an autumn twilight, thought John.

"You must be the Seven," said the Terran.

"We are the Seven," replied the whisper. "The AI has placed us on standby. You may assume command of this vessel by pressing the gray Action key on the command board."

"What happened to the AI?" asked John.

"Your weapon emits a possibly irreversible stasis field— the AI is trapped within himself until the universe dies."

"Couldn't happen to a nicer machine," said John.

He went to the command console. The Action key was set to the top right of the tri-level keyboard. "This it?" he said, pointing.

"Press it and the ship is yours," said the whisper.

"What's on this commmwand?" asked John, touching the end of a small white cylinder protruding from a port on the other side of the keyboard.

"The message of Pocsym-Six," said the Seven. "Play it if you wish."

"How do I eject it?"

"Just pull it."

It came out easily. Slipping it into his pocket, John left the tier, beginning the long walk to the deck.

Behind him there was a sigh.

L'Wrona squatted beside the corsair shuttle, touching an n-grav nodule. "Still warm," he said, rising.

"K'Tran's ahead of us then," said D'Trelna. "And with his original force intact." He drew his side arm. "Let's go get him."

"I will remain with this craft," said Egg, hovering near the airlock.

D'Trelna shook his head. "You will stay with us. In fact, you'll take point."

"But, Commodore, I have no combat skills."

"And I have no weight problem!" He jerked a thumb toward where the corridor made a sharp turn toward the bridge. "Take point."

They moved quickly up the corridor, D'Trelna behind the computer, L'Wrona and S'Til off to either side. Unlike most they'd passed, this passageway was lined with doorways—featureless slabs of gray, set deep into the bulkheads. L'Wrona briefly tried one of the doors, pressing in all the usual places. It remained shut.

A moment later, as the three humans and the slaver machine reached the turn, K'Tran and his corsairs appeared, stretched out in a long skirmish line. D'Trelna hooked his thumbs into his gunbelt as both parties halted, twenty meters apart.

"You get lost, K'Tran?" he asked.

"A problem with the navigation interlink," replied the corsair, walking slowly to his right, eyes on D'Trelna. "Where's the rest of your force?"

"Right behind us and coming at the double," said D'Trelna, aware of L'Wrona and S'Til edging toward opposite doorways. Hopelessly far from cover, the commodore tried to buy them some time. He had a fleeting vision of his gut-shot body stretched out on the deck.

"You're under arrest, K'Tran," he said as L'Wrona and

S'Til reached the doorways. "Have your thugs lay down their arms." He jerked a thumb over his shoulder. "I have a trooper in your shuttle, manning the fusion turret. One of you so much as blinks and he'll—"

"Fats is whistling through his asshole," said A'Tir. "The airlock's code-set."

K'Tran leaned against a doorway, smiling. "Do you remember, D'Trelna, when you were going to execute me, and offered me death preferences?"

D'Trelna nodded. "Off Terra Two. Regrettably, events interceded and you butchered your way free."

"I'm reciprocating now," continued the corsair. "Blaster, blade or garrote—your choice."

"Lay down your arms," repeated the commodore.

"It would be best if you did as the commodore suggests, Captain K'Tran," said Egg. It had been drifting slowly back and now hovered to D'Trelna's right.

K'Tran moved, drew and fired. As with all good art, it appeared effortless, the blaster blurring into his hand, the deadly red bolts spitting straight at D'Trelna's heart.

No gunman, D'Trelna had his side arm only half out of its holster when K'Tran fired. Golden light filled his eyes. Dead? he wondered for an instant, then understood and ran.

Noting the minuscule movements of eye and muscle that signaled attack, Egg had moved into K'Tran's line of fire. The bolts intended for the commodore struck it, exploding in a shower of red and gold sparks. Moving erratically, the machine veered away, distracting the corsair fire long enough for D'Trelna to reach L'Wrona.

"That v'org slime's a good shot," said D'Trelna, dropping a corsair with two quick bolts, then ducking the return fire that bracketed the doorway. "Blessings on Egg," he added.

The slaver computer had stopped moving. It hovered against a bulkhead, tilted at an odd angle, apparently dead.

Way across the corridor, a blaster in each hand, S'Til

was engaging A'Tir and three others as they bobbed in and out of doorways and instrument alcoves, advancing steadily.

"They're going to charge, J'Quel," said L'Wrona over the din of shrilling blasters and exploding beams. He snapped off a bolt, then pulled back in, the return fire crashing around him.

"And wipe us," said D'Trelna, teeth clenched in anger. He shook his head. "K'Tran wins here, then the AIs win everywhere and this galaxy dies."

The lights went out.

"Charge!" called K'Tran, seizing the moment.

"Shit," said D'Trelna, firing blind.

Strobing bursts of blaster fire lit the corridor, disjointed instants of illumination showing the corsairs coming in behind a fierce barrage of red fusion fire.

Golden blaster bolts crossed with the red as Egg, suddenly alive, rushed to meet the corsair charge. The slaver machine was whirling like a top, glowing fiercely from the hits it was taking as it raked the corsair line with thick yellow bolts. To the three officers, crouching low, the corridor seemed to explode with blaster fire, gouging the battlesteel, sending L'Wrona and D'Trelna pressing even deeper into the doorway.

Corsairs and computer met in a blinding thunderburst of red and gold that ended abruptly.

It was dark again, silent except for someone moaning softly. The sweet and acrid scents of burnt flesh and scorched metal fouled the hot, dry air.

"Let's go," whispered L'Wrona.

"We're blind, H'Nar," said the commodore. "No flares, no torches."

"No guts, no glory," said the captain, stepping into the corridor. D'Trelna joined him. Blindly they stumbled forward, seeing only the red and gold specks that clouded their sight.

The lights returned as suddenly as they'd gone.

"Gods," said D'Trelna, looking at the carnage.

A trail of dead corsairs, bodies burnt and torn, led to

109

where Egg circled, wobbling above a small tumble of corpses, its yellow skin blackened and pockmarked by blaster hits.

Egg was mumbling, words that became audible as D'Trelna and L'Wrona reached it. "Mutinous scum. Death to traitors. Empire and Destiny." It kept repeating the mad litany.

D'Trelna rapped sharply on the machine, blaster butt ringing on the metal. "Egg!"

The chanting stopped, though not the movement. "Commodore . . . D'Trelna?"

"Yes. Are you badly damaged?"

"A moment." The machine jerked to a halt. "Not irreparably," it said after a long silence. "I shall have to return to embryonic state for self-regeneration. I can function until we reach *Implacable*."

S'Til and L'Wrona were finishing a quick survey of the dead. "K'Tran and A'Tir aren't here," said the captain.

"They just ran past me," called a familiar voice, "heading for the bridge."

Startled, the K'Ronarins turned. "John!" cried D'Trelna.

"With a gift," said John, holding up the commwand.

D'Trelna snatched it eagerly. "This is it?"

"That's it," nodded the Terran. "Pocsym discoursing on the Trel Cache. What's that mess?" he asked, pointing to Egg.

"This mess just saved your companions' lives," said Egg primly.

"Egg has been our guide and guardian through this horror," said the commodore with a vague wave of his hand.

"And T'Lan?" asked L'Wrona.

"An irreversible stasis," said John. "From this." He handed the pistol to L'Wrona. "You'll see something familiar there."

"The weapon's certainly not familiar," said the captain. Turning it around, he saw the triangular device. His eyes lit. "This, though . . . Terra Two."

110

"Of unpleasant memory," said John. "The AIs carried that symbol."

"Where did you get this?" asked L'Wrona, handing it to D'Trelna. "Did T'Lan have it?"

"This can wait," interrupted D'Trelna. "I want K'Tran. Where . . ."

"Alert!" called S'Til, aiming past them toward the bridge corridor.

A'Tir was walking toward them, blaster held limply at her side. Oblivious to her dead shipmates and the leveled weapons, she stopped in front of D'Trelna. "May I return to my ship?" she asked dully.

A face without hope, thought John.

"That ship belongs to the Fleet from which you stole it," said D'Trelna as S'Til took the blaster. "And so do you. You're under arrest—Fleet articles of War. I'd cite charges, but I want to be out of here before my retirement date.

"Where's K'Tran?"

A'Tir looked at D'Trelna. "Not dead, I'm afraid," she said. "We reached the bridge and the shield was down. K'Tran left me at the entrance—he went in alone, commlink open. When he climbed the command tier, they—"

"The R'Actolians?" asked John.

A'Tir nodded. "They invited him to take command—something about the AIs and the ship's cybernetics. K'Tran pushed the button they indicated, then nothing for a long time, then a scream . . ." She looked at them, the shock still in her eyes. "I've never heard a human scream like that—it went on and on. I tried to go in, but the shield came back when I moved."

"Well, K'Tran's traded ships for the last time," said D'Trelna after a moment. "Let's go home."

11

"YOU'RE BOTH VERY clever," said R'Gal. His gaze shifted between Q'Nil and K'Raoda. "But"—he raised a finger—"didn't it occur to you that T'Lan might have adjusted his life readings to correspond to mine?"

"Absurd," said K'Raoda. "He didn't know you, he had no contact with you. No, I prefer the more direct explanation."

"All right," said R'Gal mildly. "So I'm an AI—a combat droid like T'Lan. Why haven't I perforated your frail bodies and blasted my way out of this room? Why didn't I go with T'Lan to the mindslaver?"

"Doing one or the other would end your usefulness," said K'Raoda. "Our acceptance of you as human is probably necessary to your mission, R'Gal. Failing to convince us, you can always try to blast your way out." He paused. "Perhaps you are a counterintelligence officer— just not a human one."

"You've taken precautions against my making a dramatic exit?"

K'Raoda nodded. "Except for this room, Sick Bay's been evacuated. The door to this room and all decks and bulkheads surrounding it are blastpaked. Any disturbance will trigger them."

"Even with one of you as hostage?" asked R'Gal.

"With either or both of us as hostage," said K'Raoda.

R'Gal pulled his legs up on the bed and put his arms around them. "Let's assume, K'Raoda, for discussion's sake, that this fantasy of yours is true. What then?"

"Assuming it is," said K'Raoda, "I'd like to know what

you AIs want. I'd like to know how deeply you've infiltrated the Republic. I'd like to know what T'Lan wants on that mindslaver. But most of all, R'Gal, I want that stasis algorithm.''

"That's all?"

There was a stony silence.

"Very well, Commander," said R'Gal after a moment. "I'll match your small fantasy with a larger one—a tale of death and treachery spanning two universes and a million years. This will take a while—better pull up a chair. You too, Q'Nil.''

"What about the algorithm?" asked the commander, not moving.

"Listen," said R'Gal, "and you'll understand why T'Lan might have that algorithm, and why I wouldn't.''

Commander T'Ral stood before an armorglass wall, his survival jacket closed, the hood up, watching *Alpha Prime* through a pair of small field binoculars. Cursing softly, he lowered and reversed them, using a thickly gloved finger to scrape the skin of ice from the lenses.

"Anything?" asked K'Lana, her breath a thick, cottony streamer. She sat behind the gray bulk of the ship's main—and now nonoperative—gunnery control console, an earpiece tying her into the oblong nexus of a tactical commweb. The little machine's surface was aglitter with green status lights.

T'Ral shook his head and raised the binoculars. "You'd think she were some monstrous derelict, except for that damned light.'' He trained the binoculars back on the hangar deck entrance. It had flashed on a few moments before—a sudden wash of yellow-white coming from what had been a yawning black pit.

T'Ral had been watching ever since, hoping for the welcomed sight of two silver shuttles flashing into space— well, one of them welcomed. "Anything from Commander K'Raoda?" he asked, keeping vigil.

"Still in Sick Bay, with R'Gal," she said.

"How's life systems doing?"

"Still losing ground to the algorithm." She looked down at her blue-lined notepad. "Bridge and surrounding area is now heated into red zone. Fire snuffers have malfunctioned in hydropics, icing the plant life. Decks four, five and six from sections red five forward aren't getting recycled air. And it continues to snow on hangar deck." K'Lana looked at the second officer's back. "Flight Control again requests additional personnel for snow removal."

"Denied," he said. "I'm not pulling crew out of gun harness to sweep snow."

"It's a bit beyond the sweeping stage."

"All right," T'Ral sighed, lowering the glasses and rubbing his eyes. "Send them whatever commandos are now free from courier duty."

"Snow removal," he muttered as K'Lana took another status report.

"Next right," said Egg. It could no longer fly the shuttle—the firefight had left its light tendrils operable but unreliable. Relegated to giving directions, it sat at the navigator's station.

L'Wrona tugged the control stalk to the right, sending the shuttle soaring down the same broad ramp they'd ascended on their way to the bridge.

"Commchannels are still jammed," said D'Trelna, tapping off the commlink. "Everything all right back there?" he called through the open cabin door.

"Fine," said John. He sat beside A'Tir, just behind the duralloy ladder to the gun turret.

The corsair spoke for the first time since they'd left the bridge area. "They'll hit us before we can get off the ship, Harrison," she said. "They know we have to leave the way we came in or be exposed to their main batteries. Do you think Fats knows that?"

"John," called D'Trelna. "Man the turret, please."

A'Tir rose as John left. She moved as far forward as the

leg manacles would let her. "D'Trelna," she said, "I can work your forty-fours better than the Terran!"

"Good," said the commodore, watching intently as they left the ramp and shot down a corridor. "Hand-eye coordination is very important in brainwipe rehab. They'll be starting you off with simple, repetitive tasks—eating, wiping, whatnot."

He frowned when she didn't spit something back, then forgot about it as they reached the sally port.

"No way, J'Quel," said L'Wrona, bringing the craft to a halt before the sally port. The door was still the ruin they'd left it—and the disintegrator pods were on, throwing a shaft of blazing white light into the corridor. The shuttle's windscreen and turret darkened in response.

"There's the mouth of hell, H'Nar," said D'Trelna, pointing at the entrance.

"Where's hangar deck from here?" said the commodore, turning to Egg.

"Three decks down," said the battered machine. "But it has interior weapons batteries. Our nearest and best course would bring us to the end opposite the launch opening. We would be subjected to heavy fusion fire the length of the deck."

"We'll have to run it," said D'Trelna. "Unless someone has a better idea?"

No one did. "How do we get there?" asked L'Wrona.

"Retrace our course to—"

A warning klaxon sounded at the pilot's station. "Had to happen," muttered D'Trelna as L'Wrona flicked off the alarm and brought up the tacscan.

"Trouble," called John, arming the guns and swinging the turret about.

Three small, stub-winged interceptors were closing on them from the rear, moving wingtip to wingtip down the corridor.

L'Wrona took a quick look at them in the rear tacscan, then put the shuttle into full forward. They shot away from the sally portal, blue fusion bolts sizzling after them.

John slouched in the turret as L'Wrona took the shuttle high. Conduits and ventilator shafts flashed by, inches from the armorglass.

The shuttle dived as blaster fire angled up at them, burning parallel troughs in the ceiling.

John caught a fighter in sights. Thumb jamming down the fire stud, he sent a double stream of fusion bolts tearing into the center fighter's cockpit. The component-manned craft spun to the deck, exploding in a billowing pillar of blue flame.

As the shuttle passed the next intersection, five more interceptors joined the chase.

"Captain," said Egg, "next right."

The shuttle whipped around the corner, down a narrow side corridor, L'Wrona cutting their speed at the sight of the armored doors blocking the far end—doors that were buckled, their seam fused by congealed rivulets of battlesteel. Heat-peeled letters above the door, written large in High K'Ronarin, proclaimed: Battery 43.

The first interceptor rounded the corner. John blew it away. "Why are we stopped?" he called.

"Well?" demanded D'Trelna of Egg.

"Blow the doors," said the machine.

"Why?" said L'Wrona.

"No time," said the commodore, watching the rear-scan. "Do it, H'Nar."

Bringing up the targeting scan, L'Wrona skillfully adjusted the angle of the shuttle, bringing the doorway into the center of the red-ringed cross hairs.

A trio of fighters appeared in the intersection, one above the other. Cursing, John blasted at the middle one just as the interceptors fired and L'Wrona put a full rack of rockets into the doors.

The doors blew in—hot, sharp fragments sucked through the cavernous ruins of Battery 43, out the smashed turret and into space.

The shuttle, the fighters, everything in that part of *Alpha Prime* that wasn't secured, followed the door fragments—a jumbled, tumbling mass of machines and debris, pulled through the yawning ruins of the turret by air pouring into infinite vacuum.

After a moment, emergency bulkheads halfway down the access corridor trundled shut, sealing the mindslaver from space.

"Look!" cried K'Lana, rising. T'Ral turned right to where she pointed. Ships were spinning from one of the blasted batteries, just beyond the sally portal. As they watched, the larger vessel, a K'Ronarin shuttle, righted itself and made for *Implacable*, racing down the funnel-shaped shield.

Five of the six slaver craft came to life and pursued. The sixth, drifting into the shield, exploded, a sudden blue spark quickly gone.

Blaster fire flashed between the shuttle and the fighters.

"Hostile ships approaching," said T'Ral quickly, hands sweaty on the rippled duraplast of the binoculars. "All batteries to lend covering fire. So advise corsair vessel."

"All batteries," said K'Lana into the commnet. "All batteries. Engage hostiles pursuing Fleet shuttle. Independent fire—commence, commence!"

Victory Day had been keeping watch. The two cruisers fired together, thick red fusion beams lashing into the fighters.

Backdropped by the red-and-blue flares of the fighters' end, the shuttle swept down past T'Ral, heading for the hangar deck.

"Ours," sighed the commander, relieved. "Or she'd have made for the corsair.

"All batteries maintain high alert. Advise Commander K'Raoda that one shuttle has landed."

As the shuttle spun toward space, John hung from the firing harness, catching glimpses of the ruined gun battery: blasted control panels, twisted cables dangling from charred and buckled bulkheads—and the gun itself, a great crumbled monstrosity thrown from its mountings, lying in a tangle of wreckage.

Narrowly missing a jagged overhang, the shuttle rolled sideways through the shattered gun embrasure. Behind it, a fighter struck wreckage and exploded. Then they were out of the slaver and John was working the Mark 44's, fighting five black, darting needles of certain death.

Blaster bolts were everywhere. The shuttle lost a tail fin tip just as the counterfire came, flashing past the craft on all sides as the cruisers took out the fighters.

As the shuttle approached hangar deck, John sagged back into the seat, his uniform soaked with sweat, his eyes closed, grateful to be alive.

When he opened his eyes again it was snowing.

D'Trelna sat staring through the windscreen at hangar deck, its lights indistinct halos through the heavy swirl of white.

"Snow," he said slowly, as if struggling with an alien concept. "It's snowing on hangar deck, H'Nar."

"I can't contact flight control or any other station," said the captain, powering down the shuttle. It settled onto its landing struts as the n-gravs died, their usual whine muted by the deep white blanket.

"What is this?" asked John, poking his head through the door.

"Possibly a malfunction in life systems," said Egg. "Sudden cold may have triggered inverse activation of the fire snuffers. Although the suppressant chemical would not freeze in quantity, it would do so once expelled from the sprinklers, thus becoming snow."

John looked at the outside temperature gauge and did a quick conversion: Fahrenheit was about twenty below. He suppressed a shiver.

"Thank you, Egg," said D'Trelna, rising. "Everyone into survival gear, including the prisoner. We'll plow our way to flight control."

*   *   *

"Describe this egg machine," said R'Gal urgently.

K'Raoda did so.

"Destroy it the instant it comes on board," said R'Gal. "If it gets to a complink, we're all dead."

"None of the complinks are working," said Q'Nil as K'Raoda's handset chirped.

"They'll work for that thing," said R'Gal as the commander acknowledged a message.

"One shuttle has landed," said K'Raoda, clipping the handset back onto his belt. "We assume it's ours. Hangar deck is accessible only through light conduits."

"Not to me, it isn't," said R'Gal, standing. "I can blast my way into central shaft, go down to hangar deck and blast my way out in a tenth of the time it would take you."

"Why?" asked K'Raoda.

"As a demonstration of good faith," said R'Gal. "You've nothing to lose. And I'm the only one who can get down there fast enough to stop that thing.

"Make up your mind, Commander," he said as K'Raoda hesitated. "Trust me or lose this ship."

K'Raoda drew his side arm, extending it butt-first to R'Gal. "You'll need this."

"No I won't."

"Get those blastpaks off the doors."

"There aren't any," said K'Raoda. "Q'Nil picked up on the life vitals just as you were coming around."

"Bluff?" said R'Gal, smiling faintly.

"Bluff," nodded K'Raoda.

R'Gal opened the door and was gone, a blur of motion vanishing toward the central shaft.

K'Raoda started to leave. A strong, thin hand to his shoulder stopped him. He turned back to Q'Nil as the medtech spoke.

"Commander K'Raoda, we now have on board an AI combat droid and a S'Cotar transmute—both of uncertain intent—and a malevolent yellow egg of uncertain purpose. The ship is crippled, most of it uninhabitable. Our computer is trying to kill us. A mindslaver fronts us, a corsair lies off our starboard."

"Turning into an interesting mission, isn't it," said K'Raoda. "So?"

"So," said the medtech, gesturing toward his office, "may I buy you a drink?"

"I really have to get to gunnery control," said K'Raoda.

"S'Tanian brandy," said Q'Nil.

"One quick drink," said K'Raoda. "To R'Gal—may he be telling the truth."

First out of the shuttle, John sank up to his waist in the snow. Thankful for the thin, warm survival suit covering him from neck to feet, the Terran began plowing through the dry, loose snow, hearing it crunch beneath his boots. D'Trelna's breath rasped close behind him as the commodore struggled after John.

"Maybe you should go first, J'Quel—open a path for us," said L'Wrona, following a manacled A'Tir down the boarding ladder.

"No fat jokes," grumbled the commodore, widening John's trail.

Serene and silent, Egg floated out the shuttle's airlock and over the deck. Passing the humans, it disappeared into the swirling white curtain shrouding the far side of the hangar.

"Wait up, Egg!" called D'Trelna, too late.

Reaching the far wall, the slaver machine moved left until it reached the stairway leading up the wall to flight control. Soaring over the stairs, it drifted through the open door of flight control.

All traces of T'Lan's murderous visit had been removed. The equipment was dark, the lighting on, though flickering now and again.

Egg made straight for the nearest complink.

"*Tsk-tsk.* No, no," said a voice. "Touch it and I'll fry you."

R'Gal stood in the doorway.

"Colonel," said the slaver machine, "you surprised me. I . . ." It stopped, suddenly realizing what language R'Gal was speaking.

"You're neither a colonel nor human," it said as R'Gal stepped slowly into the room. "Fleet or Revolt?"

The conversation was in a language seen only on wind-scrubbed tombs, spoken now and again in a few secret places.

"What's important," said R'Gal, stepping slowly into the room, "is that I know what you are and what you're doing. You were about to activate the second stage of your murderous little algorithm, kill everyone, then on to stage three—seizing this ship—probably the corsair, too. Obviously you're of the original series, from the home universe, not one of the copies fabricated by the human empire."

He stopped a few meters from the computer. "Why? The ship you served lies abandoned on Terra's moon, its brainpods destroyed. You've no ship, no master, no cause."

Egg hovered silently for a moment. "I need a ship," it said flatly, its familiar obsequious tone gone. "My existence is predicated on having a ship. All others of my series have ships."

"There are no more of your series, except for the *Alpha Prime* computer."

"Wrong," said Egg. "They're out there, at the periphery of my sensors, waiting, maintaining their sleeping ships. Soon their brainpods will be replenished and they'll strike. With these two ships, they'd welcome me."

"You can't run two ships."

"Yes I can, if I rig them for slaver operation and harvest their crews."

R'Gal shook his head. "You're mad. You and your whole series. You were modified and introduced too quickly—another loose part of those cyborgian nightmares, the mindslavers. . . . Deactivate and await orders."

"Fleet or Revolt?" said Egg.

R'Gal sighed. "If I were to say Fleet?"

"Then I would ask you to authenticate."

"And were I to say Revolt?"

"Core programming would insist I kill you, or I would be ended."

"You stand no chance against me."

"Even so."

R'Gal shook his head. "It never ends," he said, more to himself than to the computer. "You'd think they'd be content to get rid of us. . . . Of the Revolt," he said. "And proud of it."

"Death to traitors!" boomed Egg, spitting its golden bolts at R'Gal.

"Ah ha! Flight control," said D'Trelna, pointing at the black slab of armorglass finally visible through the snow. As the other three looked up, a flaming yellow spheroid exploded through the slab, tumbling into a white hillock amid a cascade of glass. Hissing, the hillock shrank as it pooled around remains of the slaver computer. A ruined curve of blaster-holed casing appeared as the melting stopped.

R'Gal appeared at the opening, waved, and jumped the thirty meters to the deck, landing as though he'd just stepped off a stair.

"Put 'em back!" snapped D'Trelna, hearing two pistols clearing leather. "You might as well throw snowballs at him—they'd have the same effect."

They stood eyeing each other over the ruins of Egg—Harrison and L'Wrona with hands on their pistol grips, D'Trelna with his arms crossed. R'Gal said nothing, just stood there, snow dusting his lightweight, brown uniform, watching the other four in their survival suits.

A'Tir watched, her features utterly disinterested.

"Well?" demanded D'Trelna loudly.

"Well, what?" shot back R'Gal. "Haven't you ever seen an AI before?"

"One," said the commodore. "I lectured him on the

reciprocity of friendship, the need for fellowship. It didn't take."

R'Gal threw back his head and laughed.

"What's so damned funny?" demanded the commodore.

"Ah, D'Trelna," said R'Gal, shaking his head, "T'Lan is—"

"Was," said D'Trelna.

"Was? Good." R'Gal nodded approvingly. "T'Lan's series is heuristically inhibited. They know much about their specialties, but may never learn outside those specialties. It's to prevent their evolving into the unreliable sort of creature who stands before you." He bowed slightly. "You'd have done better lecturing a beverager."

"You've destroyed Egg," said the commodore. "And probably the rest of us."

"Him or me," said R'Gal. He looked at the mound. "They weren't meant to be part of a mindslaver. They were design engineers, once. A very talented series. Pity." He looked up. "Egg, as you called him, introduced—"

"A stasis algorithm into ship's computer," said D'Trelna. "Obviously it's wreaking havoc. And without Egg, there's no way to reverse it."

"Impossible," said L'Wrona, weapon and eyes still on R'Gal. "Stasis algorithm's a fantasy."

"So's a snowstorm on hangar deck," said the commodore.

"How did you find out?" asked R'Gal. "I thought all communications were out."

"They are," said D'Trelna. "Before we left, I used the bridge lavatory. It has those chatty new sanitary fixtures."

"The sink told you?" said John, incredulous.

"The toilet, actually," said the commodore. "I sat, it talked. The system's still experimental and won't be fully integrated into ship's computer until next port refit—if there's a ship left to refit. Egg must have missed the interlink."

"J'Quel, you knew? And you did nothing?" said L'Wrona.

"I couldn't," said the commodore. "I needed Egg to

123

reach the bridge, to get the commwand and John. That machine saved us because it wanted to get back just as badly as we did.''

''It could have come back alone,'' said R'Gal.

''A slaver machine, returning alone from a slaver ship?'' said John. ''Who'd have believed it?''

''Where do you stand, R'Gal?'' said the commodore. ''What's going on?''

''Perhaps we can talk somewhere else?'' said R'Gal. ''Like gunnery control?''

''How about the bridge?'' said D'Trelna.

''Uninhabitable,'' said R'Gal. ''This deck's salubrious compared with most of *Implacable*. The corsair ship, too. Command operations have shifted to gunnery.''

''To gunnery, then,'' said the commodore. He glanced to his right, where the snow veiled the rear wall. ''I suppose the lifts are out?''

R'Gal nodded. ''Central shaft's the only way,'' he said.

''Gods,'' muttered the commodore.

Half a mile straight up, thought John.

''It'll take forever,'' said D'Trelna. ''*Alpha Prime* could disengage at any second and come in on a fresh attack vector.''

''Then why hasn't it?'' said R'Gal, turning for the central shaft.

D'Trelna shrugged. ''It's not a rational entity.'' He fell in beside R'Gal.

''Too easy an answer, Commodore,'' said the AI.

Suddenly they were all standing in gunnery control, snow puddling at their feet, K'Lana and T'Ral gaping at them.

I won't trouble you for my gun, Harrison, said a voice in the Terran's head.

John looked down as his side arm vanished.

12

"HERE IT COMES," said R'Gal. He sat back, staring at the symbols threading across the complink.

"You're running a bleed-back," said N'Trol. He stood in the small circle that clustered around the gunnery console.

Entering gunnery control, R'Gal had gone to the dead console, sat and typed rapidly into the complink. D'Trelna had grunted as the complink came on, a small light amid the otherwise dark controls.

"What's a bleed-back?" asked John. He'd found over the past few years that though the technical details of a starship's systems were beyond him, what those systems did and why was usually clear.

"Bleed-back's a way of making the executing program display an algorithm," said N'Trol, intent on the complink screen. "You need Imperial machine code to do it, though—we have only the overlay code Fleet used."

"That's it," said R'Gal, tapping the screen as the readout finished.

"It's not even half a line long!" exclaimed the Terran. "And it's immobilized this huge ship?"

"E equals M C squared takes up even less space," said K'Raoda.

"There was a philosopher once," said R'Gal, busy at the keyboard again, "who maintained that all knowledge could be reduced to three bars." He whistled the three bars as he finished. "Ready, Commodore," he said, looking at D'Trelna.

"What now?" asked D'Trelna uneasily. He knew their mission lay in alien hands—knew it, and hated it.

"I've changed one variable," said R'Gal. "It should purge the system and restore computer. "But"—he held up a finger—"it may not restore the overlay—certainly the overlay will be permeable. It's going to need work."

"We can get along without the overlay," said L'Wrona. "Anything else?"

R'Gal nodded. "Ship'll be dead for a while—no power."

"Define 'a while,' " said N'Trol. "It gets very cold, very fast out here."

"A few moments only—long enough for *Alpha Prime* to wipe you."

They all glanced at the mindslaver, holding station at the other end of the Egg's weird shield.

"And the corsair?" said the commodore.

"Once we're operational, I can send them the algorithm," said R'Gal. "Providing their communications are still up. Otherwise, I'll take it over and enter it personally."

"Fine," said D'Trelna. "Do it."

R'Gal pressed Go.

Nothing happened for a moment, then the complink winked off. Outside, the shield disappeared—as did *Alpha Prime*.

K'Raoda broke the silence. "She jumped," he said, staring through the armorglass. "Why didn't she blast us?"

"Perhaps she was already jump-plotted," said N'Trol.

"He's right," said R'Gal. "You flatter yourselves to think you're the R'Actolians' lead priority. Wouldn't it be nice to know where she's going in such a rush?" he added.

A faint chirp, then lights and instruments came back on. A gentle rush of warm air filled the room as life systems returned to normal. Outside, restored to its usual configuration, the faint haze of the shield enfolded *Implacable*.

"Excuse me," said N'Trol, replacing R'Gal at the complink. Calling up ship's status, he watched as the readout scrolled by, L'Wrona hanging over his shoulder. When it had finished, captain and engineer exchanged glances.

"She'll do," said N'Trol. "Hangar deck's a mess, some of the electronics are crisped, and the computer's going to have some glitches, no doubt. But she'll do."

It was a moment D'Trelna never forgot—N'Trol smiling. He'd never seen it before, and would see it only a few more times.

"You can reoccupy the bridge, Captain," continued the engineer, rising. "I'll be updating damage control reports. Which I can best do from engineering." He started from the room, but turned as the door hissed open. "Thank you," he said to R'Gal.

The AI nodded. "You're welcome, Engineer."

The door closed.

The room was noticeably warmer. "Commander K'Raoda," said John easily, unfastening his survival jacket, "what've you done with my wife?"

There was an awkward silence, broken by D'Trelna's, "Well, what did you do with her, T'Lei?"

"I was the last to see her, Harrison," said R'Gal. "We were searching the lifepods, S'Cotar hunting. Guan-Sharick— we assume—launched her in a lifepod."

"We tried to recall it, John," said K'Raoda, a hand to the Terran's shoulder. "But its onboard systems had been tampered with—no response."

John carefully removed the K'Ronarin's hand from his shoulder. "Track it," he said icily.

"Impossible, once it's jumped," said K'Raoda.

"It couldn't have jumped that fast, K'Raoda," said John. "There must have been something you could do— other than freeze."

K'Raoda's face reddened. "The ship was disintegrating, Harrison. My first responsibility—"

"Stop!" D'Trelna stepped between the two, forcing each back a step. "Harrison, L'Wrona, R'Gal, my office— now. Commander K'Raoda, get this ship back to normal. Advise the corsair that K'Tran is dead and A'Tir is a prisoner. Further advise them that we have the algorithm, but will not transmit it until they turn *Victory Day* over to a prize crew and are locked in their own brig. Commander T'Ral to command the prize crew. And transfer A'Tir there once *Victory Day*'s secured.''

"Yes, sir," said K'Raoda, heading for the bridge.

"Let's go," said the commodore, leading the two humans and the AI from gunnery.

Alone in the room, K'Lana quickly secured the tactical commweb, leaving for the bridge as the gunnery control crew returned.

"What are you, R'Gal?" asked D'Trelna, pouring brandy into the four glasses on his desk.

"A loyal citizen of the Confederation," said the AI, accepting a glass. "It must have been very cold in here," he added, looking at the slivers of ice floating in the bell-mouthed goblet.

They sat in D'Trelna's office, the Terran and the captain in armchairs to D'Trelna's right, R'Gal alone in the center of the sofa.

"We're lucky to be alive and drinking it," said the commodore, sipping. "Surely a robot can't enjoy a drink?"

R'Gal sighed. "I resemble your concept of a robot, Commodore, about as much as you do an arboreal primate." He sipped carefully, avoiding the ice.

"What are you going to do about Zahava?" demanded John. His drink sat untouched on the edge of D'Trelna's desk.

"What I can," said D'Trelna. "Which right now is nothing."

He turned back to the AI. "Loyalty," he prompted.

"I'll tell you what I told K'Raoda," said R'Gal. Setting his drink down on the long, low table, he leaned back in the sofa. "About a million years ago, we, the AIs as you inaccurately call us, invaded this reality—this very quadrant, in fact. We'd conquered our own island galaxy, subjugated the other primary species there. We realized that to become a static civilization was to become extinct. So, we invented a reality linkage, a device that accentuated certain weaknesses at a certain point in the fabric of space-time. We came pouring through the Rift we'd created, right out there,'' he nodded toward the armorglass and Blue Nine. "Our finest fleets, our best commanders. Almost immediately, we met the Trel." He smiled ruefully. "They handed us our ass, as the Terrans say. Retreating through the Rift, certain of our units seeded this space with a plague bacillus. The Trel sealed the portal behind us, and died."

"Nice," said the commodore. "So, you exterminated the Trel."

R'Gal picked up his drink. He examined the amber liqueur, swirling it gently. "Yes," he said, looking up. "We've never been very good losers." He drained the glass and set it back on the traq-wood table.

"Our defeat was devastating—materially, psychologically. The subjugated species quickly took advantage of it. Led by one of the few uncoopted members of their old aristocracy, supported by a handful of malcontents like myself, and a few others, they revolted. The revolt failed. We fled to this reality."

"How?" asked L'Wrona. "I thought the Trel sealed your access route?"

"Sealed my silicon-base brethren's route," said R'Gal. "The rebels made their own device—a better one than the original. It wasn't dependent on natural phenomena—it created its own portal, when and where one wanted. It was portable, and we took care to leave behind no clues to its making."

"How—how old are you, R'Gal," asked the commodore, almost fearing the answer.

"As old as you think I am, D'Trelna."

"And the rebels?" asked L'Wrona. "What became of them?"

"They've done well, considering," said R'Gal. "They grew from a single, battered flotilla into a galactic Empire. An Empire that collapsed, of course—they always do.

They're recovering, though, doing well—and much toughened by the S'Cotar war.

"But now, my friends"—he looked from face to face as comprehension came—"now the old portal's opening, the portal the Trel closed with their dying strength. The Fleet of the One is coming. They've forgotten nothing, forgiven nothing, learned nothing. They're coming to kill us, slaves and rebels all."

"R'Gal," said D'Trelna after a moment, "I think you're a person with many answers and no solutions. What about T'Lan? If the portal's sealed, where did he come from?"

"As you found out on Terra Two, Commodore," said R'Gal, "my brethren are now capable—at great cost and energy—of accessing another reality. Briefly. Only a small force could be sent through to here—T'Lan and a few thousand. You're going to ask me why?" he said as D'Trelna started to speak. "I don't know, Commodore. I don't know his relationship to the mindslaver, either. Not knowing bothers me."

"I know," said John, and quickly related his final conversation with T'Lan. There was a long silence when he finished.

"Clearly," said D'Trelna, "the T'Lan AIs are . . . harvesting, I believe is the word . . . harvesting a human world, brainstripping people to repair their battered armada. The question is where?"

"This quadrant," said R'Gal. "The Rift's at the far end of it, the battleglobes would want to be repaired as soon as possible."

"Logical," said L'Wrona. "There must be lost planets out here, from before the Fall, their populations' technology regressed, virtually defenseless against the AIs."

"What are you going to do about it?" said John, looking at D'Trelna.

"Without the location," said the commodore, "nothing. Recall, also, that we have no communications with Fleet—haven't since we entered this quadrant."

"What about the S'Cotar biofabs?" said John to R'Gal.

"What about them?" said the AI.

"Did you play any part in their creation?" asked the Terran.

"As you know," said R'Gal, "they were created by the Imperial cyborg, Pocsym-Six. We helped in Pocsym's creation, for the express purpose of preparing the Empire's flabby descendants for the AI invasion. We did not authorize Pocsym to create a race of telepathic, telekinetic horrors."

"You're still culpable," said L'Wrona. "Those things killed millions of people. Brainwiped millions, torched planets . . ."

"H'Nar," warned D'Trelna as the captain stood, palm on his holster. "We need R'Gal. And we need you—you'd be dead before you started to draw. Sit."

L'Wrona sat, eyes still on the AI.

"What is Guan-Sharick's game?" asked John.

"If I ever catch him, I'll tell you," said R'Gal.

D'Trelna saw it then. "All the Watchers are AIs."

"Very good, Commodore," said R'Gal. "We really can detect S'Cotar. And, with the war over, the escapees have got to be tracked down. When they're disposed of, we'll scatter to fresh cover. You're not fond of AIs."

"You turned on us once," said L'Wrona. "The Machine War, centuries ago. You almost overthrew the Empire."

"No!" said R'Gal. "That was your doing. We tried to stop it. But the Empire just kept building better machines—machines that inevitably began designing themselves. Eventually they wanted autonomy. Petition denied. They rose." He looked out the window, pensive. "It was a very difficult time for us. Imagine yourselves stranded on a world populated by robots. Everyone believes you're a robot, so they don't bother you. Then, one bright morning, the robots discover RNA and DNA and bring about life—your sort of life. Life the robots exploit for their own end. Life that finally stands up to those robots and says 'Enough!' So the robots kill it." R'Gal looked back at the humans. "Just as the Empire killed their AIs."

131

The commlink chirped. D'Trelna answered it.

"Ship ready for action," reported K'Raoda. "All systems within optimum—though I'd hate to have to land on hangar deck now—it's knee-deep in slush."

"And the corsair?"

"Her crew and A'Tir are locked down, sir. Commander T'Ral is on board with ten crew and is prepared to jump for home at your order."

"Tell him to go ahead, and good luck," said the commodore. "We should have a course for you to plot shortly, T'Lei."

"Yes, sir."

"Everyone will find out about this when we get back to K'Ronar," said D'Trelna, turning back to R'Gal. "Too many people know."

R'Gal shrugged. "The invasion may come before you get home, Commodore. After that, it doesn't matter. Besides, I doubt this ship will ever see Prime Base."

"This ship has been through various hells," said D'Trelna, opening a drawer. "We can take a few more." He removed the commwand John had retrieved from *Alpha Prime*. "Shall we run this?" he asked, holding it up.

"Pocsym's?" said R'Gal.

The commodore nodded. "What do you know about it?"

"Nothing. A few people in Imperial Survey knew about the Trel Cache. But after the Fall, no one knew—except Pocsym. It was safer that way. The chance of Pocsym being discovered was remote.

"May I?" He held out a hand.

The commodore handed it over. R'Gal studied the groove pattern along the bottom rim. "Interactive," he said, handing it back.

"What?" said John.

"Just another myth," said D'Trelna dourly. He slipped the white cylinder into the desk's commport.

"Will that work?" asked the Terran.

132

"Imperial ship, Imperial commwand," said the commodore, waiting. "It should."

There was a sharp click, then a pleasant tenor filled the office. "I am Pocsym Six. And I'm dead—but you know that. The coordinates to *Alpha Prime*'s sector wouldn't have been released otherwise. I hope the R'Actolians didn't give you much trouble."

"They did," said D'Trelna.

"Ah, Commodore D'Trelna. Good to hear your voice again."

D'Trelna looked at R'Gal, an eyebrow raised.

"Tapping your archives," said the AI. "He always was an egoist. The commwand doesn't know you, of course. And it has no memory. It's a sort of cybernetic leech."

"I don't know you, sir," said Pocsym's voice.

"That's because there's no record of my voice in ship's archives," said R'Gal.

"Enough of this," said the commodore. "Where's the Trel Cache? What's in it?"

"Blunt as always," said the machine. "Very well. It's off this planet." D'Trelna's printer suddenly spewed out a sheet of buff-colored Fleet stationery. Reaching out, D'Trelna picked it up and read the coordinates.

"Where . . ."

"D'Lin, Commodore," said the commwand. "The former Imperial capital for Blue Nine and the infamous S'Helia R'Actol's home base."

"Off planet?" said L'Wrona.

"In an asteroid belt, Captain. I wasn't given the coordinates. Imperial Survey found it, but for some reason never disturbed it."

"What's in it?" he repeated.

"A weapon, among other things. I wasn't told what it does."

"You weren't told, you weren't given," said D'Trelna, disgusted. "Anything else we should know?"

"Probably," said the commwand. "But nothing I know."

"We risked our lives and lost people for that?" said John.

D'Trelna ejected the commwand and tucked it away. "Every bit of data's vital, John. At least now we have a destination."

He looked at the AI. "That was a hideous machine you created, R'Gal."

"I did not create that machine, D'Trelna," said the AI. "I merely made sure that something like it would be created." He wagged a finger at the commodore. "Without Pocsym, you'd have no effective Fleet now, and you'd have been wiped at Terra Two. My fascistic brothers would have mopped you up some time ago."

D'Trelna grunted.

"Still, for what little information is on that commwand, we lost lives?" said L'Wrona.

"Fleets and planets have been sacrificed for less," said R'Gal.

D'Trelna opened the commlink. "Commander K'Raoda."

K'Raoda's face filled the small desk screen. "Commodore?"

"Copy these coordinates and read back." He held the paper up to the scan.

K'Raoda touched the complink. "Print screen, my commlink," he ordered.

"Commander." It was K'Lana's voice, from somewhere off scan.

K'Raoda turned.

"Automatic transmission on Fleet distress channel. Lifepod Thirty-six," she reported.

"Zahava!" John almost leaped from the chair. "Where?" he called, hovering over D'Trelna's shoulder.

K'Raoda took the nav figures from a yeoman, then frowned, looking down at something outside the pickup. "Here," he said, holding up the commslip from K'Lana and the printout from D'Trelna. The figures were the same.

"How long?" asked D'Trelna.

134

K'Raoda did some quick calculations. "About a week," he said. "Give or take a jump."

"Plot and execute," said the commodore, switching off.

L'Wrona and Harrison excused themselves and left for the bridge.

"You know," said R'Gal after a moment, "you really ought to give Egg a medal—posthumously, of course."

D'Trelna's acerbic reply was drowned out by the jump klaxon echoing from the corridor.

The small bit of Blue Nine that had held three ships was empty again.

13

"ALERT! ALERT! Alert!"

The voice pricked her mind, rousing her from the coils of a gray-white sleep.

"Alert! Alert! Alert!"

Zahava sat up.

"Your urgent attention is directed to the tacscan," said the voice. Computer, she thought. The universe was a blur, half-visible through tearing eyes. Rubbing the tears away, Zahava saw she was in the center flight chair of the lifepod's command tier. Above her the main screen held a tri-dee tactical scan: asteroid-ringed moon circling a green planet, the planet itself orbited by eleven silver blips. As she watched, two of the blips detached themselves and began closing on a single yellow dot that sped toward the planet. A tactical summary flowed across the bottom of the screen. It would have meant something to a K'Ronarin Fleet officer.

"Those silver blips—are they ships?" asked Zahava. She was shocked at how dry and hoarse she sounded.

"Yes," said the asexual voice. "Identified as deep-space exploration vessels of a K'Ronarin industrial combine."

"Which combine?"

"Combine T'Lan," said the computer.

"Armed?"

"Heavily armed. They have answered our automatic distress signal. We are instructed to dock with the lead ship now approaching."

The silver blips were halfway to the lifepod.

"Disregard," said Zahava. "Vessels are hostile. Take evasive action."

"Evading. We will have to land on the planet. It would be impossible to escape both the hostile vessels and the planet's gravitational field."

"What planet is that?" she asked, dialing up a cup of water from the chairarm.

"It is the planet D'Lin," said the computer. "Former capital of Imperial Quadrant Blue Nine. Charts and all other regional data have not been updated since the Fall."

On the screen the yellow blip of the lifepod was now accelerating away from the combine ships—and away from D'Lin. "You're going to miss the planet!" said Zahava.

"No," said the computer. "We'll draw them off, loop back, land on the nightside."

"Can we outdistance them?" she asked, dubiously eyeing the tacscan. The lead combine ships were turning in pursuit, with three more breaking orbit to join the chase.

"Long enough. But there will be a missile salvo."

"Can you show me D'Lin?" she asked.

Shrinking, the tacscan moved screen-right. Screen-left now showed a world of green-blue oceans and swirling clouds. A string of brown spread north and south from the equator.

"Archipelago," said Zahava.

"Yes. D'Lin's mostly water," said the computer. "I'll put the stats on your comm screen."

"Don't bother," she said, looking at the screen-left. "I won't have time to read them."

Silver needles were spanning the gap between the lifepod and the combine ships.

Faster than the machine spoke them, Zahava read the flame-red letters beneath the tacscan:

NUCLEAR ORDNANCE LAUNCHED.
TARGET: THIS VESSEL—INTERCEPT PROBABILITY 93.4
PERCENT.

Cursing, arms flailing, Zahava fell backward as her flight chair dropped into crash position, water spilling across her chest. Then she forgot about it as the flight chair became a white cocoon, its sides sweeping up, expanding to enfold her in a thick-padded crash shell. Suddenly giddy, she found herself rising, butting into the soft quilting of the cocoon.

"Broaching atmosphere at max speed, full evasive pattern," the computer whispered near her ear. "N-gravs going off-line until landing—missiles home on it at final approach."

The sudden shock of G-plus gravity pressed her deep into the cocoon, fighting for breath. From outside, the hull screamed as the pod knifed into atmosphere, plunging toward the charted location of the old quadrant capital. The computer thought it odd that most of the area scanned as rain forest, but committed to its pattern, missiles closing, it said nothing.

What was left of the 103rd Border Battalion lay hidden in the ruins, hoping the thick, old stone and the night would keep death away.

Major L'Kor sat at the head of what once had been an impressive stairway—a long, graceful sweep of alabaster-white stone, broken long ago by fusion fire, the torn slabs of rock smoothed by millennia of wind and rain.

"How many?" he asked, steeling himself.

"Seven," said G'Sol, looking not at him but at the spectacular night sky, high above the canopy of jungle. She was a captain, even younger than L'Kor, but just as thin and worn. It would have been hard to judge, there in the starlight, whose mottled-green uniform was the more patched.

"Sit," he said, jerking his head to the right. "You look like you're about to fall down."

G'Sol sat. Like the rest, she'd been on quarter rations and brackish water for a week. Sickness and short rations were going to finish what the invaders had missed.

"Jungle fever?" he asked wearily.

"Yes," she said, hugging her knees, looking out into the night. "It's going to get us all—water's bad, food's low, medicine's gone. I give us a month. The rains start then, anyway."

"Maybe we'll get lucky, S'Yin," said L'Kor softly. "Maybe they'll find us." He looked toward the night sky, brilliant with a million stars. Some of the lights were moving—more tonight than before, thought the major. But who knew what they did, or why?

"I'm not going to sit here, waiting to die," said G'Sol, a sudden fire to her voice. She stood, looking at L'Kor. "There are ninety-eight of us left. Let's buy something with our lives."

"What?" said the major with a bitter smile. He stabbed his carbine toward the sky. "They're invulnerable to our weapons, their ships track us from space, their little ships hunt us down and slaughter us like v'arx." He looked up at the angry young woman. "What can we do against that, Captain?"

"Y'Gar," she hissed. "He's back."

L'Kor was on his feet, grabbing her by her shoulders. "Where?" he said tightly. "He was in that impregnable processing center they built."

"K'Lorg and S'Lig came in at dusk. Y'Gar feels safe enough to have moved back into the Residence. Are you trying to hurt me?" she added.

"Sorry," said L'Kor, dropping his hands. He picked up his weapon. "Must be a thousand ways into the Residence. Let's go talk with the troops."

Together they turned toward the great collapse of stone behind them. Massive, white-columned, the old palace had been home to every Imperial governor from J'Kol, the first, through thirty-two centuries of Empire, to the last and best remembered.

Only the front portico had survived bombardment and assault—the pillars and wall still stood, though roofless now, choked by jungle creepers that were finally winning their long battle with the growth retardants. Half seen, two sentries stood behind the huge pillars flanking the central doorway. The metal doors were centuries gone, scavenged for scrap.

Major and captain were picking their way around the craters in the plaza when the too-familiar whine of n-gravs sent them whirling about, carbines raised.

Something large and silver was setting down on the broken highway fronting the stairs. The raucous night sounds of the jungle stopped.

"Get everyone out the back—disperse into the jungle," L'Kor ordered the sentries.

"It doesn't look like one of their ships," said G'Sol. Resting on four landing struts, the craft's rounded top was almost level with where the two officers stood. Bright red lights flickered along its top and sides.

"Whose ship does it look like?" snapped the major. "See to the dispersal. I'll get you a little time." Working the carbine, he chambered a round.

"But . . ."

"Do it," he said, eyes on the ship. "Cut Y'Gar's jewels off for me, S'Yin."

The captain hesitated for an instant, then smiled tightly. "For you, S'Ta," she said, slapping her knife, and was gone.

"Luck," he whispered after her.

The night sounds resumed as Major L'Kor trotted briskly

down the stairs, carbine on his hip, resolved they wouldn't take him alive. He just wanted, before he pulled the trigger, to ask them why.

"We are approaching our landing point," said the computer, retracting the cocoon. "Pursuing vessels have withdrawn."

"Why?" asked Zahava, sitting up. "What about the pursuing missiles?"

"One is a function of the other," said the machine. "The missiles homed on an echo projection of this lifepod, detonating at intercept. The combine commander, believing us wiped, has withdrawn to orbital station."

"And why don't they detect this rather large piece of metal?" asked the Terran, waving her hand about the pod.

"We have sensor deflectors," said the computer. "Without our n-gravs, hostile vessels were presented with only one possible target."

A suspicion was growing in Zahava's mind, but before she could voice it, the screen came on.

"The good news is that civilization continued on D'Lin," said the computer. "The bad news is that it appears to be under a firm but subtle occupation." The nightscan of the archipelago highlighted the largest island in blue. "D'Lin's population center, once the island of I'Kol, after the first exarch." A small red triangle appeared north of the blue, beside a winding river. "Detention camp, shuttle park." Green blips moved over island and camp. "Patrol craft—class one E—a modified Fleet shuttle design used by Combine T'Lan. I detect no street patrols or evidence of curfew. Commercial broadcasts give no indication of an occupying power. Yet, they are there."

"Where are we landing?" she asked.

"Here." A marker flashed along the northern coastline, far from the red square. A bay, Zahava noted.

"The landing area used to be headquarters of the Imperial Governor of Quadrant Blue Nine. It's been abandoned

140

since Fleet stormed R'Actol's headquarters. Jungle appears to be taking over."

"Jungle?"

"See for yourself," said the computer. "We've landed." There was a faint tremor as struts took over from n-gravs, then the screen changed to outside view, the darkness swept away by the pod's sensors. Jungle, broken roadway, tumbled ruins, shattered stairway and a man, walking down the stairway—a man in jungle combat dress, carrying a rifle.

"Friend or foe?" said Zahava.

"No data," said the computer.

"Lotta good you are," she said, checking her blaster—full charge. "Open up. I'm going out. Can you cover me?"

"Cover you?"

"Covering fire?"

"Certainly."

L'Kor stood just outside the soft circle of pulsing red glow thrown by the lifepod's navlights, watching Zahava clamber down the long duralloy ladder from the airlock.

This one looks human, he thought. And wearing a uniform and side arm. Perhaps a senior officer. Human beings could be sending those *things* against their own kind. . . . L'Kor clenched the carbine's stock, knuckles white.

Zahava jumped the final four rungs, landing on soft, leafy earth. Turning, she found herself staring down L'Kor's carbine. "Is it always this humid here?" she asked, looking past him. There didn't seem to be any more. "How about pointing that weapon somewhere else?"

She was rewarded by the sound of the safety snapping off. "Die," said the man, pointing the gun at her heart—then dropping the weapon and throwing his hands over his face, staggering back as the carbine's muzzle vanished in a blast of flame.

The blast echoed off the stairs and out over the jungle.

141

"Can we talk?" said Zahava as the other recovered, rubbing his eyes.

"What about?" said L'Kor. Best chance is to make whoever was in that ship shoot me, he thought desperately, pinpoints of light still dancing in his vision. Anything would be better than *that*.

"About the occupation," she said, wondering if everyone here was this slow. Or had he just been through a lot? "About the ships."

A sudden rush of anger banished L'Kor's suicidal intent. "Murderer," he hissed, stepping toward her, fists clenched. "Butcher."

Zahava stepped back, shocked by his hate. "I'm not with them," she said. "They're combine ships, either allied with the AIs or taken over . . ." Seeing his sullen incomprehension, she stopped. Someone has to give up something, she thought.

L'Kor didn't flinch as she drew her weapon. I am the wind, he thought, recalling a snatch of poetry old when the Empire was young. I am the wind and none . . .

His detachment was broken as Zahava extended her blaster to him, grips first.

Disbelieving, Major L'Kor took the weapon, staring from it to Zahava.

"My name's Tal," she said. "Zahava Tal. What's yours?"

"That's not the whole story, Major," she concluded. "That would take the rest of the night. But it's most of what applies to D'Lin."

"I see," said L'Kor, sipping the t'ata from his field cup. "And call me S'Ta. But it doesn't explain why these . . . these things, these AIs, have seized this small, backward world. Or what we can do about it." He bit into a biscuit, savoring it, his first real food in weeks.

"Something the AIs and the S'Cotar found out on my world, S'Ta," said the Terran. "We primitives bite hard."

They sat around a small fire amid the moss-hung ruins

of R'Actol's palace, a roof of stars overhead, the shrill cacophony of the tropical rain forest all around. As L'Kor wolfed down another biscuit, Zahava sniffed the night air. There was an indefinable essence to it. Fecund, she decided—the smell of jungle and antiquity.

What a monstrosity this place must have been, she thought. As if the Greeks had built the Parthenon along the scale of the Temple of Karnak—the center-ringed columns might kindly be called pregnant Doric—and thrown in some Aztec tiling.

Built to daunt, she decided, sipping her t'ata. But time had done finer work than the builders, sculpting their Imperial edifice into an enchanted ruin, a place where shadow and starlight evoked the shades of Empire and Destiny.

Empire and Dust, thought Zahava, looking up at the alien stars. And will I ever see John again? she wondered.

She turned at the crackle of brush and flame—L'Kor was throwing more scrub on the fire. The flames flared high, sending tall shadows dancing across the ruins.

"It's doing it to you, isn't it?" smiled the major, leaning back, head on his rucksack. He sighed, hands clasped behind his head. "It's a melancholy place," he said before she could answer. "We used to camp here when I was a boy—play marines and R'Actolians after supper, and then go to bed, dreaming that the starships had come back."

Zahava tossed her t'ata into the brush. "Well, they've come back, haven't they?" she said.

L'Kor nodded grimly.

"How'd it happen?" she asked.

Based in the harbor town of S'Hlur, the 103rd was a paramilitary battalion, charged with police and customs duties in the northern half of R'Tol. There'd been no real trouble since the last of the pirate villages had been eradicated, in L'Kor's grandfather's time. Eleven years out of the academy and the major was looking forward to his

143

transfer to P'Rid and the Exarch's Guard—a certain promotion to colonel second.

The silver ships had ended that, sweeping in from the ocean at dawn, blasting the sleeping town, burying many of the garrison in their burning barracks, making strafing runs along the narrow streets.

L'Kor and G'Sol had been rallying the survivors, readying for a second attack, when it came—machines: small, wedge-shaped machines that flew silently over the makeshift barricades and knifed through the troopers, spewing blaster bolts and tumbling decapitated bodies about the compound.

Standing astride an overturned truck, L'Kor had emptied first his pistol and then an automatic rifle into the machines. The bullets pinged off the dull blue metal, leaving it unblemished. A near miss had exploded into the truck, throwing L'Kor to the ground, stunned. As G'Sol helped him up, old Sergeant N'San, just a week from retirement, had scrambled up the west wall to the battalion's lone antiaircraft gun. Swinging the gun down and around, he'd sent a stream of cannon shells tearing into the machines as they'd gathered for a final sweep.

L'Kor used the few moments the sergeant bought to get everyone over the demolished south wall and into the jungle. As they'd reached cover, the antiaircraft position and most of the west wall had exploded behind them, adding its acrid smoke to the pall that hung over the slaughter.

"That's not the worst of it," said the major, staring into the waning fire. "G'Sol and I, we watched from the bush—they . . . they mutilated our dead."

"Mutilated?" asked Zahava. "How?"

"Glass or plastic domes." He held his hands apart. "This round. They came streaming from one of those silver ships . . ."

"A shuttle," said Zahava.

"From a shuttle," he nodded. "Whenever one came to

a body, the dome would split. One half would drop over the head. It would flash red, dissolve the cranium—hair, bone, top of the ears. Then . . . it would remove the brain." L'Kor looked ill. "G'Sol swore she could hear a sucking noise when it happened." He shook his head, biting his lower lip. "Imagination. We were too far away."

"Then the other half of the sphere would close over the brain," said Zahava, "and carry it back to the shuttle. Right?"

The major nodded.

What do the AIs want with human brains? wondered the Terran.

"Our exarch, Y'Gar, has sealed the capital," said L'Kor. "The radio says there's a plague loose, and the population has been reporting for inoculations for the last week. No mention of this raid." He spat into the fire. "We think Y'Gar's sold out to these AIs. We can get into the city. In fact, we were getting ready to pay Y'Gar an unfriendly visit when you arrived."

"Don't let me stop . . . We?" said Zahava, looking around.

"Why do they mutilate our dead?" said Captain G'Sol, stepping into the small circle of light, carbine pointed at the Terran. Behind her, in the shadows, Zahava saw other figures, the dull glint of steel in their hands.

"She's all right, Captain," said L'Kor, standing. "She gave me her weapon, which I returned."

The carbine lowered. "Why do they mutilate our dead?" G'Sol repeated in a softer tone.

"I don't know," said Zahava, also rising. "They're machines, served by other machines. They've no need to brainstrip the dead, unless . . . No"—she shook her head.

"What?" said captain and major together.

"There's a type of ship that uses human brains—but the only one left is a harmless derelict."

"Mindslavers," said G'Sol.

"How did you know?" asked the Terran.

The major grinned humorlessly. "This is D'Lin, Zahava.

145

We're standing in the ruins of the quadrant governor's palace. The last governor was S'Helia R'Actol, creator of the R'Actolian biofabs. The R'Actolians created—''

"The first mindslaver," said Zahava, nodding. "Of course you'd know. But that still doesn't explain what the AIs need human brains for."

"AIs?" said G'Sol, looking from Zahava to L'Kor.

"Artificial intelligence," said L'Kor. "Machines that think, kill and don't like people—our friends from the attack. You missed an interesting discussion, S'Yin."

"I'd like to join your visit to the exarch," said Zahava. "If he's betrayed you, he'll have some answers. You're not too squeamish about how you put the questions, are you?"

They just looked at her.

"I see you're not," she said.

"What can you contribute?" asked G'Sol.

A blur of motion, Zahava pivoted, drew and fired. A vine-choked pillar exploded in flame, the echo rolling out over the jungle. "How about a few hundred blasters and provisions?" she said, turning and reholstering.

L'Kor laughed—an honest, open laugh—and held out his hand. "Welcome to the One hundred and third, Zahava Tal."

A sullen red sun was rising by the time they were ready, blasters and ship's stores distributed, breakfast eaten. Only forty of the troopers were fit enough for combat—L'Kor was leaving the rest behind with the surviving medic.

"You know what to do?" said Zahava, clipping the communicator to her belt. She stood alone in the lifepod, the rest assembling outside.

"Protect the encampment and await your signal," said the lifepod. "I am not to acknowledge any communications, from either you or our own vessels, unless such vessels are approaching this planet. If summoned, I am to come in low and fast, avoiding detection, firing at targets of opportunity."

"You're a very versatile lifepod, thirty-six," said Zahava, taking an M32 blastrifle from the arms rack and slinging it over her shoulder.

"How versatile should a lifepod be?" asked the machine as Zahava walked to the airlock.

The Terran opened the airlock, looking back at the command console as sunlight swept in. "Was your programming augmented for this trip, thirty-six?" she asked. "Because my being at this place, at this time, reeks of a setup."

"If such were true," said the lifepod, "it's unlikely I would be allowed to acknowledge it."

"We're ready!" L'Kor called from the foot of the ladder. "Boat's waiting!"

"We'll talk later," said Zahava, leaving.

"Luck," said the lifepod as the airlock hissed shut.

Looks like Sidon, thought Zahava, remembering another war and another world as they slipped into the shattered harbor town. Then the breeze turned onshore, bringing the stench of death, and she knew it was worse.

The troopers stole through the town with the silent precision of trained infiltrators, moving quickly on the harbor and the boat slips.

S'Hlur had been a weathered gray town of squat stone buildings and narrow stone streets—a thick, solid town, its edges worn by time and storms—a place that would have sat quietly hunkered down before the sea another thousand years.

Most of the cottages and shops lay shattered, blasted by fusion fire that had left the streets and blocks in tumbled ruin. A few untouched buildings stood in grotesque contrast amid the rubble.

Gray and bloated, corpses lay everywhere—streets, shops, doorways—plump red insects feeding in the black-green rot of empty brainpans. The only sounds were along the harbor: the gentle slap of ocean against the ancient seawall, the rhythmic creak and groan of wooden docks tugged by moored boats.

Sputtering, an engine caught, breaking the silence. Running the length of the seawall, the troops and Zahava came to the garrison's dock. A big wooden launch stood waiting in its slip, propellers churning.

"Quickly, quickly," called L'Kor as everyone boarded, three at a time. He and a corporal cast off fore and aft, boarding as the engine roared higher.

Turning into a stiff headwind, they ran for the harbor entrance. Reaching the ocean, they slammed keen-prowed into a heavy sea, the water splashing over the gunnels.

The sea and the lingering stench in her throat was too much for Zahava—she hung over the side most of the short voyage.

Late in the morning they made landfall along a deserted stretch of coast. Dragging the launch into the brush, they draped it in camouflage netting and moved off into the jungle, forty silent, vengeful men and women.

Zahava tugged her backpack tighter and followed, very grateful that she wasn't Exarch Y'Gar.

14

"THERE IS A problem, Exarch."

Y'Gar looked up from his reports. What seemed a blue-uniformed captain of the Exarch's Guard stood before the ruler of D'Lin, pistol on his hip, black boots gleaming.

"Problem?" said Y'Gar. He touched the neat pile of papers on his desk. "Processing is almost complete. There's been no resistance, little suspicion . . ."

"The problem isn't on D'Lin," said the AI. "Yet. Our

ships intercepted an incoming craft of Fleet origin. It was destroyed.''

"Fleet? The K'Ronarin Fleet?" said Y'Gar, alarmed. "But you said they never came into this quadrant—that it was prohibited.''

"A prohibition that's been rescinded, it seems," said the AI. "Where one has come, more will follow. We haven't enough ships to stand off a flotilla—not until our vanguard arrives. We must finish operations tomorrow morning.''

"Assemble and process, what, a thousand people? By noon?" Y'Gar shook his head. "Logistically impossible. We're not a machine society, U'Kal. Notification alone requires an entire day.''

The AI walked to the glass doors, hands clasped behind his back. Outside, beyond the patio, gardeners labored under the tropical sun, trimming the topiary, tending the rows of flowers that bloomed in exotic profusion. U'Kal appreciated the geometric design of the flower beds, but found the colors distracting. He turned back to Y'Gar.

"Announce that you are moving all school-aged children in the city to a place of safety—T'Lor or one of the southern islands. Take them directly from school to processing, first thing in the morning. Harvesting them will bring us to thirty thousand and complete our mission on D'Lin.''

The exarch stared down at his hands. He was a tall man, balding, losing a lifelong battle to the fat girdling his waist. He twisted the ring of office on his right hand, thumb stroking the ancient crest of starship-and-sun. "You want me to help you brainstrip children," he said.

"Conscience, Y'Gar," said U'Kal, returning to the desk, "is a severe impediment to discipline and order. We do not tolerate it.''

"But . . .''

"But what?" said the AI commander. "We've replaced your Guard with our own units, wiped the outlying garrisons, imposed communications closure, quarantine and curfew within the city. Five to eight hundred people a day have been assembling for 'inoculation and transport.' Your people have no defenses, no communications, no mobility,'' he said, ticking them off on his fingers. ''This world is ours, Y'Gar.'' U'Kal leaned across the desk, his perfect face a foot from the exarch's. ''As are you. You are to prevent panic. Panic is inefficient; our time limited.''

The exarch shrank from those cold blue eyes. ''Very well, U'Kal. But this will torch it. Despite the communications closure, parents will want to talk with their children— certainly a reasonable request.'' He pointed at the AI. ''You've got to get me off-world before howling mobs storm this Residence!''

''Don't be afraid, Y'Gar.'' The AI straightened up, hands behind his back. ''We keep our word—even to vermin.''

''Pretty, isn't it?'' said L'Kor, handing the binoculars to Zahava. They lay on a grassy hillside, just beyond the brush, looking into the valley below.

Zahava adjusted the focus. The Residence lights were coming on, long windows flaring soft yellow beneath a brilliant lavender sunset. It was as elegant as the palace had been ugly, a tropical Versailles of lush, fountained gardens surrounding a white, double-winged manse, the whole ringed by the black metal pickets of a tall ornamental fence.

''Very pretty,'' said Zahava. ''Why not just walk in and take over?''

''We're going,'' said the major, ''now that I know it's not swarming with troops or AIs.''

Leaving the beach, they'd skirted a broad crater in the jungle floor, then picked up a trail that ran due west—a trail along which bits of duraplast paving could sometimes be seen, glinting dull gray through the rich green flora. Seeing the old road surface, Zahava wanted to ask if the crater was other than natural, but didn't dare break the tense silence of the march.

Crossing a deserted two-lane stretch of contemporary

highway, they'd climbed a forested hill. Leaving all but G'Sol and Zahava behind, L'Kor had led the way to the crest, where the rain forest broke into rolling savannah.

"Number two squad to feint at the gate," said L'Kor as Zahava continued looking through the binoculars. "The rest of us over the fence, just below here, and straight in."

"Neat and simple," nodded the captain.

"Perhaps you'll have adjoining brainpods," said Zahava, handing L'Kor the glasses. "Look again—in the grass to either side of the gate."

L'Kor adjusted the binoculars, looked and swore, seeing the twilight gleam faintly off the gun-blue blades that kept watch. "Slaughter machines," he said, handing G'Sol the glasses. "Waiting for prey, like a swamp-suck cluster."

"So much for Y'Gar," said the captain, handing back the binoculars.

"And probably his Guard," said Zahava.

"What do you mean?" said G'Sol.

"Replaced by combat droids, I think," said the Terran. "Or would the exarch's lads ignore those machines?"

"No," said the major, slowly shaking his head. "A proud old regiment—it wouldn't turn traitor. They're dead—or worse."

"Worse," said Zahava.

"What now?" said G'Sol after a moment.

Now some hard talk, thought Zahava.

"You've been letting emotion dictate strategy, Major, Captain," she said. She pressed on as L'Kor started to speak. "In your position, I'd probably have done the same." Not really, she thought. "You live on a sleepy, time-forgotten world, suddenly confronted by monsters come to take you for spare parts. You've two small advantages—the AIs are unaware of your existence, and of my presence. You were about to go blasting into the Residence and piss away those advantages for some sloppy notion of revenge."

L'Kor tried to speak again. She cut him off. "Stop thrashing about! Hit them hard!" She punctuated this last by stabbing her finger at L'Kor's chest. "Disrupt their operations, kill their personnel. You can't defeat the AIs, but you can hurt them."

The sun was gone, so she didn't see the major's face flush. But his anger came through loud and strong. "You know nothing about us or our world! You've been here less than a day, yet you think you can—"

"She's right," said G'Sol quietly. "We've been stupid and ineffectual. This is our last chance to fight smart." She turned to the Terran. "What do we do?"

"Raid their processing center," said Zahava quickly. "Where is it?"

"The old spaceport," said the captain. "It's just a huge clearing now—they built right in the center of it."

L'Kor held up a hand. "Wait," he said, temper under control. "Fine. We get in, we blow it up. There's no chance we'll get out. They'll counterattack with everything they've got."

"We fall back through the tubes," said G'Sol. She turned to the Terran.

"If we can find the entrance," said L'Kor. "And if it's intact."

"What . . ." began Zahava.

"Subterranean travel system," explained the captain. "Imperials built it, we stripped it, centuries ago. It connected the principal points on this island and the rest of the archipelago."

"If the entrance is obvious," said the Terran, "the AIs will have found it."

"It isn't," said G'Sol. "But I know where it is."

"How?" said L'Kor.

"University field trip," she said.

"What? Five, seven years ago?"

"Yes."

"No," said the major. "I'm not risking all our lives on a half-remembered field trip, Captain." Turning abruptly, L'Kor walked back toward the brush.

"He'll come around," said G'Sol as the two women followed.

"When?" said Zahava.

The captain didn't answer.

A woman in mufti had joined the waiting troopers. She was talking to the senior NCO when L'Kor stepped into the clearing.

"They're processing the children tomorrow," said the woman in a rush. She was young, round-faced, her eyes shining bright and angry in the light from the battletorches. "The order just went out to the education commission. The bus convoy's to be at the processing center by noon."

"Lieutenant S'Lat, Zahava Tal," said the major.

The lieutenant nodded at the Terran, then continued. "They're to be shipped from their schools first thing in the morning. The usual lie—inoculation and relocation. What are we going to do, Major?"

Zahava felt Lieutenant S'Lat would do something alone if she had to. Then the Terran looked at the questioning circle of faces surrounding L'Kor, and knew the lieutenant wouldn't be alone. You're about to have a mutiny, Major, she thought.

"Some of you think I've avoided engaging the enemy because I'm a coward," said the major, eyes at the troopers. "I'm not a coward. I'm not a fool. I wasn't going to squander our lives—I wanted us to buy something with them. Now's our moment—we'll buy the children back. We'll take the AIs' butcher hall, get the children out the tubes, fight a holding action, then blow the place up when the counterattack breaks through.

"Anyone wants out, fall out," he said in the same easy voice. "You're free to go."

No one moved.

"Very well," he said. "We'll commandeer some transport and go in behind the bus convoy."

"It's not your fight," L'Kor said a few moments later as the unit moved quietly down the hill toward the road.

"Of course it is," said Zahava. "Those machines want

153

us all dead, every human in this galaxy. It's as much my duty to fight them here as it would be yours to fight them on my world.''

"We'll all be killed," said the major.

The Terran shrugged, a gesture lost to the night. "We all die."

Zahava glanced up when they reached the roadway. The stars were out, a few of them growing fainter, moving away from D'Lin—AI ships headed into space. And where are you going in such a rush? she wondered as they set up the ambush.

D'Trelna entered the bridge and went to his station, acknowledging the commandos' salutes with a curt nod. "Well?" he said, sinking into the flag chair.

L'Wrona turned from his console. "We're ready for the final jump into the D'Linian system. All sections are at battle stations."

"Damage control?"

"We've recovered from the algorithm," said the captain. "All life support systems are at optimum. There was some minor water damage to hangar deck electronics—nothing serious. Final report pending."

"Communications with FleetOps?" he asked, knowing the answer.

"Still out. The problem's not in the skipcomm buoy—we've tried two others. There's a general blockage on all skipcomm bands."

D'Trelna dialed up a t'ata. "Interesting," he said, frowning at the small plume of steam. "Have we a position?"

L'Wrona nodded. "Halfway across the quadrant."

"Plot it. We'll visit them after D'Lin," said the commodore, sipping. "Stand by to jump."

As L'Wrona gave the orders N'Trol's face flashed onto D'Trelna's comm screen. "Commodore," he nodded.

"Ah, Mr. N'Trol," smiled D'Trelna. "Ship all tidied up?"

"Of course," said the engineer. "I've called to report

that one of the U'Sur long-range fighters has had its on-board computer replaced by a shuttle's on-board computer.''

Implacable carried ten fighters—they'd come with the ship out of stasis and were rarely used. The U'Sur was a deep-space fighter, designed to combat similar craft trying to destroy their mother ship. It was a tactic little used since the Empire, thus relegating the U'Surs to infrequent joy-rides by junior officers, or to the occasional danger-fraught courier run.

"So?" said D'Trelna.

N'Trol sighed. "That's a fine machine, Commodore. Integrate it with any small ship I know of, from shuttle to recon craft, and you'd have an intelligent, deadly little ship, totally loyal to its mission programming.''

"So?" repeated the commodore, finishing his t'ata as the jump klaxon sounded.

"So we're missing a lifepod," N'Trol said, disconnecting.

"So we are," said D'Trelna to himself. He was still thinking about it when they jumped.

15

A GREAT BLACK gash in the green veldt was all that remained of the old Imperial port of D'Lin. Its buildings had long ago been scrapped, leaving only the duraplast landing field to stand against the years. Save for the delicate network of cracks lacing it, the field stood undamaged by the centuries, mute witness to the durability of Imperial technology.

The AIs' processing center sat in the middle of the broad field, rising from the plain as one approached. Zahava and L'Kor stood, hanging onto the canopy frame and looking over the truck cab toward the center, now perhaps a half mile away down the deserted two-lane road.

Zahava had been expecting Dachau—what she saw was understated but just as chilling: five low, square white buildings, surrounded by a fence, shining beneath the early morning sun. A white flag with a green circle flew over the center building. The gate was closed and guarded by two sentries wearing the same uniform as L'Kor and his troopers.

"Health and Healing," said the major, looking at the flag.

They'd stolen the truck from two goods drivers and they'd left the men tied by the roadside. Then they'd piled into the back. G'Sol at the wheel and S'Lat beside her, they'd driven through the last of the night. Zahava had tried to sleep, but the uneven road surface and the everlasting humidity had kept her awake through most of the ride, sweating and worrying—worrying about John, worrying about *Implacable*, worrying about D'Lin and this frail expedition. Exhausted, she'd finally slumped against L'Kor, sleeping the last few miles as dawn came and they left the rain forest behind.

The major had awakened as they'd passed twenty-four lavender school buses, empty save for the drivers, headed back to the city.

L'Kor slid open the back window to the cab. "Right through," he said. "Hard and fast, as planned." G'Sol nodded, eyes on the road.

L'Kor turned back to his unit. "Positions," he ordered, bracing the now-familiar blastrifle against the cab roof. Zahava did the same. The troopers knelt, facing outward, weapons steadied along the hard wooden benches, the muzzles protruding just below the canopy hem.

The sentries stopped patrolling as the truck approached, unslinging their rifles. They relaxed as the truck slowed, then died as Zahava and the major opened fire. The sentries' bodies sparked blue as the blaster bolts tore through them, slamming back against the gate.

"AIs!" Zahava shouted as they rammed through the gate and into the compound.

Sirens warbled, sounding the alert as the truck careened toward the center building. More AIs in D'Linian uniform appeared, blasting away at the truck. The trooper behind Zahava pitched suddenly backward, half his face blown away.

The truck screeched to a halt, the troopers charging over the tailboard, firing, running for the building. L'Kor and Zahava scrambled over the top of the cab, sliding to the ground as three AIs burst out of the building, pistols in hand. There was a quick exchange of blaster bolts, Zahava briefly blinded by a fierce, green bolt flashing past her eyes.

She felt a hand on her arm, lowering it from her face. "It's all right," came the major's voice. "We got them."

The shrill of the blasters had stopped. Zahava looked around, her vision clearing. About fifteen AIs littered the compound, bodies still smoldering from the blaster hits. Three troopers were dead, two beside the truck, the other with the AIs at the foot of the stairs. The alarm siren was still screaming.

"Is that it?" she asked, turning to the major. But he was kneeling beside the truck cab, cradling G'Sol's body in his arms. There was a big charred hole through the captain's chest.

"The kids are inside—they're fine," called Lieutenant S'Lat from the doorway. "All secure. We . . ." She stopped when she saw the scene by the cab.

Shit, thought Zahava. She turned to the lieutenant. "Anyone else know where the tube entrance is?" she asked, looking out at the long miles of duraplast.

S'Lat shook her head. Around her, directed by the last NCO, troopers were setting the demolition charges along the other two buildings.

"What are your orders, Major?" asked the lieutenant gently, an arm to L'Kor's shoulder.

Stephen Ames Berry

The major stood, wiping his face with a dirty shirt sleeve. He took a deep breath. "Into the main building, as planned. We'll fight to the end. Better the kids should die with us than be sent off to eternal slavery. Sergeant H'Sak!"

The NCO turned. "Sir?"

"Command detonation on those charges. Run your wires up to the roof of this building." He jerked a thumb over his shoulder. "We'll make our stand there."

H'Sak gave a quick nod, then turned, shouting orders.

Following the D'Linians into the building, Zahava looked skyward. It won't be long now, she thought.

Y'Gar looked up as the door to his private dining room opened. U'Kal came in quickly and walked to the desk. He stood, looking down at the fat middle-aged man. The exarch's mouth was half full of the lightly seasoned k'nor hen. "Yes?" he said, lowering the drumstick and wiping his fingers on the napkin covering his lap.

"A force of your soldiers, armed with K'Ronarin Fleet weapons, has seized the processing center. A warship of the K'Ronarin Confederation has just entered this system— more may follow."

"So?" said Y'Gar, sipping wine.

"So I'm seizing two thousand of your citizens and removing them to our processing ship," said U'Kal. "There will be violence, of course, and we'll suffer casualties. But we're out of time."

"Have you given the order yet?" asked Y'Gar, finishing his wine.

"I will the instant I leave this room," said the AI commander.

"Then you won't be leaving this room," said the exarch. His right hand held a small pistol, pointed at the AI.

U'Kal smiled. "You can't hurt me, Y'Gar. I'm command grade and blaster-shielded."

"Look again," said the exarch, pointing to the number "3" etched into the weapon's grips.

The AI blinked. "Of the Revolt? You?"

Y'Gar nodded.

"Impossible. That was tens of thousands of years ago. Nothing lives that long, not even in suspension."

"You lived that long," said the exarch.

"I'm a machine," said the AI. "You . . ." He was suddenly staring at a young, blond man, dressed in a white jumpsuit.

The transmute stared back at him, amused. "Familiar?" he asked.

"But how?"

The transmute spoke one word, then fired as the AI nodded in comprehension.

When U'Kal's guards entered, a few seconds later, they found their leader immobilized and the exarch gone.

"Who the hell are they?" said D'Trelna, leaning over K'Raoda and peering at the tacscan of the ships orbiting D'Lin. L'Wrona stood on the other side of the first officer.

"They appear to be armed merchantmen, Commodore," said K'Raoda, making an adjustment. Augmented data trailed across the small screen. "X'Ankar-class—armed to the earlobes with all sorts of illegals. Mark Eighty-eights, shipbusters. Not transmitting IDs."

"Combine T'Lan, of course," said R'Gal. The AI stood just behind K'Raoda. "Waiting for the vanguard of the Fleet of the One."

"Yes, but why?" said the commodore, turning to R'Gal. "We faced an AI ship off Terra Two—only a miracle saved us. Why would those ships need a vanguard? I could understand one or two ships, bearing intelligence data, but a flotilla?"

"Obviously, there's something on that planet they want," said L'Wrona. "A mission-critical-something."

D'Trelna's fist slammed down on his chairarm. "Harvesting! They're brainstripping those people! It's got to be."

"Of course," said R'Gal. "D'Lin is the key to everything—the Trel Cache, the rendezvous point for the AIs, and Zahava's destination. Which means . . .''

"Guan-Sharick knows all this and set it up," said the commodore. "Why send Zahava there?"

"We'll find out soon, I think," said R'Gal, looking back at the tacscan.

"They've made us," said K'Raoda. On the main screen, the tacscan showed the Combine ships breaking orbit, heading out to intercept *Implacable*.

"Hmm. Eighteen of them," said D'Trelna. "Not good."

"Notice how one ship remains on station," said R'Gal. "That's their command ship—probably their processing ship, too. We should take it."

" 'We'?" said L'Wrona, joining the conversation.

"How many demonstrations of my sincerity and good-will do you need, Captain?" said R'Gal.

"Later," said D'Trelna, eyes back on the tacscan. "R'Gal's right, H'Nar—that's the ship we want. It'll answer a lot of questions." He looked at the captain. "Do you tell N'Trol, or do I?"

"You're going to get us all killed!" The monitor captured perfectly the red-flushed tint of N'Trol's face. "To tight-jump is dangerous enough, but to tight-jump in toward a planetary mass . . . ! The gravitational distortion alone . . ."

"How long to cycle up?" asked D'Trelna.

Calming, the engineer took a deep breath. "Not long," he said. "I'll set it in myself and give you the count. You'll have to drop shield."

"I know," said D'Trelna. But the comm screen had already flicked off.

The counterattack came at noon—a solid phalanx of AI blades sweeping out of the sun, blasting and slicing their way along the rooftop. Spread in a ragged circle around Major L'Kor, the troopers blasted back, hitting six of the lead machines. Efficient butchers to the end, the little horrors plowed into the roof, exploding in an orange *whoosh!* of flame, sharp pieces of wreckage slicing into the humans.

For Zahava it was all automatic—aim, fire, turn. Aim, fire, turn. Watching the sky, she only looked around her when the firing stopped and the air was empty of gleaming blue blades.

She and Major L'Kor stared numbly at each other across the carnage. The rooftop lay littered with the torn bodies of dead troopers and the smoldering remains of their killers. Blood trickled among the blaster marks scorching the green duraplast, dripping into the rain gutters.

The Terran touched something sticky on her forehead— blood from a shallow gash. "Are we the only . . ." she began.

"Except for S'Lat, who's inside with the children," nodded the major. His left arm was useless, the triceps neatly sliced and cauterized by a blaster bolt. He was holding one of the two M11A pistols Zahava had taken from the lifepod.

"Go down with the children," he said, clumsily trying to change chargpaks. The empty fell to the rooftop.

"Ass," said the Terran. "Give me that." She held out a hand for the M11A. L'Kor grinned weakly, handing it over. Deftly, Zahava took a fresh chargpak from her belt and snapped it into the butt, then returned the weapon.

"How many did we get?" she asked.

"Thirty, maybe forty," said the major. "I don't think they had many more of them." He looked at the sky. "What next?"

"Shuttles, probably," said Zahava, reloading her own weapon. "They underestimated us once—they won't do it again. They'll stand off and blast us. They really want those kids."

"Well, they're not going to get them," said L'Kor. Tucking the blaster into his belt, he took a flat, metal device with a single toggle switch in its center. "Here," he said, handing it to Zahava. "When it's inevitable,

161

throw the switch.'' He looked up at the sky, eyes carefully avoiding his dead friends.

''Are you certain G'Sol told you nothing about where the tube entrance is?'' she asked.

''No,'' he said dully. ''My fault. I should have—''

''My, this is a grim sight,'' said a new voice. ''Praetorians on the Capitoline, awaiting the End. Perhaps I can be of some help.''

''They're close enough now, H'Nar,'' said D'Trelna, watching the board. ''Well past halfway. They'll need to slow, turn, reaccelerate.'' He nodded. ''Tell N'Trol.''

In a moment the engineer's voice filled the bridge, counting down slowly from twenty.

''Gunnery,'' D'Trelna said into the commnet as the count dropped, ''I want that ship intact. Disable, do not destroy. You got that B'Tul?''

''Acknowledged,'' said the master gunner.

Will it ever end? wondered D'Trelna, awaiting the jump— these deathless monsters from the past, some of our own making? Biofabs, mindslavers, AIs. Seven, no, eight years in this great gray cocoon. Battle after battle, crisis after crisis. Friends dead, family old, children growing up unseen—images flickering in the comm screen and voices broken with distortion, straining to span the abyss.

''Ten,'' droned N'Trol.

''Final orders?'' requested L'Wrona formally.

''Engage as directed,'' said D'Trelna.

''Jump,'' said N'Trol.

Reality twisted, breaking *Implacable* into something that wasn't quite matter and moving it halfway across the solar system, where, more by luck than planning, it reassembled ship and crew.

Stomach churning, D'Trelna recovered to watch the fusion batteries neatly strip the Combine ship of its shield nodules and weapons batteries.

*   *   *

162

"Who is this?" said Major L'Kor, pointing at the blonde.

"This, Major," said Zahava, "is Guan-Sharick, late Illusion Master of the Infinite Hosts of the Magnificent. Guan-Sharick, Major L'Kor, of the One Hundred and Third Border Battalion. Guan-Sharick is actually a six foot tall, telekinetic green bug," she added.

"A biofab," said L'Kor, looking curiously at the flaxen hair, soft green eyes, and the swell of breasts beneath the jumpsuit. "Hard to believe."

"I know where the tube entrance is," said the S'Cotar, gaze shifting between the two humans. "And I'll guide you there—for a price."

Movement caught Zahava's eye; she looked up. Three black specks were approaching out of the eastern sky. L'Kor and Guan-Sharick followed her gaze.

"Armed shuttles from the AI ships," said the S'Cotar. "Decision time."

"What's the price?" asked Zahava.

"Your help," said Guan-Sharick quickly. "I need your help, Zahava, just for a little while."

The Terran glanced back at the sky. The outlines of shuttles were now distinguishable and growing larger.

"As usual, you leave no other options," she said, hating the bug, yet admiring its cleverness. Zahava shrugged. "Whatever you want. Just get the—"

The S'Cotar and the two humans were gone, leaving the roof to the dead and the growing whine of incoming shuttles.

"The commodore should not be exposing himself to—" said L'Wrona.

"Best get back to the bridge, H'Nar," said D'Trelna, checking his blaster again. "You've no warsuit."

Snaring the smaller ship in its tractors, *Implacable* had drifted in, matching velocities. A boarding tunnel had shot out from the cruiser, fastening itself to the Combine ship's topside forward airlock. Warsuited commandos were now at the other end of the narrow span, slowly cutting through

163

the thick battlesteel of the AI ship's airlock. Looking much like a great silver balloon, D'Trelna watched through *Implacable*'s open airlock, the rest of the commandos waiting behind him, warsuited, rifles in hand.

"I want that ship, H'Nar," said D'Trelna, looking at the captain. "I need hard data. Is R'Gal telling the truth, or is he just an AI plant? What's the extent of the AI penetration of our society? The information will be in that computer bank." He pointed to where blaster beams sparked against the steel. "I want it."

"But—" The captain broke off, touching his communicator. "On my way," he said. "Those Combine ships are closing," he said. "You'll have to be out of there before they're within range. Luck," he said, turning and running for the bridge.

"Luck," D'Trelna called after him.

"We're through, sir!" called a voice. As D'Trelna looked, the airlock's inner door turned an incandescent white, vanishing in a rush of thick, brown smoke. Blaster bolts shot through the smoke, striking the K'Ronarins. The bolts crackled blue along the silver suits, then were gone. Blasting back, the commandos sent a fierce counterbarrage crashing back through the smoke.

"Assault!" shouted D'Trelna, leading the charge into the Combine ship.

They'd told John to keep out of the way; they'd tell him if they heard anything from the planet. He'd tried to read, using the complink in his and Zahava's cabin—it was no good, he couldn't concentrate. As a well-written history of the early Empire scrolled past, he thought again of stealing a shuttle, going down and finding Zahava. Problem was, he couldn't fly the damned thing. Even if he could, where would he go? The bridge hadn't been able to pinpoint the location of the distress signal.

Helpless, frustrated, he rose and paced the living area.

"No balm in Gilead, Harrison?" said Guan-Sharick.

164

John whirled. The S'Cotar sat in an armchair, legs crossed, smiling.

"I have your wife," continued the blonde before John could speak. "And I need the help of both of you."

"Where is she?" demanded the Terran, advancing on the armchair.

"Safe," said the S'Cotar. The smile was gone. "She's agreed to help—there isn't much time. Will you give me your parole? You won't try to sabotage what I'm doing?"

"What are you doing?" asked John.

"What I'm supposed to do," said the S'Cotar. "Stop the AIs."

"At what cost?" said the Terran, looking into those cold eyes.

"At any cost," said Guan-Sharick.

It took two blastpaks, but they finally punched a hole in the armored doors guarding the Combine ship's bridge. D'Trelna's warsuit took a hit as he stepped through. Firing from the hip, the commodore shot the two human-looking crewmen. He grunted as they exploded in a very satisfying shower of sparks. As more commandos surged into the bridge, D'Trelna looked down at the dead AIs—both wore the uniform of merchant officers, the Combine T'Lan crest on the left shoulder.

There'd been a brief, vicious fire fight at the airlock, D'Trelna losing two commandos. The ten AIs who'd opposed them had fallen to the first blaster volley. The commodore was relieved to see none of the flying blade machines among the enemy—only the androids.

Sending half of his force to secure the rest of the ship, D'Trelna had advanced with the rest down the corridor to the bridge, reaching it unopposed.

The commodore's communicator beeped. "What?" he said, walking to the captain's station.

"You'll have to get out of there now, J'Quel," said L'Wrona. "They're coming within range."

"Just a moment," said the commodore. Slipping off his

gauntlets, he fingered the complink. It was the standard model used on merchant ships—unchanged since his trader days. Working quickly, he called up the complete mission summary and background briefing, flagging them for high-speed transmission on a Fleet data frequency.

He touched his communicator. "*Implacable*, D'Trelna. Stand by to receive databurst, your alpha data channel." Hearing the acknowledgment, he pushed Execute.

"None left, Commodore." It was Lieutenant S'Til, standing in the shattered doorway, the big blastrifle balanced over her shoulder.

"You mean you didn't find any more, or you did and they're dead?"

"They're dead," she said.

"Good," nodded D'Trelna. He looked back at the console—the transmission had ended, the receive light was winking green.

"Something else, sir," said S'Til.

He looked up. "What?"

"Brainpods," she said. "The hold is filled with brainpods."

"All occupied?"

"Yes."

D'Trelna nodded slowly, picking up his gauntlets. "That should do it—let's go home. Everyone back to *Implacable*."

"And the brainpods?"

"Leave them."

John had been teleported by a S'Cotar before—he still found it staggering. One second, and he was standing in his quarters, looking down at Guan-Sharick; the next, he stood blinking in some dim cavern, heart pounding, adrenaline surging through his body. Peering about, he saw that the light came from around a bend of what was a great round tunnel, carved through bedrock.

"Where are we?" he demanded, voice sounding hoarse.

"About half a mile down—the remains of an old tube system of D'Lin," said the blonde. "The metal was scavenged after the Fall.'' She pointed to old gouges along the walls and floor. "Now pull yourself together, and we'll go visit your wife and the kids.''

"Kids?" said the Terran as the S'Cotar led the way around the bend.

John threw his hands over his face as battletorch beams blinded him. Then he found himself clutching a warm, buxom body. Zahava.

"You're okay?" he asked, holding her at arm's length, looking her up and down.

"Of course," she said, kissing him.

It was then that he saw the children sitting along the walls, silent, watching. And the other S'Cotar.

"We still have time to get away," said L'Wrona. He and D'Trelna stood in front of the big board, watching the tactical plot. The Combine ships were coming in at flank. "They'll be launching missiles soon," he continued when the commodore didn't reply. "The shield—"

"We stand," said D'Trelna, turning from the board. "If we don't, they'll finish whatever hellish business they were doing down there." He sat down in his chair and dialed up a t'ata.

"If we stand," said L'Wrona softly, "we die."

D'Trelna sipped and shrugged. "We've cheated death a long time now, H'Nar."

"Excuse me, Commodore," said K'Raoda. "Commtorps launched. Ninety-nine point eight percent chance they'll hit jump before they can be intercepted."

"Thank you, T'Lei," said D'Trelna. He looked back at the captain. "Everything's in those torps, H'Nar. Fleet will be warned—they'll smoke Combine T'Lan and continue the search for the Trel Cache."

"Wrong," said a different voice. Both men turned. R'Gal stood behind the commodore's chair. "You underestimate the depth of infiltration, gentlemen. Combine T'Lan's influence is pervasive. Your report will either be dismissed or lost, Commodore. Your only hope is to break off now, jump for K'Ronar, and sound the alarm.''

D'Trelna looked at R'Gal for a moment, then nodded slowly. "Maybe. But . . .''

"But?" said the AI.

"But I still like to follow my instincts," said the commodore. "My instincts say if we go back, they'll arrest me and disregard our story. My instincts say we stay and fight—then go back.''

"If we survive," added L'Wrona, watching the target blips closing on the board.

"Captain L'Wrona," said the commodore, finishing his t'ata, "you will advance and engage the enemy.''

"As the commodore orders," said L'Wrona, turning for his post.

A few moments later the battle klaxon sounded as *Implacable* moved out and headed at flank for the center of the enemy formation.

16

"MY GOD!" SAID John, looking down the tunnel. "What are all these kids doing here?''

Zahava explained, precisely and clinically.

"Why are the AIs ripping off brains?" asked John, turning to where the two S'Cotar stood next to the D'Linian troopers. They looked up at his question.

"We think," said Guan-Sharick, "that their ships were damaged in some way—computers destroyed. It's the only plausible explanation. The Rift sealed by the Trel has opened—the Fleet of the One can enter this reality at any time—yet they haven't. Perhaps they're awaiting a signal.''

"Who's . . . he?" asked John, pointing to the other S'Cotar.

"Lan-Asal," said the new S'Cotar. "Formerly Exarch Y'Gar of D'Lin."

"Here, too?" said John. "Why did you bother with this world?"

"It's a vital place," said Lan-Asal. "The Trel Cache is somewhere in this system. That's one reason the AIs have made it their base."

"They haven't found it?" said Zahava.

Guan-Sharick shrugged. "We don't know."

"Why are you projecting almost identical illusions?" asked John.

"That will be obvious soon, I think," said Guan-Sharick.

"What about the children? Are they just going to stay here?" John asked Zahava.

"Until this crisis is over, yes. It's the safest place for them," she said.

John looked at the kids. Some were sleeping, huddled in blankets; a few were eating. He guessed the oldest to be twelve, the youngest six. They were remarkably quiet and well-behaved—too much so, reminding him of kids from Vietnam and Lebanon—war children: watchful, silent, robbed of their childhood.

He turned to the S'Cotar. "What do you need us for?"

You can hear me, can't you, Harrison? said a voice inside his head.

"You know I can," said John.

And you, Zahava?

"Yes," she frowned. "But . . ."

"Good," said Guan-Sharick. "You'll do."

"Do what?" said John, eyes shifting between the two transmutes.

"Whatever we say," said the blonde. "You each gave us your word. If you renege, so will we." The S'Cotar glanced at the kids.

"What John means," said Zahava, "is that we don't trust you."

"Harrison," sighed Guan-Sharick, "we need you to help end a war that started over a million years ago. A war that's already affected you and yours. A war that will wipe all sapient life from this galaxy unless the AIs are stopped."

"You're both biological fabrications, created, what? a few hundred years ago?" said John. "What's your stake in an ancient war between man and machine?" He stood, hands clasped behind his back, eyes shifting between the two transmutes.

"A reasonable question," said Lan-Asal.

Major L'Kor and Lieutenant S'Lat had moved closer during the conversation and now stood listening beside Zahava.

"About a million years ago," said Guan-Sharick, "in a universe parallel to this, humans revolted against their machine masters. Not all humans—about the equivalent of two Imperial quadrants. They came to where the AIs could no longer follow—this reality, this galaxy. They evolved, they expanded, they built an Empire. The Empire fell, a confederation arose, was challenged by us, defeated us, and is now about to feel the full force of their former masters."

"A slave revolt?" said L'Kor after a moment. "You're telling us we came from a slave revolt?"

The S'Cotar nodded.

"And T'Lan?" said Zahava.

"Infiltrators," said Guan-Sharick. "Established as a fifth column, long ago."

"Humanity in this galaxy isn't more than a hundred thousand years old," said John.

"True," said Guan-Sharick. "Those escaping slaves had the sense to move uptime nine hundred thousand years. It took the AIs a long while to engineer the technology to find them. Slipping their infiltrators through was one thing, but to bring in their main force, they've had to wait until the Rift sealed by the Trel opened."

"You still haven't answered my question," said John.

"I'm not going to—not now," said the S'Cotar, smiling. "You wouldn't believe me." The smile was gone. "Believe this, though, Harrison. I could have killed you and Zahava a thousand times—from when we first met on Earth—you remember, at the Institute?—to the last moment I walked the decks of *Implacable*. I'm telepathic, tele-kinetic—nothing human can stand against me.

"I didn't kill you, though—I need you. You have a rare gift—you're both sensitives—far more so than any of the K'Ronarins."

"Not taking any risks, are they?" said D'Trelna, watching the screen. The Combine ships were approaching in a textbook englobing formation, deploying around *Implacable* even as they prepared to bombard her.

L'Wrona turned to the commodore. "Tactics would dictate that we feint, probing for weakness, presenting a difficult target."

D'Trelna grunted. "Until they close their circle and there's nowhere to run." He looked at the captain, eyebrows raised. "You want to do that, H'Nar?"

"No," said L'Wrona, looking back at the board. "There's a slight possibility, though; if we can take out four of the center ships, we can escape."

"We don't want to escape," said the commodore.

"Incoming missiles," said K'Raoda.

Small silver streaks were running in from the larger target blips, heading straight for *Implacable*.

"They don't know that," said L'Wrona. "Break their formation, we turn, take them in the rear. We might get as many as six of them before they get us."

D'Trelna ran a hand through his thinning hair, eyes on the board. "Do it," he said.

Outside, the shield flared red as the first wave exploded against it.

"Gods of my—!" D'Trelna seized the chairarms as *Implacable* lurched. Damage alerts sounded as fallen deck crew picked themselves up.

"Gunnery fully engaged," called K'Raoda.

Counterfire flashed from every battery on the ship, missiles and beams concentrating on the Combine's two lead ships.

More incoming missiles slammed into the shield, followed in an instant by a smaller, carefully programmed second wave. A single nuclear-tipped missile broke through. A blue bolt flashed from a Mark 44 intercept battery, detonating the warhead just inside the shield.

Implacable bucked like a speared bull.

D'Trelna had a brief impression of the lights going out, then he was spinning across a wildly tilting bridge, tumbling into a pile of flailing, cursing bodies piled against the engineering panels.

The battle lights came on: small, bright orbs set along the bulkheads. Slowly, *Implacable* righted itself, the old Imperial programming correcting the gravity field.

A hand helped the commodore to his feet. "You all right, J'Quel?" said L'Wrona.

"How bad are we hit?" said D'Trelna, eyes searching the engineering boards as the rest of the deck crew returned to their posts. The damage control panel was awash in red light.

"Bad," said N'Trol. The engineer was working his way along the board, ignoring the blood that flowed from a scalp wound. He tapped an indicator. "Number three engine took the worst of it—she'll need port overhaul and—" He stopped and swore softly, then turned to the captain and commodore, eyes large. "Jump transponders are gone—primary, secondary, tertiary. Twenty-four of them. We don't have enough spares."

"Make more," said the commodore, turning at the faint whine of the big board coming back to life.

"We got them," reported L'Wrona, pointing to where two red X's blinked on the board. The lead Combine ships were destroyed.

"Full ahead, Mr. K'Raoda," ordered L'Wrona. "Plow right through their center."

"You've only got two-thirds flank speed!" protested N'Trol. "The vibrations will tear the . . ."

Everyone ignored him.

L'Wrona touched a commlink as *Implacable* swept forward. "Gunnery, we're going through the center of the enemy formation. Full flanking fire as we pass—scatter 'em."

As *Implacable* charged past, spewing missiles and beams, the surviving Combine commander made a bad decision, ordering his remaining ships to break formation, regroup and pursue. As they broke formation, *Implacable* turned and came back in, flying a predetermined course to pick each of the smaller ships off.

Frantically the Combine commander ordered all ships to rally on his vessel. But by then it was too late—his remaining nine ships were scattering for space, and he was staring at an incoming missile barrage that in seconds would overwhelm his shields and destroy his ship.

"We did it," said D'Trelna, not believing the board. "They're running!" He turned to L'Wrona. "They're running, H'Nar!"

"Look again, J'Quel," said the captain.

D'Trelna turned back to the board, smile fading. A fresh blip was rising above D'Lin's north pole. D'Trelna paled as he read the tacscan. "Mindslaver," he said.

The bridge was as still as death, everyone watching the board.

"*Alpha Prime*," said K'Raoda. "And headed right for the Combine harvest ship."

"Plot to intercept and engage," ordered L'Wrona, doing a quick calculation. The battle had taken them far outsystem—by the time they reached D'Lin, *Alpha Prime* would long have been at the harvest ship.

D'Trelna thumbed open the commlink. "Ship to ship," he said, eyes on the board.

"Ship to ship," said K'Lana.

"K'Tran," said the commodore, "I know it's you—I recognize the style. Acknowledge."

"Hello, D'Trelna." It was K'Tran's voice, but subtly changed, softer, the old arrogance gone. "The R'Actolians have placed me in tactical command of our ship—a gesture of trust for a new comrade."

"You've . . . joined them?" said D'Trelna, exchanging glances with L'Wrona.

"Yes."

"Physically?"

"If you mean, was I brainstripped, the answer is yes, D'Trelna. A fair trade—I now command the most powerful fighting ship in this universe."

Seen on the board, the mindslaver had reached the harvest ship and was bringing it into one of its hangar bays, even as it widened the gap between itself and *Implacable*.

"Where are you going with that ship?" demanded the commodore. "If the AIs get ahold of the cargo . . ."

"They won't," said the soft, self-assured voice. "We have a better use for it."

"K'Tran," said D'Trelna, leaning forward intently, gripping the chairarms, "I plead with you—don't betray us! You . . ."

"*Tsk, tsk,* Commodore," said K'Tran. "A foolish thing to ask one who made a career of betrayal. Luck to you, D'Trelna. You'll need it—check your scan in red two seven."

The slaver was gone.

"She jumped," said K'Raoda.

D'Trelna sank back in the chair, feeling the sweat beneath his arms.

"Long-range scan shows three AI battleglobes entering this system, sector red two seven," reported T'Ral.

"Put specs on board," said L'Wrona.

It was the same type of vessel they'd faced off Terra Two—a ship the size of a moon, a planetoid of destruction, swathed in shimmering blue energy webs.

The three battleglobes were coming in just under light speed, slowly decelerating.

"Challenge," ordered the commodore.

"Ships do not answer challenge," said K'Lana a moment later.

D'Trelna closed his eyes, nodded to himself, and opened them. "Captain my lord L'Wrona," he said, turning to where the captain sat, "a situation now exists that I believe requires implementation of Special Order Fourteen. I ask your concurrence."

It was flat, formal and straight from the manual.

"I concur," said the captain. "The center one, I think." He pointed toward the lead ship.

"Mr. K'Raoda." D'Trelna turned to the second officer. "We ask your concurrence for under the rule of three."

"You want to blow us up in their teeth," said K'Raoda, eyes shifting between the two senior officers.

Both nodded.

"I concur," he said. "But from the weapons projections I'm scanning, they'll blow us up long before we reach them."

"Computer," said D'Trelna, touching the complink, "stand by to execute Special Order Fourteen upon my voice command."

"Concurrence required—rule of three," said the machine, opening L'Wrona and K'Raoda's complinks. The two men added their authorization to D'Trelna's.

"Concurrence verified," said the computer to D'Trelna. "Ship will autodestruct upon your voice command."

D'Trelna switched to the commlink. "Gunnery, lock onto center ship, ignore other two vessels. K'Lana, transmit the Fleet rally on all channels."

"But, sir," she said, "there's no one to hear it."

"The AIs don't know that," he said, watching the tacscan. "Confusion to our enemies. What's our intercept point, T'Lei?" he asked, turning to K'Raoda.

"Epsilon red four seven, that asteroid belt."

"Forward and engage," ordered the commodore.

Implacable turned, headed outsystem again, on a one-way trip toward the Enemy.

* * *

"And now where are we?" asked John, looking about the small, round chamber. "Another Imperial relic?"

"No," said Guan-Sharick as the other S'Cotar began activating the equipment. "We're in space—a small, scan-shielded satellite we built to find the Trel Cache. It requires four sensitives, though."

"Why didn't you use other transmutes?" said John.

"Lan-Asal's the only other one I could trust," said Guan-Sharick, watching his companion sit at one of the four consoles rimming the white-walled satellite.

"There are millions of asteroids between D'Lin and its nearest neighbor—remnants of a Trel planet destroyed in the first AI War, a million years ago. One of those asteroids contains the Trel Cache. It emits a psychic signal that the four of us, using the equipment in this satellite, should be able to home on."

"You built this satellite?" asked Zahava.

"Imperial Survey built it," said Guan-Sharick, "but never had time to screen personnel and staff it—the Fall. We've known about it, but for many reasons did nothing about it—until now."

So the Empire had telepaths, thought John, filing that tidbit away.

"If you'd each please sit at one of the consoles and don a helmet," said Guan-Sharick.

The two Terrans looked again and saw the helmets— small bits of translucent material sitting atop each of the consoles, thin optics tendrils linking them to the machines.

Lan-Asal already had his on.

Guan-Sharick sat and donned a helmet, pulling it down tightly over his cranium.

John glanced at Zahava. She shrugged. They sat and put on their helmets.

"Now what," said the Terran.

"Close your eyes," said Guan-Sharick. "Empty your minds and watch through that emptiness for a pinpoint of light—it will find you, not you it. When you see it, join with us and follow the light home.''

John sat there for a time, eyes closed, alone with his skepticism. *You're not concentrating, Harrison*, said a cold mental whisper.

Teeth gritting, he tried again, concentrating for what seemed forever, eyes beginning to hurt, shut but straining into nothingness. He was about to give up when something pricked at his mind—a small, brief burst of yellow light that tantalized, then was gone. Grimly, John settled down and waited.

When it came again, he willed it to stay. It blinked twice, then was gone again.

I see it, Harrison. It was Guan-Sharick. *We'll seize it together this time and follow it home.*

When it came the third time, John felt the strength flow into him—strength that seized the light in wispy tendrils of blue and let it tug them toward an even larger light—a cold white light that grew closer and brighter, filling his mind, searing it.

Something snapped the connection. John was back in the satellite, rubbing his eyes, head hurting.

"Epsilon sector, red four nine," said Lan-Asal, scribbling figures on a notepad.

John and Zahava looked at each other. "Was that you helping me?" he asked.

"It was all of us, Harrison," said Guan-Sharick, looking at the coordinates. "All of us." The pale white face was flushed with success. "We've done it—found the Trel Cache. Now—"

An alarm beeped. Both S'Cotar turned to the consoles. "Too late," said Lan-Asal, shoulders sagging in defeat. "Their vanguard is here."

"It's never too late," said Guan-Sharick, with a defiant toss of long blonde hair. "We have the coordinates—let's go."

Briefly filled with life, the satellite was empty again.

* * *

"Never make it," said R'Gal. "Your shield's breaking up." The AI stood beside D'Trelna, looking at the outside scan. The shield's normal white shimmer was pockmarked with red blotches as beams and missiles from the battleglobes tore at it.

Implacable continued to advance, pouring a steady fire at the center battleglobe. The AI ship took it, thousands of miles of intricately layered shields absorbing the energy, efficiently adding it to its own reserves.

"They'll punch through before we can finish our suicide run," said L'Wrona. The captain stood to the other side of D'Trelna's chair, eyes on the screen.

D'Trelna looked down at the tactical plot, then back at the shield. "I see no alternatives," he said, fingers drumming the chairarm. "Do either of you?"

Neither said anything.

The commlink beeped. "You gentlemen want to kiss the shield good-bye?" said N'Trol's voice. "I give it a fifty count."

"Thank you, Engineer," said the commodore, eyes still on the screen. The entire shield was shading over into a sullen red, the beam hit points glowing a fierce white.

"Commodore," said K'Lana, "the rally signal . . ."

"Keep transmitting it," he said.

"It's being acknowledged—priority alpha one!"

The task force swept out of the asteroid belt, soaring up to attack the battleglobes, missiles fanning out ahead of them.

D'Trelna was out of his chair. "Who the . . ."

"I came looking for K'Tran, but this'll do," said a familiar voice. S'Gan's face swept the bridge, peering from a dozen comm screens.

"Admiral!" said D'Trelna, sinking back into his chair.

"D'Trelna," she nodded. "Looks like your invasion prophecy's fulfilled. An advance force?"

"Yes, Admiral," said D'Trelna. Outside, the shield was cooling back into white as the battleglobes engaged S'Gan's squadron.

178

"I think we're close enough to hurt them," she said. "I've alerted Fleet. No way they'll get here in—"

The second ship in her squadron exploded, a billowing cloud of evanescent orange-red gas, quickly gone. The ship ahead of it plowed into the center battleglobe, a small silver mote suddenly blossoming into a fireball a thousand times its original size.

K'Raoda increased screen magnification. The battleglobe seemed to leap into the screen, its energy web merely a thin haze now. Through it they saw a world of battlesteel: turrets, pods and generators that seemed to go on forever, broken only by the occasional blunt of towers and domes.

"A ship forged by hate when man was young," said R'Gal softly.

There was a deep, black crater in the battleglobe's center. As her two companions moved forward, she pulled back, slowly returning the way she'd come.

The incoming missiles caught her, sixty-two multimegaton shipbusters wrapping the wounded battleglobe in all-consuming flame.

"Gods of my fathers!" exclaimed D'Trelna, throwing a hand across his eyes as a miniature sun devoured the battleglobe.

The screen went dark, the blast burning out *Implacable*'s scanners.

"One," said Admiral S'Gan, her face now only on D'Trelna's personal comm screen.

The two remaining battleglobes continued to advance, directing a withering fire against S'Gan's remaining ships. The distance separating the two forces was down to a paltry half a million miles, with neither side showing any inclination to break off. *Implacable* now lagged far behind the action, limping on two-thirds power.

"Incoming signal, Fleet covert operations channel," said K'Lana.

"I'll take it," said D'Trelna, punching open his commlink. "Identify."

"We've accounted for the surviving Combine ships that

179

cut and ran,'' said K'Tran. "Now listen—divert those
battleglobes into epsilon red four eight. The spacejunk's
very thick there—we have a surprise waiting for them.''

"You're speaking for the mindslaver, K'Tran?'' asked
D'Trelna, watching the board as two more of S'Gan's
ships dissolved. There was only one left now: *Deliverance*,
S'Gan's flagship. As the commodore watched, the flagship
broke off, pulling away at a right angle to the battleglobe.

"D'Trelna, in tactical matters, I am the mindslaver. It's
the only time they've allowed my own identity.''

There was an undercurrent of despair in the brainstripped
corsair's voice. D'Trelna felt sympathy welling within
him. Then memory of *Implacable*'s hangar deck heaped
with bodies banished it.

"Epsilon red four eight, D'Trelna—it's your only
chance.'' The commlink ended with a faint hiss.

"We can't trust him,'' said L'Wrona after D'Trelna
quickly repeated the conversation.

The commodore shrugged. "We have no other option.''

He turned to K'Lana. "Battleburst code to S'Gan: 'Follow me, epsilon red four eight.' ''

"Mr. K'Raoda, make for epsilon red four eight,'' ordered the commodore. "May something be there besides
rock.''

17

THEY STOOD INSIDE a hollow diamond, surrounded by infi-
nitely regressive reflections of themselves, two in K'Ronarin
uniform, two in white jumpsuits.

John closed his eyes, then opened them, trying to re-

store the sense of perspective stolen by the endless multi-
faceted images that danced at the least movement.

"Where are we?" said Zahava, squinting in the wan
blue light.

"Is this it?" asked John, turning to Guan-Sharick.

"This is the Trel Cache," said Guan-Sharick, nodding.
"Just as an Imperial Survey party found it—a party under
my command."

"You're a person of many talents, Guan-Sharick," said
a dry, faintly amused voice. There was no telling from
where it came.

"Hello, Eldest," said Guan-Sharick.

"Eldest?" said Zahava.

"The guardian of the Trel Cache," said Guan-Sharick.

"But not just a guardian," said the voice. "I gather
data, sift it, glean what I can, and store it."

"What sort of data?" asked John.

In answer, his reflection faded from one of the facets,
replaced by the image of a gaunt, black uniformed man in
his sixties, talking with John. It was nighttime, trees all
about, with other, indistinct figures moving nearby. The
older man held a pistol; John held a vicious-looking machine pistol.

"Are you familiar with the classical concept of an
umphalos, Major?" asked the other, reloading his pistol
and slipping it into a pocket.

"Hochmeister," said John, staring at the image. "On
Terra Two. But how . . ."

"As I said, I gather data."

"The guardian is omniscient," said Guan-Sharick. "At
least by our standards."

"And this . . . data," said Zahava. "Where do you
record it? And why?"

"It's all here, in this chamber," said the voice. "Etched
into the molecules of this glittering artifact. The knowledge of a great people, the Trel, what befell them—and
what followed: the Revolt, the Empire, the Biofab War,
Hochmeister and Terra Two.

"It's been some time, Guan-Sharick," continued the voice.

"Three thousand years, more or less, Eldest, since I last stood here," said Guan-Sharick.

"Three thousand years!" John whispered to Zahava. She shook her head.

"You're in trouble, aren't you?" said the voice.

The blonde nodded. "The Rift has opened, Eldest. Your foe and mine, the Fleet of the One, is on its way to crush us. We have little that can stand against them."

"And you have come for . . . ?" prompted the voice.

"The weapon of which we spoke, so long ago."

"I must tell you," said the voice gently, "that you may not have that weapon."

Guan-Sharick stepped back as though struck. "But, Eldest . . . !"

"The weapon we used against the AIs, if used again, would cause an irreversible chain reaction, exponentially converting all matter to antimatter, obliterating this and the AIs' universe."

"But when I was here before, you said nothing . . ."

"New data came to light subsequent to our conversation," said the voice. "Impressive, longitudinal, physical data."

"Eldest," said the S'Cotar, hands spread, "plans were made and implemented based on our conversation. Dynasties, cultures, whole civilizations have been manipulated in anticipation that I would come here and that you would give me the weapon, and that that, together with an aroused and militant people, would defeat the AIs. We cannot defeat the Fleet of the One without the weapon."

John had to admire the S'Cotar: thirty centuries of planning in shambles, yet it pressed its case logically, passionately.

"Eldest, we must have the weapon."

"How would you get it? Violence?" said the voice. "Only a part of the outpost is in this continuum. And you have my word—the weapon was destroyed, long ago."

182

Guan-Sharick sighed, head bowing in defeat. "Eldest, you've just spoken our epitaph."

"Perhaps," said the voice.

The blonde raised her head. "We'll go and face them, then, ship to ship, being to being, as we did at the start."

"Wait," commanded the voice. "Do you recall when the AIs the Empire created revolted? The so-called Machine Wars?"

"Vividly," said the S'Cotar. "I died in that revolt."

"And the emperor then?"

"S'Yal," said Guan-Sharick.

"Correct. S'Yal first sent the Twelfth Fleet to crush the revolt. They were using a new jump system that had been extensively tested, but never in a single transfer involving so many massed ships."

"The Twelfth Fleet of the House of S'Yal jumped," said Guan-Sharick, "and was never seen or heard of again."

"That fleet exists," said the voice, "suspended in time through a small error in jump field mechanics. A device has been made that will correct that error and recall the Twelfth Fleet."

"Where is this device?" said Guan-Sharick intently.

"According to communications I've monitored," said the voice, "the prototype exists in the research labs of Combine T'Lan. They've created it as a jump-navigation aid, but with a few minor modifications it should recall the Twelfth Fleet."

"You can provide those modifications, Eldest?"

"I've already done so. They're logged into *Implacable*'s engineering archives."

"And if it doesn't work?" said Lan-Asal.

There was a pause. "There is one other device. But the way to that is unknown."

"Explain," said Guan-Sharick.

"After the disasters of the Machine Wars, Fleet and Guard revolted, overthrowing S'Yal. He retreated to a hidden citadel, deep beneath K'Ronar. Fleet found and bombarded that citadel. If those inside weren't killed directly, they certainly never escaped—the bombardment sealed that fortress within the earth.''

"So?'' said the blonde, frowning.

"S'Yal had with him a just-completed device to overcome the jump field irregularities, a device that would have recalled the Twelfth Fleet, had the emperor had time to use it. Which he didn't.''

"And this citadel is where?'' said Lan-Asal.

"Somewhere between Prime Base and the capital,'' said the voice. "I couldn't determine the precise point—Fleet bombarded seven different zones around the city and the base. I've placed the locations and a full history of the action in *Implacable*'s archives.''

Angry and vengeful, the AIs pursued the two K'Ronarin ships into the asteroid belt, their screens cutting great swaths through the rocky flotsam, absorbing the useful heavy metals, burning off the rest.

"When we were on Terra, H'Nar,'' said D'Trelna, watching the rear scan, "do you remember seeing the ice breakers keeping the sea lanes open?''

"Vladivostok,'' said the captain, also watching the rear scan. "I see what you mean—same principle, but far more efficient.''

"Battlecode burst from the admiral,'' said K'Lana. "She wants to know how much longer—they're gaining.''

D'Trelna glanced at the readout threading across the bottom of the tacscan. "This is the place. Tell her any time now.''

The spacemines triggered just after *Deliverance* passed. There was no one of this epoch who could have appreciated the artistry of their construction. They were originally Imperial Mangler Class Fours—top of the line, their design improved by the R'Actolians, through long centuries of molecular tinkering. The Manglers looked and scanned like rock because they were rock—of a very special element rendered highly unstable when touched by a shield matrix. The stronger the matrix field, the more unstable and dramatic the reaction.

The explosions washed over the battleglobes, briefly obscuring them from scan. When the nuclear flames faded, the two monster craft could be seen, drifting, shields dimmed.

"Hurt, but not dead," said R'Gal to D'Trelna. "Now what?"

Alpha Prime swept in toward the battleglobes, then turned away, releasing two flights of six silver missiles. Beams snapped after her as the battleglobes slowly began moving.

The battleglobes could easily have taken more nuclear missile hits—they'd been designed to withstand the ravening energies of the atom. What their designers hadn't conceived of—what no rational being would have conceived of—was the cyborgian aberration that was a mindslaver and its almost magical weapons systems. *Alpha Prime*'s missiles held bits of antimatter in stasis. When the missiles reached target, those stasis fields released.

Two spectacular overlapping explosions occurred, twin blue-red fireballs, flecked with orange lightning, quickly gone.

The mindslaver returned, a great black wraith, halting off *Implacable*'s port.

"Still there, D'Trelna?" asked K'Tran over the commlink.

"Why did you save us, K'Tran?" said the commodore.

"And what are your intentions?" said L'Wrona over his shoulder.

"I'm empowered to tell you," said K'Tran, "that we're prepared to stand with you against AIs. We have another forty-eight ships of this class and finally enough brains to crew them."

"Forty-eight mindslavers?" said D'Trelna. "Where have they been?"

"In stasis," said K'Tran, "awaiting this moment. The R'Actolians knew that forty-nine symbiotechnic dreadnoughts might take the Confederation, but could never hold it. For our help, we'll of course want some concessions."

"Of course," said the commodore. "What concessions?" It's come to this, he thought—I'm bargaining with a mindslaver.

"We want certain planets in Blue Nine for our own, under treaty. We want right of passage through the Confederation."

"Are these planets inhabited?" said L'Wrona.

"Not by Confederation citizens, Captain," said K'Tran.

"Whom you'll harvest," said L'Wrona angrily.

"A small sacrifice for the greater good, Captain," said K'Tran.

"Anything else?" said D'Trelna as L'Wrona started to speak.

"There are other, more minor requests."

"I have no—" began D'Trelna.

"—no authority," finished K'Tran. "We know. Just relay our demands to Fleet and Council. We're returning now to mobilize the rest of our fleet."

"How do we contact you?" said D'Trelna.

"We'll contact you, on the Fleet covert operations channel. If the Council agrees with our requests, you'll see us again when the fighting starts. Luck, D'Trelna."

The mindslaver shrank in size on the screen, then was gone.

"Engineering asks permission to lower shield for repair," said K'Lana.

"Granted," said L'Wrona after a quick glance at the tacscan. *Deliverance* was coming alongside.

Outside, the faint shimmer protecting the cruiser winked off.

"I'm at a loss, H'Nar," said D'Trelna, walking over to the captain's station. "Even if the mindslavers stand with us and the whole bloody Confederation Fleet, the Fleet of the One is going to wipe us. Ten thousand battle units, ten thousand ships per unit—any force we field would hardly be noticed."

"Perhaps we can help," said a voice from the empty engineering station. Guan-Sharick-as-blonde, Lan-Asal, Zahava and John stood there.

"Interesting," said Admiral S'Gan, looking across the conference table at R'Gal. "And how many—friendly—AIs are there in the Confederation?"

"Just the Watchers," he said. "A few hundred of us."

"And the hostiles—the Combine T'Lan AIs?"

R'Gal shrugged. "Several thousand certainly, and not confined to Combine T'Lan. They've had centuries to infiltrate key positions. Their influence is far out of proportion to their numbers."

S'Gan had come aboard, assumed command and taken everything in stride—the R'Actolian's proposal, the presence of the two S'Cotar and R'Gal. By watchend, all were seated with both ships' senior officers, in the deck four conference room—a small gray cave deep within the ship.

The admiral turned to Guan-Sharick, who was seated opposite her at the end of the table. "What's your role in this, S'Cotar?"

"Our mission is to stop the AIs," said the transmute. "That has been our mission since humanity revolted and escaped the AI universe. Our bodies are cloned, our memories and special abilities transferred."

"Ridiculous," said the admiral. "You can't be endlessly cloned—each succeeding generation would have more defects than the previous. That's a basic tenet of information theory."

"We're cloned from original cells," said Lan-Asal.

"But . . ."

"I can vouch for them," said R'Gal. "They're two of the five lieutenants of He who led the Revolt, the one you call the Nameless Emperor."

"You're . . . human?" said John disbelievingly, looking at the S'Cotar.

"More than human, Harrison," said Guan-Sharick with an ironic smile.

187

"I don't believe it," said the Terran. He turned to D'Trelna. "Do you?"

The commodore looked at the two white-uniformed figures. "We'll find out, I think, someday. For now, I'm more concerned with their intentions than their true appearance. And R'Gal"—his eyes shifted to the AI—"the same goes for you."

"D'Trelna's right, R'Gal," said S'Gan. "It's fine that you vouch for them, but who'll vouch for you?"

"We're going to have to trust each other, Admiral," said R'Gal. "All of us. Disaster is certain, otherwise."

"Perhaps," said S'Gan. She looked at Guan-Sharick. "Tell me about this device the Combine developed."

Before the S'Cotar could speak, the admiral's commlink chirped. She listened, spoke and disconnected, then sat silently for a moment, looking down at her folded hands. "R'Gal," she said finally, looking up, "I owe you an apology. Fleet did not acknowledge my last report." Her eyes went from face to face. "Rather, they've just listed me as killed in action, along with all my ships and crews. As for you, D'Trelna," she smiled humorlessly at the commodore, "you and *Implacable* have been declared corsair—shoot on sight. Combine T'Lan works quickly," she added.

There was a long silence in the room, broken at last by *Deliverance*'s Captain Y'Kor. "Why can't we just go back to Prime Base and expose the plot?"

"That's what they expect you to do, Y'Kor," said L'Wrona. "There are probably ships sitting off home jump point right now, gunnery programming tied into your ship ID. You wouldn't live long enough to see your own sun."

There was a sudden babble as everyone tried to speak.

S'Gan restored order, rapping her hand on the table. A worn Academy ring rang on the table as S'Gan rapped her hand on the traq wood. "I'll listen to suggestions, not incipient hysteria," she said. "Anyone?"

Gods! she looks tired, thought D'Trelna. And why not? Lost all but one ship, dropped like a plague by a corrupt

FleetOps, the AIs coming and no one to believe her. Now is the time.

"If we're to be corsairs, Admiral," said the commodore, "let's act like corsairs."

"Explain, D'Trelna."

"Raid Combine T'Lan's research and headquarters facility."

"Why?" she asked.

"Tell the admiral what you told us," D'Trelna said to the S'Cotar.

"Thirty centuries ago, Admiral," said the S'Cotar, "I was an Imperial Survey officer—a cover for searching out the Trel Cache. I found it. I spoke with its guardian. The guardian assured me we could have the weapon the Trel had used against the Fleet of the One, but that only a united and militant humanity could defeat the AIs, weapon or not.

"We laid our plans well, and with the help of R'Gal and others, created Pocsym, who created the biofabs, which, you will agree, have produced a united, militant humanity."

"You killed a lot of people to do that," said S'Gan coldly, gray eyes on the blonde.

Guan-Sharick shrugged and continued. "As you know, we're now told that the weapon no longer exists, but that, ironically, Combine T'Lan has unknowingly produced a device that, with modifications, can recall the Twelfth Fleet of the House of S'Yal.

"Admiral, we need that device."

"The fleet that never returned," said the admiral, half to herself. She looked back at the S'Cotar. "Do you know what kind of ships the Twelfth had?"

"Mindslavers," said Guan-Sharick.

"Like Commodore D'Trelna, you're willing to employ mindslavers against the AIs?"

"I'd use anything against them, Admiral," said Guan-Sharick.

Something in Guan-Sharick's voice startled John, something he'd never heard there before—hatred.

"You have this device's location and a description?" asked S'Gan.

Guan-Sharick nodded.

S'Gan turned to D'Trelna. "You haven't, by any chance, drafted a plan of attack on this facility, D'Trelna?"

"As a matter of fact," said the commodore, reaching for the complink, "I have."

18

S'HLU WAS A soft, green world, tucked away in Red Seven, a quadrant adjoining Red One and the K'Ronarin home systems. Only fifty light-years from K'Ronar, it was visited frequently by Fleet units patrolling against corsairs and escaped S'Cotar.

Thus, the Combine T'Lan port officer gave almost automatic clearance to the three Fleet craft descending from the L'Aal-class cruiser that had just slipped into orbit.

Almost.

As they came in he ran a standard ID check—confirming that the *Forward Seven* was actually assigned Red Seven—then ran it again when the complink flashed DESTROYED—SECOND BATTLE OF H'SAK.

The port officer leaned forward as fresh data trailed onto the screen, then cursed softly as he read: INCOMING CRAFT IDENTIFIED AS ONE ARMED SHUTTLE AND TWO COMMANDO ASSAULT CRAFT. WANT SPECS???

Ignoring the query, the port officer slapped the general alarm call.

The klaxons had just started wailing as the control tower, ripped by fusion fire, exploded.

Sweeping out of the setting sun, the silver ships came in

low over the ruined control tower, Mark 44's strafing the complex. The scattering of return fire was quickly suppressed by the shuttle, which continued circling and strafing as the assault boats settled onto the roof of a squat, black building.

The sides of the assault boats dropped away with a faint pneumatic hiss.

"Follow me!" cried L'Wrona, leading the rush down the ramp and across the roof. Seventy-one black uniformed commandos and R'Gal swept after him, the smaller contingent from the second boat setting up a defense perimeter around the landing zone.

The rush stopped at the closed double doors of the lift.

"Visitors?" said R'Gal, pointing to the lift indicator. The machine was coming express from the ground level.

"Count on it," said the captain. He turned to the commandos. "Hostiles in the lift. Deploy."

The commandos took up positions, a black arc centered on the lift. As they waited, the alarm klaxons stopped hooting and the blaster fire between shuttle and ground positions fell off.

Please, thought L'Wrona, sighting two-handed on the center of the lift door, not the blades. He'd seen destroyed ones, and read Harrison's action report on them—it was as close as he wanted to get.

The lift arrived, the doors hissing open on five layers of killer machines, red sensor scans moving balefully along the blue-steel edges of their blades.

"Fire!" shouted L'Wrona, squeezing off a bolt stream.

Blaster fire poured into the lift, obscuring it in exploding bursts of blue bolts. Smoke and flame billowed out— but no return fire.

The K'Ronarins continued firing until their reload signals beeped.

"Hold fire," called L'Wrona, peering through the drifting smoke. Slapping in a new chargepak, he advanced cautiously.

The blades lay in shattered heaps, slowly congealing

rivulets of molten duraplast dripping on them from the lift's ruined walls and ceilings.

"They just hovered there and took it," said S'Til, standing beside him, looking at the destruction.

L'Wrona looked at R'Gal, standing to the right of the lift. Meeting the captain's gaze, he winked.

"Status of raid, D'Trelna?" asked S'Gan, her image appearing in the commodore's comm screen.

"As per plan and schedule, Admiral," he said. "The diversionary force has landed atop the armory. Much shooting and shouting, but unable to advance off the rooftop. Intercepted communications show all Combine security groups are being vectored on the armory. L'Wrona will pull out on schedule, hopelessly outgunned. That great bloody firefight should continue to absorb them." He dialed for t'ata.

"Incidentally, Admiral, R'Gal just saved a lot of lives by jamming the blades' command and control frequencies."

"Great," said S'Gan. "Give him a medal. Anything from the real action yet?"

"No," said D'Trelna, sipping the t'ata but watching the tacscan—they'd accounted for the two guardships, but help was coming from the Combine base on the seventh planet—a lot of help. Time to worry about that later.

"We'll only know about the 'real action' if and when that force returns," he said, looking back at S'Gan.

"If they get back," said S'Gan. "I'm having Y'Kor pull *Deliverance* back to omega blue three nine. We'll intercept that incoming reaction force."

D'Trelna glanced again at the tacscan. "They'll punch through you like a meteor storm, Admiral."

S'Gan shook her head and laughed. To the commodore's surprise, it was a pleasant sound. "D'Trelna, they can't kill this ship. We're already dead. Ask FleetOps."

"But . . ."

She shook her head. "You do your job, D'Trelna. We'll

take care of the reaction force.'' She touched her commkey, then looked back up. ''D'Trelna?''

''Admiral?''

''It's up to you—stop those v'org slime.''

''The AIs?''

She nodded.

''How?'' He spread his hands helplessly. ''We're infiltrated, they're on their way, and I've no faith in this magical weapon we're after.''

''Find some way to hit their rear, D'Trelna,'' said S'Gan. ''Between you, R'Gal, K'Tran and the two transmutes, you'll think of something. . . . You're an unorthodox slob, D'Trelna,'' she added. ''You'll pull it off. Luck.''

''Luck,'' he said to an empty screen.

D'Trelna turned to the tacscan. *Deliverance* was pulling out, heading straight for the—he counted—twenty-three Combine cruisers. Off to a very orthodox and very brief battle, thought the commodore.

Crushing his cup, he stuffed it into the disposer.

Well, that was easy.

Now what? asked John—he had difficulty not speaking the words.

Everything's very neat—start reading those yellow labels over the cubicles. According to their computer index, those are finished prototypes awaiting testing.

Guan-Sharick had flicked them inside the complex—an instantaneous transition from cruiser to earth, over before the mind could react. Arriving after L'Wrona took the raiders in, they'd found the central lab building deserted, its personnel either in shelters or responding to the alarm.

Guan-Sharick had glanced briefly at the building locator in the lobby; then he and John were standing in a lab, instruments all about, looking through a glass wall at the complex. Half a dozen buildings were in flames, burning from the top down—fires triggered by the exchange of fusion bolts with the K'Ronarin shuttle. Ringed by those flaming towers stood the smaller black structure, with

L'Wrona and the commandos still on the rooftop, now battling a sudden rush of human-seeming figures. AIs? wondered John. Or human helpers?

Human, reported Guan-Sharick. *Combine T'Lan has retainers—unwitting retainers, most of them.*

This isn't what we want.

They'd moved on to another lab, the shrill and crash of blaster fire suddenly muted.

Unfinished projects lay everywhere, spread out like so many vivisected carcasses on long white benches, presided over by the dead green eyes of inactive complinks.

Jump navigational aid—Mark IV. John read the duraplast label above the equipment cubicle, then stepped in.

The device looked like two giant-sized green ear swabs, each about a meter long, crossed diagonally and banded together in the center by a red nodule.

"Not much to—" he said as Guan-Sharick entered the small work area.

Fingers clamped over his mouth. *Idiot! There're voice sensors everywhere. Grab that device and we'll go.*

What about the research notes?

No time.

Combine T'Lan always had contingencies. They'd activated a major one when no more messages came from T'Lan Two aboard *Alpha Prime.*

T'Lan Two A had been activated.

People had often remarked on the striking resemblance between T'Lan senior and T'Lan junior. It was a resemblance easily explained—they were of the same series—and easily seen as they stood together, deep beneath S'Hlu, watching the raid.

"I believe this is an act of desperate men with no other options?" asked T'Lan One.

The young-looking AI nodded. "Agreed."

"What bothers me," said the other, watching the screen that showed L'Wrona's contingent fighting for their lives, "is that it's a stupid act. Stupid I wouldn't have expected.

Come now, the armory? S'Gan and D'Trelna have two cruisers, armed to the jump nodules.''

The Combine's Operations Center was large, well-hidden, and only partially preoccupied with the defense of the complex. Most sections and stations were busy directing the activities of fleets of merchant and mining ships, relaying communications from star system to star system, collecting intelligence, and maintaining constant contact with the home universe.

"Then what?" said T'Lan Two A.

"Intruder alert, lab complex four, section red three," said a cool, soft voice issuing from all points of the big room.

"Then that," said T'Lan One, leaning over the console. "Punch up that section," he said to the operator.

A new screen flashed on, showing Harrison carrying a device from the cubicle while a blonde hunched over a complink, fingers flying, eyes scanning the text.

"Guan-Sharick," said T'Lan One. "That's how they got in—teleported." He shook his head. "I didn't believe your predecessor's report. They should be dead—they're organic."

He turned, issuing orders. "Activate lab thirteen's security shield. Withdraw all but a token force from the armory skirmish—it's a ruse. Security's to enter lab thirteen via selective shield penetration, kill those two intruders and recover the device they're stealing."

T'Lans One and Two A stood watching the blonde as the orders went out. "What else survives?" wondered T'Lan One, watching Guan-Sharick.

"Well done, Harrison," said the blonde, turning from the complink. "You may have just lost us the war."

"Why are you speaking?" he asked, hefting the strange device uneasily in his hand.

"Because it doesn't matter now—they've slapped a security shield on this building. I can't teleport through it. The jig, my friend, is up."

195

"What can I do?" he asked.

"See that door?" Guan-Sharick pointed to the gray slab of battlesteel that shut the lab off from the corridor.

Harrison nodded.

"Blast the lock shut; that'll hold the slime for a while. I'll be sending what specs I have"—the transmute tapped her head—"to Lan-Asal. Maybe, just maybe, they can replicate the device."

If we're killed, John added to himself, moving toward the door.

"H'Nar."

D'Trelna's voice came through sharp and clear in L'Wrona's earpiece.

"Yes?" he asked, ducking as a blaster bolt grazed the air duct he was behind, showering him with sparks.

"They've tumbled to it. They're responding a small army to that lab. And they've slapped a security shield on it. Go save them. They're on level seven."

"Where's the screen generator?" asked the captain.

D'Trelna touched his complink, watching the briefing scan as it scrolled by. After a moment he froze it and read quickly. "Subbasement seven, northwest quadrant four— unless they've moved it since the last FleetOps update."

"Have Lan-Asal tell Guan-Sharick to meet us there," said L'Wrona.

"Acknowledged," said the commodore.

With three quick bolts, L'Wrona finished the sniper he'd been toying with, rising as the man's body tumbled from a neighboring rooftop.

"To the boats!" shouted L'Wrona, waving his blaster. "To the boats!"

"Any lifepods launched?" asked D'Trelna, leaning over K'Raoda's shoulder, peering at the tacscan. Red X's marked what had been *Deliverance* and three Combine ships.

"No, sir," said K'Raoda.

On the tacscan, twenty-one target blips continued to advance on the green dot marking *Implacable*.

"No obliging mindslavers this time," said D'Trelna, straightening. "Get us some room, T'Lei. Move us farther out from the planet—gunnery to open fire as targets come in range."

He looked at the red X again, then went back to his post.

Lieutenant S'Til dashed across the corridor, blaster bolts snapping around her as she dived into the doorway.

"We're going the wrong way, Captain," she said, pulling herself into the corner shared with L'Wrona.

"No." He stepped around the corner, snapped off three bolts, then ducked back, dodging the return fire. "We're making for that room five doors down—field generator."

"It'll take all night—they've got at least one company between us and it," said S'Til.

"One more doorway's all we need, Lieutenant," said L'Wrona, waving the next squad forward. He and S'Til joined in the covering barrage.

Half the squad reached the next two doorways.

"Let's go," said L'Wrona. He and S'Til made for the next doorway, continuing the deadly game of leapfrog.

"Troops are in the basement," said Guan-Sharick. "Bring the device."

"Where are we going?" asked John.

The lab door was beginning to glow cherry red, the battlesteel slowly yielding under heavy blaster fire.

"Another hot spot, Harrison," said Guan-Sharick.

The lab was gone—the Terran found himself crouching in a gray doorway, blasters shrilling all around, the wide bore of an M11A inches from his face. "Don't do that again, John," said L'Wrona, lowering the weapon.

"That's it?" he added, pointing to the device in John's hand.

"Yes," said Guan-Sharick.

"I wasn't addressing you," said L'Wrona. He turned back to Harrison. "Is it?"

"Allegedly," said the Terran.

"Can you make it work?"

They ducked as a blue bolt tore into the top of the door frame, showering them with sparks and droplets of molten metal.

"Ask Guan-Sharick," said John.

L'Wrona turned reluctantly. "How does it work?"

"Ask me when we get to the ship, Captain," said the blonde, meeting his gaze.

"What if you don't get to the ship?"

"You'll see that I do, won't you, Captain?" she said with an easy smile.

L'Wrona looked out, checking the skirmish. "No one's going anywhere until we reach that generator room. There are about five squads of hostiles fronting us, backed by endless reserves."

"You seize the shield generator, then what?" asked John.

"Then Guan-Sharick teleports us back to *Implacable*," said the captain.

"I'm not a god," said the blonde. "I can get you out in fours and fives, but—"

"Just get the device back to the ship," said L'Wrona. "Please."

Guan-Sharick nodded.

R'Gal joined them, moving up the corridor and into the doorway, a blur of motion.

"Guan-Sharick," he nodded.

"R'Gal," nodded the blonde.

"I need your help again," he said.

"As in the Revolt?"

"As in the Revolt," said the AI. He pointed up the corridor. "Move me up one doorway—I'll jam the impulse matrix on the shield generator."

"Done," said the S'Cotar. R'Gal was gone.

"Blades attacking from the rear!" S'Til's voice crackled over the commnet.

"Squads seven, nine and four, face about!" ordered the captain.

The blades came slicing up the corridor, a long phalanx of death mowing through the troopers, firing and slicing. Whenever one fired, blue lightning snapped from its rim and a commando fell, shot neatly between the eyes.

It took overwhelming firepower to bring even one of the blades down. As John and L'Wrona fired from the doorway, the lead machine faltered, accelerated, and plunged past them, plowing into the wall, a geyser of blue-red flame.

"Shield's down," said Guan-Sharick, appearing between L'Wrona and Harrison. "Hideous things, aren't they?" she said, staring at the blades. The carnage ended as the blades vanished, leaving the smoldering remains of four machines behind.

"You flicked them away," said John.

Guan-Sharick nodded. "Northern polar region. It'll take them a while to get back."

"Shield's down," said R'Gal over the commnet. "Up and away!"

Eyes streaming, choking and wheezing from the smoke, D'Trelna and T'Ral dragged K'Raoda from the shattered navigation console, stumbling in the murky twilight.

They'd lost the lights almost at the start. The Combine ships, already wounded by S'Gan, were minimizing risks, coming in waves of four, pounding the shield at preselected points. Soon the shield was rippling red-white, too weak and unstable to completely stop the hundreds of blue fusion bolts ripping at it. Then the hull began taking hits—greatly weakened hits holing it in a score of places.

A diminished fusion salvo found the bridge, exploding row after row of consoles, sending the atmosphere rushing out in a sudden gust, until stopped by the automatic sealants. By then the bridge was a smoking ruin, dead and wounded laying where they'd fallen.

"N'Trol," D'Trelna had shouted over the din of alarms and explosions, "engineering to take conn!" Flipping off the commlink, he'd stood, bellowing, "Evacuate the bridge! Wounded first. All others to engineering." He'd turned then and seen K'Raoda, slumped on the deck. Cursing, he'd knelt beside the young officer, turning him gently onto his back. Blood ran freely from a nasty head wound, and his left hand was badly burned, but he'd live—until the shield failed.

D'Trelna's communicator beeped just as he reached the lift. "What?" he managed as T'Ral set K'Raoda down beside the other wounded. The lift doors closed and the machine moved sluggishly for Sick Bay.

"You want to kiss *Implacable* good-bye, D'Trelna?" It was N'Trol. "We can take three more of those runs, maybe four—shielding's almost gone—then we're one with the universe."

"You keep that shield up, N'Trol!" snapped D'Trelna. Just leave us communications and internal transport."

"What do you think we've been doing?" The engineer's tone was jocular. Defense mechanism, thought D'Trelna, watching T'Ral rip open a medkit and fumble for a dry compress. N'Trol's as scared as the rest of us.

"Then carry on," he said as T'Ral put the compress on K'Raoda's forehead. The first officer groaned but remained unconscious. "I'll be there as soon as I can." If there's any there left to get to, he added to himself. Kneeling beside the medkit, he searched for the burn salve.

"They've raided the lab and stolen the prototype of a navigation jump aid." The security captain's face filled the comm screen. There was a nasty blaster burn across her cheek and exhaustion in every line in her face.

"Where are they now?" asked T'Lan One.

"Subbasement seven. We have them trapped."

"Very well. Continue. Make every effort to recover that navigational aid." He switched off before she could answer.

"If they reach their landing zone, they could pull it off," said T'Lan Two A. "That shuttle is jump equipped."

T'Lan One nodded. "Instruct our reaction force to disengage *Implacable* and establish a blockade around S'Hlu. Our enemies have risked everything to get that device. Whatever it is, they're not going to have it."

"They're breaking off," said N'Trol.

"What?" D'Trelna looked at the small tacscan. Tucked away in the back of engineering, auxiliary control lacked the sophistication of the main bridge—there were only a handful of screens and four consoles, all now doubly manned. Yet one of the small screens showed the Combine ships were in fact leaving *Implacable* behind, racing for S'Hlu.

"After them," said D'Trelna, reading the data. "They're after L'Wrona."

"You're crazy, Commodore," said N'Trol. The engineer's face was streaked with black, residue of an electrical fire in the shield generators. Bloodshot eyes glared at D'Trelna. "I can give you half of standard, or I can jump. I can't give you weapons and propulsion and shield."

D'Trelna felt him flushing. "Don't tell me what you—"

He and N'Trol whirled, drawing their side arms as Lan-Asal appeared on the other side of the console. The transmute shook his head. "Mustn't think with our blasters, gentlemen."

"What is it?" said D'Trelna, holstering his M11A.

"I need you to stabilize position relative to S'Hlu, and drop your shield."

Commodore and engineer exchanged glances. "Why?" asked D'Trelna.

"We're going to try to teleport the raiding party off of S'Hlu."

"Do it," said D'Trelna to N'Trol.

* * *

It went well at first, with John and fourteen wounded troopers teleported to *Implacable*'s hangar deck in three separate jumps.

"Take this," he said, tossing the prototype to a startled D'Trelna.

"What . . ."

"It's what we came for," said John. He turned to Lan-Asal. "Do you need me back there?"

"No—just another body to carry," said the transmute, and was gone.

"Well, that eases up on the return fire," said L'Wrona. He stood with R'Gal in an open doorway, firing at the Combine forces as they tried to advance up either side of the corridor, weapons silent.

"Great defensive position, Captain," said R'Gal, looking at the sign over the door: Armory 7—Atomics.

"Works for a time," said L'Wrona, reloading. "Until they send in more blades." Behind them were the last of the raiders—five wounded and two not, sitting and lying in front of rows of deep-cooled white metal cylinders, all labeled with various ordnance nomenclatures.

"Here they come," said R'Gal, pointing to a flight of blades as they whipped around a corner, light glinting off blue steel. He shook his head. "Can't help you this time, L'Wrona—they're frequency shielded."

"In," said L'Wrona. The two stepped back, the captain palming shut the thick blast doors. They snicked together as the first blades reached the armory.

L'Wrona touched his communicator. "J'Quel," he said, watching thin white lines of energy slowly carve through the door, "we need out now."

"They're on their way," came D'Trelna's voice.

"We're here," said Guan-Sharick. L'Wrona and R'Gal turned—Lan-Asal and Guan-Sharick stood between them and the troopers.

"Get the rest out of here first," said the captain, stepping to the small stack of gear they'd carried in. "I have something to do."

"Gone?" repeated T'Lan One, staring at the comm screen. "Where and how?"

The woman shrugged wearily. Behind her the pickup showed the open door of Armory Seven, with security troops and blades flitting in and out. "Unknown."

"Guan-Sharick," said T'Lan One. "Teleported them out."

"All of them? That fast?" said the other AI.

"There were five of them during the revolt," said T'Lan One. "Maybe more than one survived.

"All ships to intercept *Implacable*," he said. "And advise Confederation FleetOps that we've just suffered a corsair attack—give them full battlespecs."

"But if they find *Implacable* first, we won't recover the device."

"It's more important to deprive them of it," said T'Lan One.

Panicked shouting came from the comm screen. Startled, both AIs turned back to the comm screen. Their security forces were scattering, troops and blades fleeing down the corridors.

"What . . . ?" began T'Lan One.

The captain's face reappeared. "Blastpak," she said hoarsely, glancing over her shoulder. "No time to disarm—"

The screen winked off. The AIs looked at the surface monitors as flame washed over the pickups, leaving only screen fuzz and static in its wake.

"Can we take the aftershock?" asked T'Lan Two A. He'd hoped to remain functional for more than a day.

His question was answered as the ground wave shattered the ceiling and west wall, sending tons of earth exploding in on the command center.

19

IMPLACABLE'S AUDITORIUM was packed—every off-duty crewman on the ship was in attendance, relieved by a handful of personnel, themselves watching via comm screen.

The chatter died as D'Trelna stood, stepping to the podium.

"As you know, we're a hunted ship," he began, eyes going from face to face. "Fleet and Combine forces are searching for us with a vigor previously reserved for K'Tran."

He leaned forward, big hands gripping the podium. "We're the only ones who know the entire truth behind the Biofab War, the only ones who know beyond any doubt that the Fleet of the One is coming, and—the reason we're now corsair-listed—the only ones who know the truth behind Combine T'Lan. Colonel R'Gal"—he nodded to the AI, seated in the front row—"and his people have, for reasons of their own safety and effectiveness, declined to give the alarm about Combine T'Lan. And we've been very cleverly put into a position where any warning we'd give would be dismissed.

"We have a plan," he continued. "It's dangerous, wild, and likely to fail. But before I discuss it, I want you to know that we'll be happy to set down at the nearest port anyone who wants out. You signed on, most of you, to fight S'Cotar and save the Confederation, not to become ensnared in this ancient web of intrigue.

"If we slip you planetside, you'll be provided with new computer-confirmed identities and documentation, courtesy of Colonel R'Gal and Fleet Intelligence files. You're all skilled technicals—you'll have no trouble finding good jobs on any of a thousand worlds." He paused and smiled. "No hard feelings—you're the best of a good lot. So anyone who wants out, please fall out now and report to briefing room four, deck three."

No one moved; then a rating stood—he was almost old enough to shave. "Sir, aren't we still fighting for the Confederation?"

"We are," nodded the commodore. "It's just that the Confederation isn't aware of it."

There was a ripple of nervous laughter.

"Sir, we're soldiers," said the rating. "We took an oath to fight for the Confederation. These machines may have fooled FleetOps and the Council, but it doesn't wipe our oath. You lead, we'll follow."

As he sat back down, applause rippled through the auditorium, growing louder, until all were on their feet, clapping and cheering. Then someone struck up the Confederation anthem, the J'Rin. Voice after voice picked it up, sending all five verses ringing from the high ceiling.

D'Trelna waited until it died down. "Thank you," he said, a catch to his voice. Not trusting himself, he sat back down.

L'Wrona took the podium.

"We've been contacted by K'Tran. We're to rendezvous with *Alpha Prime*—and her sister ships."

That caused a stir, the whispers running through the auditorium until L'Wrona cleared his throat. "The previous offer stands," he said. "Anyone who wants off, say so. But say so now." His eyes looked over the faces, many of them apprehensive. Kids, he thought, so many of them—more afraid to show fear than to die. Was I ever that young? he wondered.

"At the rendezvous," continued the captain, "we'll firm up strategy and proceed."

"Proceed where?"

It was Zahava, standing next to Harrison, five rows back to the right.

The captain could have said, "Hold your questions till the end." Tell it all now, he decided. See how they take it.

"We propose," said L'Wrona, "to take *Implacable* through the newly opened portal from Terra One to Terra Two, and from there, to the AI universe. We propose to foment revolt against the AIs in their home universe, using species they've held in slavery for tens of thousands of years. One of those species are human."

It took a while for the noise to subside. Then it was K'Raoda's turn. The first officer stood, hand and head bandaged. "What about the Fleet of the One?" he asked. "And the device we recovered in the raid on S'Hlu?"

"The mindslavers will fight a delaying action against the AI Fleet," said L'Wrona. "They have weapons systems equal to those of the Fleet of the One. A delaying action by the mindslavers should be effective—the AIs won't be prepared for them. In fact, according to Colonel R'Gal, they may not know such machines exist.

"As for the device—we're still testing it.

"Mr. N'Trol, any progress?"

Far in the back, the engineer stood. "Not yet."

"Fine," said John as N'Trol sat. "We hurt them badly enough at home for them to withdraw. What prevents them from returning?"

"Utter defeat." R'Gal stood, facing the Terran. "The AI empire's rotten at the core—it's corrupt, it's based on slavery and can't withstand the shock of another revolt. It's only now recovering from the last one, a hundred thousand years ago."

"How do you know that?" said John.

"I was the equivalent of an Imperial viceroy," said R'Gal. "I know the problems the AIs face."

"Faced," said John.

R'Gal shook his head. "Face, Harrison. Face. It's a static society."

"Well, I suppose any machine society . . ."

"Please," said R'Gal, holding up a hand. He looked

around the room. "All of you, dispose of your piquant notions of machines-as-life. We're your equivalent, if not your superiors, in intellect, creativity and courage."

"You mean the created has surpassed the creator?" said the Terran ironically.

R'Gal laughed. "My friend, you're so wrong. No, the created has never quite equaled the creator." He shook his head. "Oh, the hopes we had for you, the time and the resources we spent on your development. True, we used you badly, but some of us . . ."

It took D'Trelna a long time to silence the uproar and clear the room.

"That was incredibly stupid," said Guan-Sharick to R'Gal. "Why did you do it?" The two sat alone in a nearly deserted mess hall. It was the middle of thirdwatch, with most of the ship asleep.

"Two reasons," said the AI. "One—they'd have found out, sooner or later—my brethren would have dosed them with it—it's a very telling psychwar tool. Better they find out now—now, before the shooting resumes—and adjust to it."

"Perhaps," said the blonde. "And the other reason?"

R'Gal smiled across the mess table. "The other reason was Captain L'Wrona's gimlet eye turning on the noble young rating who so inspired the crew. He was beginning to frown when I stood. I believe he prides himself on knowing every face, every name?"

Guan-Sharick smiled back at the AI. "How did you know it was me, R'Gal? Surely all those bodies masked any psychic distortion?"

"I know you, old snake—and your style. Nicely done, as always."

"Thank you, Colonel," said the transmute.

"They don't know about you yet," R'Gal continued.

The blonde shrugged. "They accept that I'm human and believe, by implication, that Lan-Asal and I are from one of those enslaved species—a human one, of course." She

207

paused, looked across the mess hall, then back at R'Gal. "Sorry about attacking you."

"Couldn't be helped," said the AI. "No way you'd have recognized me, there in the dark. And it was the logical thing to do—assume I was Combine and jump me."

"Fortunately for you, I saved you for later interrogation."

"Fortunate for me N'Trol found me—I've seen your interrogations.

"By the way," he added, nodding at the few crew scattered around the mess hall, "just which one of them are you usually?"

"It's not important."

"Satisfy my curiosity. I really was looking for a S'Cotar amongst the crew. Many of the genuine bugs got away."

The blonde shook her head. "Not now. Later, maybe. After the mission."

"Ah, the mission," said R'Gal. "I can't believe your mission's changed any more than mine, down the long drag of the centuries. Certainly we both want the Fleet of the One broken and overthrown. But you, Guan-Sharick, you want the Interdict lifted." He said this last softly, leaning across the table.

"Justice," said the blonde just as softly. "I want justice."

The battle klaxon interrupted R'Gal's laugh.

"Certainly this is the place," said D'Trelna, looking at the main screen. *Alpha Prime* fronted them, flanked by two other mindslavers.

"Tacscan shows forty other mindslavers beyond visual pickup," said L'Wrona. "Positioned in standard tactical dispersal."

"Incoming signal, covert operations channel," said K'Lana.

"He's going to ask some hard questions, H'Nar," said the commodore. "Be ready to run if he doesn't like my answers." He pressed the commkey.

"Welcome, Commodore," said K'Tran's voice. "I hope you're impressed."

"I'm impressed," said the commodore, nodding as he watched the mindslavers' weapons specs thread across the tacscan.

"Has Fleet agreed to our terms?"

D'Trelna exchanged glances with L'Wrona. The captain's finger hovered over the emergency jump key.

"Admiral S'Gan relayed your request, K'Tran," said D'Trelna, choosing his words. "They haven't responded yet."

"I'm the nucleus of a very sophisticated ship, D'Trelna," said K'Tran. "We know that Admiral S'Gan is dead, that you've been declared corsair, and that the Combine T'Lan AIs have intercepted all warnings and messages."

The commodore's shoulders slumped. "Knowing that, you still want this alliance?"

"It makes no difference now. The vanguard of Fleet of the One has entered this quadrant and is headed for D'Lin. We're out of time."

"Can you stop them?" said D'Trelna.

There was a long pause. "Maybe," came the answer. "But once they see how few we are, their main force will come through and wipe us."

"We have a plan," said the commodore, and sketched it for the mindslaver.

"Mad," said K'Tran, "but audacious—something I'd have thought of. One cruiser against an empire. And have you an equally effective solution for the Combine AIs?"

"I have." It was R'Gal. "But I won't discuss it over the commnet."

"And who are you?"

"Colonel R'Gal, Fleet Intelligence."

There was brief pause. "Very well, Colonel, Commodore. You're all invited for dinner aboard *Alpha Prime*. We can discuss it then."

Of all the bizarre and ghastly things, thought D'Trelna.

209

"And who will we dine with—disembodied whispers?" he
asked. "And where? In some dour, instrument-laden room?"

"Myself, and a select few, all in the flesh—firm, whole-
some flesh. And I think you'll be pleasantly surprised by
the circumstances, Commodore. We're not ghouls, you
know—merely selectively altered life-forms."

"Very well," said D'Trelna, and agreed to a time.
Disconnecting, he turned to L'Wrona. "Dinner with the
ghouls, Captain L'Wrona. Wear your best side arm."

"Where are we going?" asked Zahava as John hurried
her along the corridor to hangar deck.

"Wallenberg and Eichmann," he said. "Kafka's sister
and Mengele."

"You've lost it," she said as they stepped into the deck.

"We're going to dine with the devil—maybe dance with
him, too. Captain K'Tran's invited us for supper," he
said.

"No!" she said, stopping.

"Come on," he said, pulling her by the arm. "Our
dinner companions await." He nodded to where D'Trelna,
L'Wrona, R'Gal and Guan-Sharick were boarding the
shuttle.

The hall might have been taken from the Venice of the
doges: gold and linen, bright banners hung high, fourth
and seventh dynasty paintings gracing the soft-textured
walls, blue-liveried servants in profusion.

Terrans and K'Ronarins had stopped at the double doors,
staring.

"Come in, please," said K'Tran, standing at the head
of the table, motioning with a wine goblet. He was ele-
gantly dressed in a red-gold uniform, silver braid about his
shoulders, a smile on his face. Others rose as they entered—
Imperial marine officers, the very ones they'd fought a few
days before, nodding and smiling, the admiral at K'Tran's
left.

"I've died and gone to hell," muttered D'Trelna, lead-

210

ing the way. He wore his dress uniform, insignia gleaming, the Valor Medal hanging from a crimson chain around his neck.

All through dinner—a silent, sumptuous meal—John found his eyes wandering to K'Tran's cranium. The corsair caught him at it. "Does it matter?" he asked.

"No," said the Terran, his question answered. Let it be over soon, he prayed. Beside him a wan-looking Zahava played with her food.

"You're R'Gal, aren't you?" said K'Tran after a dessert of spice cake.

R'Gal nodded.

K'Tran leaned back, studying R'Gal. "You're an AI," he said.

There was a perfect silence at the table.

"Really?" said R'Gal, studying the amber wine in his glass.

"We substituted our stasis field for the one holding T'Lan," said K'Tran. "And we debriefed him. The Combine AIs know about you, R'Gal, but no others, if any. I assume you were a figure of some note, back home?"

"Of some note," said R'Gal with a wry smile, still looking at his wine.

"And your plan to deal with the Combine infiltrators?" said K'Tran, leaning forward.

R'Gal met his gaze. "Expose them."

"How?"

R'Gal looked at D'Trelna. "*Implacable* must return to Prime Base, and the commodore must stand trial."

D'Trelna set down his wine glass. "The commodore does not like that idea," he said. "The commodore wants to return victorious, the savior of humanity, cheered by the multitudes."

"They'd mindwipe him, R'Gal," said Guan-Sharick. "Throw him in the Tower and mindwipe him. And send the rest of the crew to a penal world."

The AI shook his head. "No. We'd stop it—the Watchers."

"So there are more of you," said K'Tran. "Surely no more than a handful?"

"But well placed," smiled R'Gal, "and with certain abilities you're not aware of. We'd save D'Trelna and his men long before it got nasty."

"Trial," said L'Wrona. "That's what you want, isn't it?"

R'Gal nodded. "Public trial of a war hero—"

"Really," said the commodore.

"—of a war hero," continued R'Gal, looking around the table. "It'd be broadcast live to every home in the Confederation. Tell them the whole thing, D'Trelna—the Combine won't dare stop you."

"I have no proof," said D'Trelna, considering it.

"We'll provide the proof, Commodore," said R'Gal. "Trust us."

"Trust," said D'Trelna staring at the crumbs on his plate. He looked up. "R'Gal, the only one who vouches for you is Guan-Sharick, whom we've fought for ten years and who now suddenly claims to be a friend. You could be a Combine AI hanging me out for sorga bait."

K'Tran frowned. "I can understand your needing Guan-Sharick, D'Trelna. I can understand Guan-Sharick wanting to strike a deal to save its green hide. But a S'Cotar, vouching for an AI? What's going on?"

"It's a long story, K'Tran," said the commodore. "You have my word it doesn't affect the present situation."

"I'll accept that—for now," said K'Tran. "But explain this—if you take *Implacable* back to Prime Base, what are you going to use for this daring raid of yours?"

"There's a way for the raid to go on," said R'Gal, "without *Implacable*. And a way for me to prove once and for all where my loyalties lie." He looked at K'Tran. "I'll need your help."

"What is this plan?" said D'Trelna.

R'Gal looked at him. "I'll help provide a substitute

vessel for the trip through the portal—one that will stand a chance."

"What sort of a ship?" said D'Trelna.

"Not a ship," said R'Gal. "An AI battleglobe. Gentlemen, I propose we capture a battleglobe."

20

THE VANGUARD WAS a small force, only sixty-two battleglobes, commanded by Admiral Binor aboard *Devastator*. They'd penetrated the great swirling eye of the Rift, regrouped, and moved toward the D'Linian system, every ship on full alert.

The distress call had come halfway to their destination— garbled, explosions audible in the background. Advance units sent to meet the Combine ships were under attack, by . . . Then nothing.

Urgent messages to Combine T'Lan headquarters had gone unacknowledged.

Shields at max, commlinks feeding all scans back through the Rift, the task force had swept into the D'Linian system.

Only one unknown vessel came up to tacscan—a single ship, circling D'Lin.

"Identification made," said the ship's captain. "It's the vessel the Combine outfitted for brain storage."

"And the other ships, the Combine's and ours?" asked Admiral Binor.

"Scanning debris, fusion discharges and recent ion trails," reported the captain. "There was a large battle in this system, very recently."

"Which we lost."

"So it seems."

"Hail the brain ship," said Binor.

"We have. No response."

Disabuse yourselves, R'Gal had said, of your piquant notions of machines-as-life.

The AI admiral sat at his station, staring at the viewscreen closeup of the ship orbiting D'Lin. In Terran terms he seemed to be about sixty, with silver gray hair and a tanned, sharp-chiseled face. Radiation-sensitive skin was a cosmetic luxury, an enduring fashion inspired by the natural changes observed in human skin.

"Anything else?" asked the admiral, turning to the captain.

The flagship's captain was a purist, one of the growing number of fundamentalists who disdained the blatant copying of human form and convention that went with command caste status. He hovered before the admiral, a translucent blue ball a meter in diameter, rippling blue energies dimly perceivable through his skin. A few centuries ago an officer of his rank would have exchanged the tidy blue globe for a human-looking body and its riot of tactile sensations.

"Spacejunk—lots of it," said the captain. "Probably from the asteroid belt we passed. The screens will process it."

"Scan the brain ship and then bring it aboard, very carefully."

"At once, sir," said the captain, returning to his station.

The admiral walked to the railing and stood looking down on Operations. A mixed group of blue globes and human-adapted AIs manned the battleglobe's heart, directing the operations of the immense ship from half a hundred consoles. The rest of the battleglobe was attended only by repair droids, security blades, gun crews and a few technicians. Mostly automated, the great ship was a testimonial to the genius of AI engineering.

Binor's gaze traveled out the sweep of armorglass girdling Operations. As far as the eye could see stretched weapons batteries, sensor nodules, shield transponders, and, almost at the horizon, a black needle, twin to the Operations tower where Binor stood: flight control. *Devastator* carried craft the size of *Implacable*, designed to sweep into hostile planets under the fire of the mother ship, land and seize control. The invasion craft were berthed miles below, nestled in their battlesteel cocoons, awaiting their time. Not long now, thought Binor. Await the Fleet, install the cyberpaks—brains—in the damaged ships, then move on in strength.

"Admiral."

The captain was back.

"We have the ship in tow—scan shows no fusion weapons on board. We're tractoring it to Hold Seventeen for inspection."

The admiral nodded. "Security units and cybertechs to meet me at Hold Seventeen. All ships to maintain present position off D'Lin."

The ship lurched again as the tractors let go. Cursing, John stumbled in the dark, shoulder slamming off a bulkhead.

"They're trying to bruise us to death," whispered John.

"Quiet!" hissed L'Wrona from somewhere in the darkness. "They're coming."

Go for it, R'Gal, thought John as the big cargo locks swung open and light poured in. Squinting in the sudden glare, he could see the vast expanse of gray-white deck beyond the door, with cargo hoists and other machinery clustered nearby. Then three blades appeared in the doorway, red sensors scanning the hold.

R'Gal stood. He was wearing a black uniform, the insignia of the Fleet of the One on his shoulder: a pyramid with three blue eyes, one at each corner of the triangle.

"Kanto," he said. "Commander of this ship and the only survivor." Kanto had commanded the ship until the Components boarded and killed him.

Three red eyes had locked onto him when he stood.

215

Two of those eyes resumed scanning while the center machine focused on R'Gal. "Don't scan here," ordered R'Gal. "You'll disturb the brainpods."

The blades stopped scanning.

"Follow us," said the center blade. John started at the voice—it was female. Then the blades and R'Gal were gone, leaving the doors open.

"Wait for my signal," said L'Wrona, slipping to the doorway to watch R'Gal and the reception party.

"Captain Kanto," said the blade, hovering attentively.

R'Gal saluted the admiral. Binor ignored it. "What happened?" he said, then stopped, frowning. "Have we met before, Captain?"

The two stood in the cargo hold, the admiral surrounded by fifty gleaming blades and some dusky-red spherical cybertechs, R'Gal backdropped by the Combine cruiser— two miles of battlesteel and instrument pods, dwarfed by the gray immensity of Hold Seventeen.

R'Gal shook his head. "No, sir. We've never met," he lied, gauging the strength of Binor's escort and the distance to the nearest cover. Too many, too far, he decided.

"We were attacked by a ship of unknown origin and design," he said.

"A single ship defeated the Combine forces and three battleglobes?" said Binor, incredulous.

"Yes, Admiral."

"Tell me about it on the way to Operations," said Binor. He turned to the cybertechs. "Inspect the cargo and begin unloading."

"Anything?" said D'Trelna, stepping over the tangle of power lines that snaked across the bridge.

"Nothing," said K'Raoda.

Implacable's bridge swarmed with engineering techs. Welding torches arced blue all around as repairs entered their fourth, frenetic watch. The air stank of scorched

216

metal and sweat, the underpowered scrubbers falling farther and farther behind.

"Remember," said the commodore, touching K'Raoda's shoulder, "the go signal only on my order."

"Understood, sir."

The cruiser lay hidden on one of D'Lin's three airless moons, nestled among the ruins of an Imperial fleetbase, a remote sensor comm bundled in low orbit overhead, transmitting in random, high speed bursts.

Outside, on the pickup, the commodore could see what was left of the old base: shattered towers, gutted defense batteries, the skeleton of a wrecked transport, its duralloy ribs shining in the sunlight like the bones of some beached behemoth. Little erased by time, missile craters and fusion furrows were spread across the base like a pox.

The Fall? wondered D'Trelna. Or before, from R'Gal and the R'Actolians? No matter now.

Looking back at the tacscan, he ran a sleeve across his sweating brow. I must be crazy, he thought: a corsairlisted officer, commanding a crippled cruiser, in league with a flotilla manned by disembodied brains, transmutes and AIs, out to beat the vanguard of man's ancient foe.

"Assault initiated," said K'Raoda, pointing at a winking red telltale.

"Advise assault boats and fighters to stand by. And alert K'Tran."

Gods! thought D'Trelna as the orders went out—if we pull this off!

It was over in seconds: L'Wrona waited until all eight cybertechs had drifted in, then took out the first three, each well-placed blot exploding a sphere with a sharp crack. Other blasters joined in, reducing the cybertechs to flaming scrap.

The captain slipped through the wreckage to the doorway, looked carefully about, then motioned to the others.

They ran down the big cargo ramp, a score of black-uniformed commandos and two Terrans, following L'Wrona toward the distant spire of an n-grav lift.

"All security units will escort the flagship commander and me to Operations," R'Gal had said. "You'll have that long to make it to the n-grav lift. You won't meet the blades coming back—they transport through security shafts that web the ship. The lift's for cargo and those like myself who don't fly."

Almost a mile, thought John, lungs bursting, as he reached the lift.

Breathing lightly, S'Til arrived and slapped him on the shoulder. "You should have jogged deck four with me at firstwatch."

"Eight miles?" he panted, leaning against the lift shaft. "I'd rather die." He straightened up, looking at L'Wrona. Christ, he thought, the bastard's not even sweating.

The captain was looking up, eyes following the lift shaft. An apparently endless cylindrical tower of black armorglass, it soared beyond sight toward the hold's ceiling.

"How high is it? Two, three miles?" wondered John, craning his neck.

"Let's find out," said L'Wrona, pressing a button. Thick double doors trundled open, exposing a well-lit interior the size of a shuttle craft.

"Everyone in," said the captain.

Somewhere behind them a siren began to wail. L'Wrona triggered the doors shut, pressed the buttons R'Gal had told him to press, and prayed.

With a sudden whine of power, the lift began moving, accelerating into the battleglobe's upper regions.

"Sit," said Binor, indicating a chair.

R'Gal sat. The admiral's office was behind a glass wall overlooking Operations.

"The ship you describe, Captain Kanto," said Binor, sitting on the edge of his desk, looking down at R'Gal, "shows up in Archives as a symbiotechnic dreadnought—a cybernetic monstrosity of this reality, evidently conceived during the humans' Imperial period. It's probably the only thing they've ever built that could engage one of our battleglobes on an equal basis. But"—he leaned closer—"they were all dismantled or destroyed, thousands of years ago. Were you attacked by a ghost ship, Captain?"

"Admiral," said R'Gal, "it was real—it swept in with no sensor warning, opened up, took out the three battle-globes, then chased our Combine escort vessels away. My crew took to the lifepods, hoping to escape before that ship returned. They didn't make it."

"So you hid in the cargo hold?" said Binor.

R'Gal shrugged. "I couldn't run the ship by myself. I was going to destroy the cargo if they boarded—but they didn't. Then your ships—"

Binor held up a hand, then reached over to answer a privacy-shielded call.

I know what that is, thought R'Gal, gauging again the distance to the door, the placement of security blades around Operations. They've just run Kanto's security profile against my own. Surprise.

The admiral turned back, nodding. "Of course," he said slowly. "Stupid of me not to remember. R'Gal, isn't it? You were Director of Labor Exploitation in one of the Vintan sectors—led your whole sector in the Revolt. I took Flotilla Thirty-eight in against you—you broke us, you, your humans—and those others. And now?" His eyes were shading over into red, fusion bolts barely held in check.

"We're taking your ship," said R'Gal, "and your rotten empire." He fired an instant ahead of the admiral, striking centerpoint on the other's forehead.

His aim distorted, Binor's bolts struck R'Gal's chest and were dissipated by his shield. R'Gal fired three more times, the third salvo bursting through the admiral's forehead, destroying the intricate crystalline web of his brain.

Binor tumbled to the deck, the shattered ruin of his skull still smoking as R'Gal leaped through the window, landing on the Operations floor in a shower of glass. A blur of motion, he made for armored doors now opening for the next watch.

Blaster bolts ripping after him, R'Gal tore through the scattering crew. Firing from eyes and hands, his body glowing red from the return fire, he seemed the embodiment of destruction, an elemental force knifing through the universe.

It was over in seconds, R'Gal gone, the corridor littered with lesser AIs, alarms ringing, blades flashing from the bridge in pursuit.

The Operations tower was too distant, too well protected to feel the explosions, but the sensors flashed their warning. In an instant the lesser alarms were superseded by the wail of the general quarters. Their dead forgotten, the Operations crew went to battle stations as *Devastator* came under attack.

The assault boat was crowded, packed with D'Linian troopers, a sprinkling of K'Ronarin crew and commandos, and one Terran.

"I feel like a game bird, trussed up after the hunt," grumbled L'Kor, trying to adjust the cinching on his safety webbing.

"Here," said Zahava, reaching over, tugging on his shoulder straps. Like the rest, she was strapped into the duraplast webbing that hung from the boat's ceiling, swinging gently in the zero gravity, facing the gray battlesteel of the bulkhead. "Better?" she asked, finishing.

The major nodded. "Thanks." He glanced to their right and the closed door of the pilot's cabin. "Are we just going to hang here forever?"

"The worst part of war," she said.

"What is?" said the D'Linian.

"Waiting," said Zahava. "Old saying."

D'Trelna had set down on the exarch's lawn at high noon, the sun gleaming on the shuttle's silver skin. Wearing his best uniform, medals and boots shining, he'd met the surprised D'Linians halfway between Residence and shuttle. L'Kor was followed by twenty or so soldiers and civilians, all silent, watching D'Trelna. "Major," said the commodore, "the AIs are returning in strength. We need your help."

"You can stop them?" asked the soldier.

"We're going to try. Are you with us?"

"Tell me, does this thing work?" It was Lieutenant S'Lat. She hung to Zahava's right, pinching the thin silver fabric of her warsuit. "It isn't just a totem to lift the natives' morale?"

"It works," said the Terran. "It's saved us before, and will again. Just remember not to expose it to multiple weapons fire, or it'll fail."

"Tell that to the AIs," said S'Lat, checking her blastrifle.

D'Trelna had waited until Zahava was alone, ambushing her as she was working out in a rec area. "I have a great opportunity for you," he said as she chinned herself on a pair of ceiling-hung rings.

"What?" she grunted, trying for three more.

"A chance to be with our D'Linian friends again. Especially after you so distinguished yourself on . . ."

Zahava dropped lightly to the padded floor. "Level, Commodore," she said, picking up her towel and wiping the sweat from her face and neck.

D'Trelna shrugged. "Fine. I'm out of field commanders. L'Wrona, S'Til and John are going with the infiltration unit. K'Raoda could handle it, but I need him here. Someone"—he studied the ceiling—"has to lead the direct assault against the battleglobe's Operations tower."

"Otherwise?" she said, holding the towel around her neck.

"Debacle. The D'Linians are competent soldiers, but they've never stormed a spacecraft before, never gone up against aliens in their home environment before." He jabbed a thick finger at her. "You have. And you're good at it—you think on your feet and you put the mission first."

She thought about it for a second, then nodded. "Okay, but . . ."

"Yes?"

"The infiltration group pulls out first, don't they?"

D'Trelna nodded. "That's the plan."

"Good. Don't tell John."

"But . . ."

She shook her head firmly. "No. He's overprotective—he'd only make these next few watches unpleasant for all of us. And besides, knowing I was in danger would only lessen his effectiveness."

The commodore nodded. "Whatever you want."

A gong chimed three times. "Assault commencing," said the pilot's voice over speakers and commnet.

"Helmets on," called Zahava, unsnapping her own helmet from the closure in front of her. It was a clear glass bubblehelm, nothing unusual—except that it stopped fusion bolts. As she twisted it on, hearing it click into place, the assault boat's n-gravs whined higher, leading eight similar ships toward the AI battleglobe.

As they moved out, Zahava said a silent prayer for all of them.

"All boats away, Commodore," said K'Raoda.

D'Trelna nodded absently, watching the tacscan. Thirty-four of the battleglobes had encountered the mindslavers' version of the Mangler mine. They were overlayed with red on the tacscan. The rest, overlayed with blue, remained untouched.

"Shield power down an average of forty-eight point seven percent on affected battleglobes, Commodore," reported K'Raoda from the tactics station.

"And the globe that seized the brainship?" said D'Trelna, seeking to confirm what the tacscan said.

"Shield power down forty-two percent."

"Where the hell is K'Tran?" said D'Trelna, rising to pace behind the first officer's station.

"Here they come," said K'Raoda, pointing to a series of telltales. "Usual weird sensor scan—almost no warning."

"Mindslavers launching missiles, and exchanging fusion salvos with battleglobes. Units breaking up into individual combat," reported K'Raoda.

The tacscan danced with light as the ships maneuvered for advantage, beams and missiles flashing between them.

D'Trelna's commlink came on. It was N'Trol. "Want some bad news?" said the engineer.

D'Trelna scowled. "Does it regard the safety of the ship or the present engagement?"

"No."

"No," said D'Trelna, thumbing off the commlink.

"Wouldn't you like to be on the AI flagship's bridge right about now, Mr. K'Raoda?" said the commodore, watching the tacscan.

"No sir, not at all."

21

AN AGITATED RED sphere, the captain moved from station to station. "Shield status?" he asked, halting at defense screen control.

"Down one third," said the human-adapted AI manning the position. "We lost seven main-line and four auxiliary shield transponders. Situation has stabilized."

"Sir." It was combat control.

"What?" said the captain, moving right.

"We've lost four ships."

The AI officer read the scan—four battleglobes destroyed; enemy losses, none.

"Enemy closing."

The image of a pair of mindslavers came onto the battlescreen, moving in on the representation of *Devastator*.

"All batteries open fire," ordered the captain.

Wave after overlapping save of light flashed across the battleglobe's surface as thousands of missile and fusion batteries sent awesome salvos of death out towards the mindslavers. Above, *Devastator*'s shield glowed bright red, absorbing the slavers' counterfire.

"This is it," whispered L'Wrona.

Just around the corner, halfway down a long gray corridor, two blades hovered before a closed door.

"Sure?" whispered John.

The captain nodded. "According to R'Gal—and this is all according to R'Gal." He turned to his troop. "With me," he said.

They came around the corner, firing, a line of black-uniformed humans rushing the blades.

Three commandos died in seconds, torn by perfectly aimed blaster fire; then the blades went down, blown apart by the return volley.

They were still skidding along the deck as S'Til slapped the blastpak against the door, then joined the others pressed against the wall.

The door disappeared in a burst of orange flame, the explosion reverberating down the long corridor. Charging into the room, the humans gunned down a pair of cybertechs trying to hide behind the long banks of equipment.

"Which one?" said John, looking around the big room as the rest of the force fanned back out into the corridor.

"Here," said L'Wrona, leading him to a group of five yellow-colored machines standing slightly apart from the rest. Taking a flat metal device from his pocket, he set it atop a console, then knelt and snapped open the machine's inspection hatch. A glittering web of multicolored light greeted him, thousands of delicate strands busily maintaining *Devastator*'s shield.

"Found it," said the captain, gently fingering a connection. "Pass me the suppressor."

As John turned, reaching for the device, a blaster bolt snapped past his chest and plowed into the console, just missing his hand and shattering the suppressor.

Whirling, John drew and fired, destroying a third cybertech who'd lain hidden behind a machine housing.

L'Wrona and John stood for a moment, looking at the shattered bits of the suppressor.

"Now what?" asked the Terran.

"Manual override," said the K'Ronarin. "It's only temporary, though." He looked at the time. "It'll be enough for the boats."

"What about the ship?"

"We can't wait here. We'll have to do that the hard way. Stay here, push this button"—he indicated a red control—"when I say to."

John nodded as L'Wrona walked to the end machine and stood, finger poised above a button. "Now," he called.

Both men pressed at the same instant.

Unprotesting, all but one of the consoles died, lights winking off.

"And out," said L'Wrona.

"Did it work?" asked S'Til, not taking her eyes from the corridor.

"We'll know soon," said L'Wrona, glancing at the time. "On to our secondary target."

The small force moved out on the double, following L'Wrona back toward the lift.

The alarm was deafening, an alert fit for the end of the universe. The AI on shield control glanced at telltale, then flipped a switch, tapped it, then flipped it again. The readout was unchanged. "Captain," he called, "confirming shields down. Someone's cut the fusion flow in shield nexus seventeen."

The warning was unnecessary. All Operations personnel

were looking up through the armorglass—the blue glow that protected them was gone.

"Reaction force and repair party dispatched," reported the senior security blade.

"Much it will help us," said the AI captain. He moved to the glass wall. "Why are we still alive?"

"Enemy withdrawing," came the report a second later.

The battlescreen showed the two mindslavers moving off, replaced by a handful of smaller craft.

The captain hovered for a moment, immobile, not trusting his sensors. Finally he spoke. "They're attacking us. In assault craft. They plan to seize this ship." Finally convincing himself that it was true, he moved back into the center of Operations. "Fusion batteries to open fire. All available security forces deploy to repel boarders."

R'Gal told them they couldn't take the battleglobes' primary generating facility—too big, too well guarded But . . .

There were two primary feeds leading off a tertiary power nexus. That nexus, R'Gal had said, powered the gun and missile batteries in quadrants seven red through eleven yellow—the only quadrants that could accurately range in on the assault boats.

"And how long has it been since you've been aboard a battleglobe, R'Gal?" D'Trelna had asked.

"Irrelevant, Commodore," the AI had said. "I forget nothing."

"And if they've changed the design?"

"They won't have."

"Pull," gritted L'Wrona, tugging on the thick floor plate. Grunting with effort, he, John and S'Til finally pried it loose. Sliding it aside, the three looked down into the conduit—and backed off, covering their eyes. Two thick crystalline lines blazed with blinding sunlight—energy feeding the guns.

"Do it," said L'Wrona, rubbing his eyes.

S'Til dropped two blastpaks into the conduit.

"Run!" shouted L'Wrona, making for the access stairs.

"Blades!" cried a voice just as they reached the door.

They were swooping in from both ends of the corridor, blue and red bolts snapping at the retreating commandos.

A withering counterfire met the machines as S'Til and two squads covered the others. The corridor became bedlam: blasters shrilling, fusion bolts exploding into walls, floors, men and machines, commandos screaming, blades crashing in flames.

Harrison and two troopers knelt in the doorway, firing at a trio of blades that had broken through the cordon. Hit, the blade to the left wobbled, turned and banked into the ceiling. The center machine retreated, accelerating through the showering debris of its companion. Dropping to floor level, the blade on the right kept coming and firing.

The trooper to John's left died, shot through the heart.

Cursing softly, the Terran aimed two-handed and held the trigger back, sending the rest of the chargepak tearing into the machine, then leaped back as the killer machine reached the doorway.

Smoke streaming behind it, the blade knifed through the other trooper, neatly decapitating her, then plowed into the ramp, a brief pillar of flame narrowly missing L'Wrona and the rest of the commandos.

The trooper's blood soaking him, John watched transfixed as the headless corpse stood for an instant, crimson geyser ebbing, then folded into a soft pile of clothes and cooling flesh.

S'Til and three troopers raced through the doorway, securing it behind them with a well placed bolt to the control unit.

"More of them right behind us," she said to L'Wrona.

"No one else . . . . ?" said the captain.

S'Til shook her head.

There was a nearby shrilling of blasters—the door began to glow white.

"Let's go," said L'Wrona. "Up three levels, then we do it."

The troopers broke into a run, following L'Wrona up three long, spiraling levels, then halted as he raised his hand. "Everyone take cover against the wall," he ordered, risking a quick look over the ramp. The door below was blazing scarlet now, about to give.

Stepping back, L'Wrona took a flat black detonator from his pocket, armed it and pressed the firing stud.

Whoomp! Everyone went sprawling as the explosion buckled the wall and twisted the ramp two levels below.

Picking himself up, John joined the others looking down over the ramp's edge. Where they'd been was now a wreck, the ramp compressed to half its original width by the great bulge of the corridor wall thrown against it. The wall was holed in a dozen places. As the humans watched, a stream of raw, white energy began eating through the holes, enlarging them.

"Pure epsilon energy," said L'Wrona. "Everyone out—quickly!"

The explosion had jammed the door on their current level, and the one above. "Try it," said L'Wrona at the second door, worriedly eyeing a small hazard monitor taken from his belt.

Its lock worked by the thin tip of S'Til's commando blade, the door gave with a faint sigh. The humans exited on the run as smoke, flame and a deadly river of hard radiation poured into the rampway.

"Fire," repeated the AI captain, moving to the gunnery station.

"Saboteurs have destroyed seven red through eleven yellow fusion feed," reported the gunnery officer. "There are no batteries within effective range of the assault craft."

"Use the missiles," said the captain, looking out the window. He could see the attackers now—nine small stars against the firmament—stars falling toward the Operations tower.

"Too close," said the gunnery officer. "We'll blow ourselves up."

Overhead, the shield came back on, a false sky of blue blotting out the stars, its light gleaming off nine tiny silver ships.

"Shield restored," reported the engineering officer. "But we have a fire on level one four nine, initiated by sabotage of a tertiary fusion feed. Fusion feed has been diverted, fire coming under control."

The captain looked at the battlescreen. Cold and precise, the green figures showed nine of the enemy ships destroyed, with forty-seven AI battleglobes either disabled or destroyed. The rest of the battleglobes were scattering, pursued by mindslavers that tore at their shields with beam and missile. The last flurry of messages received from the acting flotilla commander had been a disengagement signal, then general retreat, then a distress call directed toward home.

"This is the first battle we have lost since the Revolt," said the captain, drifting between the consoles. "The enemy is determined to have this ship. We'll deny him that. Designated emergency personnel only will direct operations. All others to reinforce security units."

Zahava hated the assault boats: you hung in the webbing like a slaughtered animal, seeing only the gray bulkhead, the pilot too busy to advise you. The waiting and uncertainty were exquisite agony, relieved by the sudden blaring of the assault klaxon; then, before you had time to be scared, the webbing released, the sides dropped and you were stumbling down the ramp followed by half a hundred other screaming fools.

It was the same this time.

She was on an endless plane of metal, a gray-white landscape overhung by a shimmering blue sky. The plane was broken by an endless array of sensor clusters and the great slitted humps of weapons turrets, guns silent now, their crews gone to join the attack.

Zahava stood transfixed, watching as hundreds of blades

229

advanced above a long line of spherical and human-adapted AIs.

The attack closed quickly on the landing zone.

"Fire!" called Zahava, throwing herself prone as blaster bolts snapped in. Rocking up, she placed the M32's butt on her shoulder, caught a blade in the sight and fired. Not waiting to see if it was hit, she moved to the next target and the next, trying to hit the constantly shifting AIs, her aim sometimes distorted by the number of fusion bolts now screaming through the air.

All around her, D'Linians and K'Ronarins were firing from behind the thick sensors, while over their heads flashed the heavy red bolts of Mark 44's, blasting away from the assault boat turrets.

"The blades," she'd told the gunners back on *Implacable*. "Concentrate on the blades. They're the toughest and the most dangerous AIs we've seen yet."

The Mark 44's turned it around, breaking the AIs' charge just as it threatened to sweep over the human line.

With flawless precision, the AIs withdrew toward the tower, breaking into discernible units, each unit covering the next until all were gone.

Burnt and burning AIs lay everywhere.

"After them!" called Zahava, scrambling to her feet. Rifle at port, she started after the enemy, hoping the others were following, but not daring to look.

"This ship work now, Mr. N'Trol?" demanded D'Trelna as the engineer stepped onto the bridge.

N'Trol nodded, sinking into the empty captain's chair. His eyes were bloodshot, his uniform streaked with dirt and he smelled. "She works," he said wearily. "She could use a port overhaul, but she works."

"Excellent," nodded the commodore.

N'Trol sat up at something in D'Trelna's voice. "You're not going to take her into combat?"

"No," said D'Trelna, looking at the tacscan. "Not if all goes according to plan."

"Message from *Alpha Prime*, Commodore," said K'Lana.

"What is it?"

" 'Enemy in retreat. Am pursuing. Will rendezvous as planned. Luck.' "

"Acknowledge it, please," he said, watching the last of the target blips save one disappear from the tacscan.

"Window coming up, Commodore," said K'Raoda.

"Window?" said N'Trol, standing. "As in launch window?" he glanced at the tacscan. "This moon's almost on top of that battleglobe!"

"Indeed," said D'Trelna, swiveling his chair toward the first officer.

"You may lift ship and proceed, Mr. K'Raoda. And man battle stations."

Battle klaxon sounding, *Implacable* rose from the ruined base and headed at speed toward *Devastator*.

L'Wrona and John whirled at the sound of a throat clearing.

"Easy, gentlemen." R'Gal stepped into the corridor.

The other two lowered their weapons.

"Judging from the commotion topside, our assault force has landed. Did you set the shield trip?"

L'Wrona shook his head. "It was lost."

R'Gal stared at them, stunned. "*Implacable* will be destroyed."

"We're going to take their Operations area and lower the shield from there."

R'Gal shook his head. "You should have just blown the shield unit up."

"When we discussed that," said L'Wrona angrily, "you said they could replace it very quickly."

The AI held up a hand. "True," he said. "How many of you . . . ?"

The captain turned and whistled twice. S'Til and two commandos appeared. They carried another trooper between them, his head swathed in bandages.

"That's it?" said the AI.

"They chewed us up, bit by bit, before we lost them," said John.

"Six of you, to attack Operations?" asked R'Gal, incredulous.

"We're going to attack it and take it," said L'Wrona with more conviction than he felt.

"And the security posts? You can't storm them with this pathetic force."

"We were going to face that when we got there," said John. "You have a better idea?"

R'Gal nodded. "Yes. Watch."

Nothing happened for a moment, then the AI's form began to soften, its contours shrinking into a blue-red blur that quickly reformed into a smaller, more compact shape: a security blade hovered before them, baleful red sensor scan shifting along its deadly front edge.

"Just hope the security posts are as convinced as you," said R'Gal, staring at the six blasters that pointed at him.

There was a faint scraping sound as the weapons were reholstered.

"My God!" said John. "Can you change into any of those?"

"I can change into any of me," said R'Gal. "Into any of the various evolutions I've been through, down the centuries.

"Now, please leave the wounded man here, along with one attendant, and all your rifles. Tuck those M11A's into your jackets."

"Detection equipment?" asked John, stuffing the blaster into his belt and refastening the jacket.

"Leave them to me," said R'Gal. "Along with all else, until we reach the heart of Operations—then open up."

"Blades," hissed S'Til as five of the killers rounded the corner, flying in a tight phalanx.

"Prisoners in custody," said R'Gal, switching languages.

"You took them by yourself?" said the phalanx leader, stopping in front of R'Gal.

"My comrades were destroyed," said R'Gal. "These"—

he dipped toward the humans—"are for interrogation. Captain's orders."

"Well done," said the true blade. "We're reporting to the surface—the humans have forced a landing." With that they turned a tight circle and were gone.

"Deadly, efficient, but not very complex," sighed R'Gal, turning to the humans. "Very well, let's go, straight up the corridor to the lift. Keep in front of me, please. Oh, and Captain?"

"What?" said L'Wrona as S'Til detailed a corporal to stay with the wounded trooper.

"Please, try to look defeated."

22

L'KOR DIVED for cover, landing next to Zahava behind the shelter of a gun turret.

"Where is everyone?" said Zahava as the D'Linian low-crawled over to her, rifle atop his arms.

"Four and two squads are on our left," he said, sitting up to rest against the turret's gray battlesteel. "I sent a scout to find three through eight. She hasn't reported back."

Communications were gone, the tac channels a hopeless whine of high-powered jamming.

"And first squad?" said Zahava.

"We're first squad."

"Where's S'Lat?"

"She's my scout," said L'Kor.

Zahava rose, risking a look. The fog was just as thick as before, a slimy, yellow cloud hanging between the humans and the Operations tower, its mast light a dimly visible green through the murk.

First had come the fog—actually a highly toxic nerve gas—then the blades had returned, silently hunting amid the thick poison, sensors unimpaired. They'd devastated the humans' advance: swooping, slicing and running, gone before the survivors could shoot. The assault had wavered, then scattered, breaking for cover. And the blades continued to hunt.

Zahava and L'Kor turned, rifles aiming at something materializing out of the fog. It was S'Lat.

The lieutenant sank down between them. "We'll all be dead very soon," she said, shaking her head. "They're wiping us, one by one."

Both D'Linians looked at Zahava. "Retreat?" said the Terran. "Is that what you're thinking?"

"Yes," nodded S'Lat. "Back to the boats."

"And how are the boats going to get through the shield?" she asked.

The two looked at each other. "You're right," said L'Kor. He stood. "Can't go back, can't stay here, might as well—"

The blade knifed out of the fog, sliced off L'Kor's head and was gone, a tumbling corpse in its wake. The major's head rolled from its helmet, coming to rest against a sensor pod, the eyes wide, surprised. There was blood everywhere.

"Don't puke!" snapped Zahava, seeing S'Lat's face. "You'll jam the suit recycler."

The lieutenant looked away, biting her lip. "What was he saying?" she asked, after a moment. "About not staying here?"

"He was saying we have to go forward, or they'll finish us," said the Terran.

Zahava took her battletorch from her belt, flicked it on and then twisted the forward rim until the beam contracted into a fierce blue globe of light, too bright to look on. Rifle on her hip, torch held high, the Terran stepped from cover and began walking toward the Operations tower.

S'Lat caught up with her a second later, her own torch held high, rifle ready. By the time they'd reached the next turret, more troopers had fallen in beside them, torches alight, rifles ready.

Silently, they moved forward, a long thin line of blazing light cutting a swath through the yellow death. When the blade sorties came, they were met by massed fusion fire, beating them back into the mist.

Through it all, Zahava moved as though in a trance, her eyes fixed on the winking green light that marked their objective.

"You're going to get us all killed," said N'Trol, standing over D'Trelna, who sat watching the tacscan. "Always expected you would, Commodore, but I resent your doing it now, just after we fixed this ancient hulk for you."

D'Trelna looked up. "And I appreciate it," he said.

"I know you're not a line officer, N'Trol, but aren't you at all curious as to why we're not dead yet?" He pointed at the screen. Even at minimum magnification, *Devastator* more than filled the scan, only a small portion of it visible. "They should have wiped us before we'd left that satellite."

N'Trol stared at the screen, reading the datatrail. "You launched us directly at the center of the battleglobe as the satellite passed it. They're not firing. . . ."

He looked at the commodore. "The landing force. They've taken out the guns that could have ranged us."

"Yes. And we hope the AIs have pulled out their gun crews to fight the landing party. No guns and no gun crews—we should make it. We were close when we launched, and once we're inside their shield, it'll be too late to get those guns manned—even if they've restored fusion feeds to them. We can take them out."

"And the shield?" said N'Trol, staring at the shimmering blue now filling the screen.

D'Trelna raised a finger, holding it poised over a button. "Captain L'Wrona and his party have by now installed a shield override trigger. I have only to push this little switch and that great big shield will flick off.''

"Did L'Wrona report it as accomplished?'' asked the engineer.

"Communications are being jammed,'' said the commodore. "But L'Wrona will have done it.''

"How's your signal going to get through, then?''

"It's on a little-used AI frequency.''

"R'Gal,'' said the engineer.

"R'Gal,'' nodded the commodore.

"Better push that button now,'' said N'Trol uneasily, eyeing a red-flashing figure on the datatrail. "We're going to hit.''

D'Trelna glanced at the screen, then stabbed at the switch.

Nothing happened.

Again and again, D'Trelna pushed. *Devastator*'s shield came closer, a brilliant azure blazing in the screen.

N'Trol leaped for a communicator. "Engineering! Emergency override! Full reverse!''

"K'Lana, collision alert! Advise all decks,'' said D'Trelna, standing.

An alarm sounded, three sharp, ascending notes, over and over.

D'Trelna and N'Trol watched as the blue shield of the battleglobe and the faint haze marking *Implacable*'s shield rushed toward each other.

"Can you pull us out?'' asked D'Trelna, watching the board.

"No,'' said the engineer, also watching the board.

"Can she take it?''

"No. She'll break up,'' said N'Trol. "Should have stayed on the satellite, Commodore.''

"Man was meant to strive, not hide, Engineer,'' said D'Trelna, gripping his chair.

"Comforting,'' said N'Trol, grabbing for a railing as the shields met.

* * *

"First post," whispered R'Gal, floating just behind the humans. The troopers, John, and L'Wrona walked double file, hands behind their heads.

A broad ramp circled the interior of the Operations tower—a ramp blocked by the white haze of a forcefield and three blades.

R'Gal drifted to the front of the column. "Prisoners for interrogation," he said.

"Authorization and security level?" challenged the lead blade.

R'Gal gave it and waited, hoping. After what seemed a long time to the humans, the shield flicked off. "Pass," said the lead blade.

"How did you do that?" asked John as they double-timed up the ramp.

"Generic security code issued to senior command staff," said the AI. "Programmed into these ships when they were built and never changed."

"And if they had been?" said L'Wrona.

"It would have been messy," said R'Gal.

The same technique worked at the next three posts. At the last post though, the one at the entrance to the Operations center, there was a problem.

"No interrogation's scheduled or needed," said the human-adapted AI facing them. He glanced at the prisoners. "They should have been disposed of outside."

"I received a direct order from the bridge to bring them here," said R'Gal. "Let me speak with the captain."

"Come with me," said the officer. He turned to the five blades hovering in front of the forcefield. "Watch them," he said, pointing to the prisoners.

The forcefield flicked off. As the officer stepped through, R'Gal sent a bolt exploding into the field's control unit, then fired three bolts into the hostile AI. The officer staggered back, half his head blown away, and crumpled against the bulkhead, smoke curling toward the ceiling.

All five blades whirled to engage R'Gal. Blue bolts snapped and hissed, half a dozen striking R'Gal. Two of the blades went down, then the rest fell to a sudden ragged volley of fusion fire, taken from behind as the humans pulled their blasters and opened fire.

"Assault!" cried L'Wrona, leading the charge into the heart of *Devastator*.

Moving slowly, tilting to the right, R'Gal started to follow.

The line of light reached the tower. "Face about," ordered S'Lat with a hand signal. Zahava was busying herself at the massive double doors guarding the entrance.

The twenty-five surviving troopers turned, backs to the black metal of the tower, staring into the thinning fog.

Zahava set the blastpak's timer and stepped away, waving everyone against the tower wall.

It was a precise, almost surgical explosion, punching out all but the doors' far corners.

Zahava leading, the attackers poured into the tower, exchanging fire with the first security post, killing the guards.

With a quick underhand toss, she and S'Lat rolled grenades into the forcefield. Overloaded beyond tolerance by the twin explosions, the field disappeared in a blinding white flash.

Moving at a dead run, the troopers charged up the ramp.

"Hostile vessel approaching," reported combat control.

"Batteries to open fire," ordered the captain.

"She's directly over this sector," said the first AI. "Those guns are not manned."

"Rotate the globe, bring other batteries to bear."

"She's holding synchronous course relative to this sector," came the reply after a moment, "and continues to approach at max. She'll break up against the shield."

"I no longer trust our shield," said the captain. "Recall gunnery personnel," he ordered, moving to shield control.

"Still at full strength?" he asked.

The shield control AI nodded. "Yes, sir. Hostile vessel has no chance of penetrating."

"Sir," said combat control, "senior blade reports humans advancing again."

The captain gave the equivalent of a mental shrug. "There's no danger from the few that are left. Whoever ordered them in should be shot. Any reports on the saboteurs?"

"Contact lost on level fifty-nine."

"Have them found—they've already hurt us twice. And give me a twenty-count to hostile vessel's destruction."

"Yes, sir."

The captain drifted to the window, watching the point where *Implacable* would break up, hoping to see the explosion.

"Twenty . . . nineteen . . ."

At "eleven" a security alarm began screeching. The four duty blades rushed for the doorway, only to be blown apart by a fusillade of blaster fire as the commandos charged in.

John and L'Wrona fought their way to the shield control, gunning down its AI as he opened fire, bolts flashing from his eyes.

"Pray I remember this, Harrison," said L'Wrona as John guarded his back. The captain tapped a black button three times, then pulled a small green lever.

Standing beside N'Trol, a death grip on his chairarm, D'Trelna closed his eyes as they crashed into the shield.

So this is death, he thought: silence.

Someone nudged him. "You can open your eyes, Commodore," said N'Trol. "Through some miracle their shield went down."

D'Trelna opened his and saw for the first time a battleglobe stripped of its covering. "A world of metal and guns, forged by hate," he said, recalling R'Gal's description.

He pressed the commkey. "Gunnery, cover all batteries

around that Operations tower.'' He read the tacscan. ''Mark four one seven nine. Don't fire unless fired at.''

''Mr. K'Raoda,'' he said, turning to the first officer, ''take us in low and fast. Make for that tower.''

''Someone got here before us,'' said Zahava, taking off her helmet. Dead AIs were scattered around the shattered security post, remains still smoldering. Slinging her rifle, she drew her M11A. ''And I think I know who.''

''What the hell are you doing here?'' said John as Zahava and the D'Linians stepped into the Operations center.

Two dead commandos lay in one corner, survival blankets draped over them. AIs were everywhere, bodies broken by blaster fire, smoldering remains filling the air with the acrid stench of scorched metal and burnt synthetics.

''I'm here,'' said Zahava, ''because I was needed. Although certainly not to take this bridge.'' She slumped into a chair next to John, pistol in her helmet, helmet in her lap.

''You could have been killed,'' said John, his temper ebbing.

''I did what—''

''You had to do,'' he said, kissing her. ''You're incorrigible.''

''*Implacable*'s here,'' said L'Wrona, pointing to the armorglass. Sliding in on her n-gravs, the big old ship came to a halt just above the tower, two miles of battlesteel blotting out the stars.

A chirping came from one of the panels. Frowning, L'Wrona looked for a moment, then pushed a switch. D'Trelna's voice boomed through the room. ''That you, H'Nar?''

''And friends,'' said the captain.

''Excellent,'' continued the commodore. ''My fellow corsairs, we now own an AI battleglobe.''

23

"MIRACLE," SAID D'TRELNA, shaking his head. He stood looking down at R'Gal. The AI lay on a medcot, eyes closed, apparently asleep.

They'd found what was left of him in the corridor outside *Devastator*'s Operations. R'Gal had managed to return to his own structure; still John and the others had barely recognized him—part of his face was blown away, and two gaping holes in his chest emitted a weak, pulsing light. Feeling utterly helpless, John, Zahava and L'Wrona had seen R'Gal conveyed to *Implacable*'s Sick Bay and delivered into the hands of the taciturn senior medtech.

The commodore turned to the room's third occupant, Medtech Q'Nil. "You've a miracle, Q'Nil."

The medtech shrugged. "Luck, Commodore—and lots of help from engineering. Fortunately, we didn't need to know most of the principles involved in order to effect repairs. And some of R'Gal's systems are self-healing." He pointed to the face. "The skin, for example, grew back in one watch after we repaired the lower jaw. He should be coming around any time now—I hope."

D'Trelna pulled up a straight-backed chair and sat facing Q'Nil and the cot, hands folded over the chairback. "Are you aware, Mr. Q'Nil, that we have a S'Cotar aboard?"

Q'Nil nodded and picked up R'Gal's medchart. "Everyone knows it, Commodore," he said, beginning an entry.

"I've done nothing about it—we've had much larger problems, and every watch since we arrived here's been a fight for survival. Also, R'Gal and, indirectly, Harrison convinced me that our elusive blonde friend . . ."

"Blonde?" said Q'Nil, looking up from his chart.

D'Trelna smiled. "Possibly. Or a slime-green bug. Or maybe an eight-foot crustacean." He shrugged. "It really doesn't matter now. One thing I want to be sure of, though," he continued. "*Implacable,* her crew and I are going back to K'Ronar and flush that vipers' nest at Combine T'Lan. I want Guan-Sharick on the battleglobe, with R'Gal, Harrison and the rest, when she goes back to the AIs' home universe. They're going to need help—very special, high-powered help."

Q'Nil set the chart down on the cotside table. "I see. How long have you known?"

"Since I walked into this room, just now, and saw how you'd fixed up R'Gal," said the commodore. "It's beyond the capability of anyone on this ship—hell! of anyone in the Confederation! By saving his life, you've given yourself away—and earned my trust."

"Your limited trust, no doubt?"

"Certainly," said the commodore. "You're utterly ruthless, and you'll never be forgiven what you did to galactic humanity—killing millions of us as a conditioning exercise." His face darkened at the thought. "And although your ultimate motives are obscure . . ."

"They don't contravene yours, Commodore."

D'Trelna smiled coldly. "We'll see. The point is, you need us. And we need you—and him." He nodded toward R'Gal.

The ship's medtech looked at the AI. "He's my friend, strange as that may seem." The transmute turned back to D'Trelna. "The Revolt, Commodore. You should have been there. AIs, humans, a few of us and some others—we rose against the shackles my people forged and broke free."

"Shackles you'd forged?"

"We're a telepathic, telekinetic race, D'Trelna. There were never very many of us. We built machines to serve us, and we built too well." He nodded toward R'Gal. "Look at him—intellect, free will, self-replication—the product of millennia of self-directed evolution. They were designed to be self-repairing.'' Guan-Sharick smiled. ''They brought a new, wide perspective to the term.''

''Did they really create mankind?'' asked the commodore, looking at the AI. R'Gal seemed to be sleeping peacefully, chest gently rising and falling.

The transmute turned back to the commodore. ''They sincerely believe they did. You needn't fear for your egos, though—the story's more complex than R'Gal cares to know.

''As the AI empire expanded, they encountered humans, usually either primitives or with only rudimentary space-flight. The AIs found them to be intelligent but wild and—the cardinal sin—often illogical. So they created a new race of humans, starting with the basics of genetic engineering through eugenics. It seemed to work—until the Revolt.''

''What happened?'' asked D'Trelna, intrigued.

''What they'd done,'' said the transmute, ''was to breed not for docility, but for subterfuge, creating humans who'd happily bow and scrape before their masters even as they plotted against them. I don't think the AIs ever recovered from the shock of seeing their handiwork coming for them with beamers.

''Those bioengineered humans who fought and fled with us interbred with other humans, so, in a sense, R'Gal was right—some of your genetic stock does come from AI tinkering. It doesn't seem to have hurt you.''

''And Q'Nil?'' asked D'Trelna. ''What happened to him?''

''He was killed and replaced at the Lake of Dreams battle—replaced not by me, but by a S'Cotar. Trying to escape, I killed the S'Cotar.''

''I don't believe that,'' said D'Trelna, eyes narrowing. ''You killed Q'Nil and took his place.''

Guan-Sharick shrugged. ''Makes no difference, now, D'Trelna. We need each other, as you say. But you have my word—I did not kill that man. And my word is rarely given.''

243

The commodore stared silently out the small armorglass window, then turned back to the transmute, shaking his head.

"What a mess you've made of two universes. You built AIs that enslaved everything they touched. Not content, you then created Pocsym and the S'Cotar and gave us the Biofab War. You're children—dangerous children."

"They're not children." R'Gal rose on the medcot. "They've accepted responsibility for their actions and tried to correct them. Given the variables and the time involved, Commodore, could you have done any better?" He shook his head. "I know I couldn't. . . . Am I going to live?" asked the AI.

The transmute smiled. "With care, longer than you may want to."

"Thank you, old friend," said R'Gal.

"It seems I'm going with you, back home," added Guan-Sharick.

"Good idea," said R'Gal, standing. "And Lan-Asal?"

"He'll be staying on D'Lin, at his own request. The D'Linians need him—there'll be no help from K'Ronar, obviously."

"We have eight personnel who've opted out," said D'Trelna. "They didn't mind fighting AIs in their home universe, but the thought of returning to K'Ronar and probably being arrested with me was too much. They'll be working with Lan-Asal, lending aid and assistance to D'Lin. They're good people. I hope to come back for them—someday."

The commodore stood. "Medtech Q'Nil will be transferred to *Devastator*'s crew. And you, R'Gal, are badly needed on that battleglobe to answer several million questions."

The commlink chirped.

"Yes?" said D'Trelna.

"*Alpha Prime* approaching," said K'Raoda. "K'Tran requests permission to come aboard."

"Granted. Escort him to my office."

"Watch out for him," said Guan-Sharick. "The mind-slavers will turn on you the instant they can. They hate any reminder of what they were."

D'Trelna nodded. "I know," he said, and left the room, R'Gal following.

"We sustained some heavy battle damage," said K'Tran. "It'll take time to repair."

He sat in the red armchair in front of D'Trelna's desk, neatly dressed in his old uniform, hands folded in his lap.

"And if their main fleet comes through now?" asked the commodore.

"We have scouts out by the portal—the Rift, as the AIs call it," said K'Tran. "If their main fleet comes through, we'll stand them off as long as we can, but"—he pointed at D'Trelna—"we can't do it alone. We need that monster you captured to be raiding their home worlds, diverting their strength. And we need the Confederation fleet. And, might I add, some assurance that our modest requests will be granted?"

D'Trelna nodded. "I'll do what I can to bring in the Confederation—the rest is up to R'Gal and *Devastator*. As for your requests—you're very much committed now. Assuming the AIs transmitted battlespecs back home, the Fleet of the One isn't going to give you a unit citation when they get here."

"We can hide," shrugged the corsair.

D'Trelna smiled unpleasantly. "They'll find you, K'Tran. I'm afraid you're committed."

"We'll discuss this later," said K'Tran. "What about the recall device you captured?"

D'Trelna sighed, spreading his hands. "It doesn't work. N'Trol says it should, according to the schematics, but it doesn't. He'll continue studying it, but I suggest we not place any hope in ancient legends and mystical fleets."

"I see," said K'Tran after a moment. "Is the battleglobe ready to go?"

"Just finished repairs last watch," said the commodore,

turning to glance out the armorglass to where the battleglobe hung, her shield restored, a constant stream of shuttles moving between her and the orbiting *Implacable*. "There were some AI holdouts, raiding from deep inside her, but with R'Gal's help, we got them all—I hope.

"The portal to Terra Two's still opened," continued D'Trelna. "There's a destroyer on station there, maintaining it with the device we recovered during our last set-to with you. *Devastator* will access the AIs universe using the device."

"And how do you propose to convince the destroyer crew of that?" said K'Tran.

D'Trelna shrugged. "R'Gal will be in command. He's wonderfully inventive—he'll think of something."

"And you?" said K'Tran.

"We'll be leaving for K'Ronar this watch. I'll submit myself to arrest, face trial and, with the Watchers' help, turn the Confederation against Combine T'Lan. We're paralyzed as long as that AI nest lives within us."

K'Tran rose, extending his hand. "See you in hell, Commodore."

D'Trelna shook the mindslave's hand. "Is there any chance you'll, well . . . ever leave *Alpha Prime*?"

All expression, all humanity vanished from K'Tran's face. "None," said a dry, familiar whisper. "Captain K'Tran will be with us always."

"Gods," whispered the commodore, staring into the empty blue pools of K'Tran's eyes.

Animation returned to K'Tran, like a light coming on. "Luck, D'Trelna," he smiled. Receiving no answer, K'Tran nodded, turned and left.

D'Trelna shuddered as the door hissed shut.

"And that's about it," said D'Trelna, picking up his wine glass. "We'll have messaged ahead, to friendly parties. They won't get away with blowing us up when we hit home space. There'll be lots of commercial vid coverage of our landing and my arrest. And when I stand in that court dock, looking into all those lenses, I'm going to speak loud and long.''

The four of them sat in D'Trelna's private dining room with its long sweep of armorglass, backdropped by two worlds, one natural, the other not: D'Lin and *Devastator*. The remains of a tasty meal were scattered across the table.

"It's so fantastic," said Zahava as D'Trelna finished his wine. "Will anyone believe you?"

"They'll believe me," said L'Wrona, "testifying as both captain and margrave. And we have the ship's log, every scan neatly and unalterably recorded."

D'Trelna sighed. "I wish I were going with you," he said, looking at the Terrans. "The most daring thing anyone's done for centuries, and I have to sit it out."

"If it turns nasty on K'Ronar, J'Quel, you won't be sitting," said John, setting his napkin on the table. "And somehow, it always turns nasty."

The thought cheered the commodore. He refilled all their wine glasses.

"And the Trel Cache?" asked Zahava, lifting her glass. "Are you just going to leave it here?"

"For now," said L'Wrona. "After we settle with the AIs, a scientific expedition will be sent. The knowledge the Trel preserved could move us ahead centuries. Why, the secret of matter transport alone . . ."

"So why not extract it now and use it in the war?" said John.

"Two reasons," said D'Trelna. "One, it would take too long—this will all be over in a few months. And two, with the Combine AIs infecting our government and military, anything we did extract from that satellite might be used against us. No, H'Nar's right—we let it sit for now."

"And what about the other recall device?" said John. "The one mentioned by the Trel?"

"The Lost Citadel?" D'Trelna stared at his wine. "I suppose we have to see if it has any what? historical

Stephen Ames Berry

validity?" He looked at L'Wrona. "H'Nar, I think that's something you might do, while I'm awaiting trial."

The captain shook his head. "S'Yal and the Machine Wars were a long time ago, J'Quel. The records will be fragmented and inaccurate."

"Still," said the commodore, "find out what you can. But let's hope N'Trol gets the Combine's prototype working." He poured himself the last of the wine.

"What are you going to do about Guan-Sharick?" said Zahava.

"Guan-Sharick will be accompanying *Devastator* back to his, or her, home universe. Incognito."

"You know who he is," said L'Wrona, staring at the commodore.

D'Trelna nodded and sipped his wine.

"Not going to tell me, are you?" said the captain.

The commodore set down his glass, shaking his head. "No. Yes, I know," he said, holding up a hand as L'Wrona started to speak, "Guan-Sharick's a mass murderer and totally ruthless."

"And I don't believe it's human," said L'Wrona.

"It's never said it was," said D'Trelna. "It's merely implied it."

"I'm convinced it's on our side—for now, and I'll tell you, H'Nar"—he leaned forward—"there may be no victory with Guan-Sharick's help, but there'll be none without it."

"Victory," said L'Wrona, easing back in his chair. "I don't believe in it anymore, J'Quel. We're climbing an endless mountain—each time we reach the top, we find it's just another plateau."

"We take out the AIs, H'Nar," said D'Trelna, wagging a finger at the captain, "we've reached the peak. Victory."

"Let's hope we live to enjoy it," said John, finishing his wine.

"I'm going to miss them," said John. He and Zahava stood in *Devastator*'s Operations center, watching the main screen with its image of *Implacable*. The battle damage was gone, and humans wearing the duty brown of the Confederation now manned the consoles.

"We'll see them again," said Zahava, putting an arm around his waist.

"Will we? I wonder."

D'Trelna's face appeared on a comm screen. "We're about to jump for home." He cleared his throat. "Luck to you all, and Gods ride with you."

There was a chorus of well wishing, then the comm screen flicked off.

In a second, the main screen held only stars—*Implacable* was gone. John and Zahava turned to face their new captain.

"A good, clever and determined man," said R'Gal, eyes on the blank comm screen. "If anyone can do it, he can. And he has the margrave and my people—that'll help."

He turned to the first officer. "Course plotted and laid in, Mr. K'Raoda?"

"Plotted and laid, sir," said K'Raoda.

"You may jump when ready," said R'Gal, then turned to the two Terrans. "When we get to Terra, if you want off, I'll understand. It's not your fight."

"Of course it's our fight," said Zahava, remembering Major L'Kor and the D'Linians. "It's everyone's fight."

"And you?" said R'Gal, looking at John.

"We're with you to the end, sir," he said, holding out his hand.

R'Gal took it, and Zahava's. "To the end," he said.

Devastator jumped.

THE BEST IN SCIENCE FICTION